CHASING RISK

BRANDT LEGG

By Brandt Legg

Chase Malone Thriller

> *Chasing Rain*
> *Chasing Fire*
> *Chasing Wind*
> *Chasing Dirt*
> *Chasing Life*
> *Chasing Kill*
> *Chasing Risk*
> *Chasing Mind*
> *Chasing Time*
> *Chasing Lies*
> *Chasing Fear*
> *Chasing Lost*

*As always, this book is dedicated to
Teakki and Ro*

Vinci Books

vinci-books.com

Published by Vinci Books Ltd in 2025

1

Copyright © Brandt Legg 2020

The author has asserted their moral right to be identified as the author of this work in accordance with the Copyright, Designs and Patents Act 1988. This work is a work of fiction. Names, characters, places and incidents are the product of the author's imagination or are used fictitiously. Any resemblance to actual persons, living or dead, places and incidents is entirely coincidental.

All rights reserved. No part of this publication may be copied, reproduced, distributed, stored in any retrieval system, or transmitted in any form or by any means, including photocopying, recording, or other electronic or mechanical methods, nor used as a source for any form of machine learning including AI datasets, without the prior written permission of the publisher.

The publisher and the author have made every effort to obtain permissions for any third party material used in this book and to comply with copyright law. Any queries in this respect should be brought to the attention of the publisher and any omissions will be corrected in future editions.

A CIP catalogue record for this book is available from the British Library.

Paperback ISBN: 9781036705268

Chapter One

"In the daydreams of our imaginations and the whimsical glow of childhood, we forget that a darkness is waiting to snatch our innocence and shatter the illusion."

Chase Malone thought about the cynical words. They had troubled him ever since a friend, called The Astronaut, had uttered them upon learning about the boy.

The Astronaut and the boy were just two of the odd collection of people Chase had accumulated since his flight from "the real world" began.

The billionaire's chiseled face softened in bewilderment and affection at seeing Tu, the little eight-year-old Chinese boy he had come to love. Searching his eyes for wonderment, joy, or any sense of whimsy, it saddened him to not see any sense of childhood excitement. Instead, the "Buddha" child often seemed like an adult, always analyzing and studying.

The product of a Chinese experiment, Tu was a special boy. While still an embryo, his genes had been edited, manipulated for increased intelligence. The results were fantastic, although disturbing. He easily worked incredibly complex math equations in his head, and could quickly reason through intricate problems with machine-like precision.

Chase, a brilliant billionaire with many patents and inventions to his credit, just wanted Tu to have a normal childhood. He looked over at Wen, the woman he shared everything with. The two of them had rescued Tu from a Chinese facility where the boy had been held since birth. Her eyes told him she was thinking the same thing.

Chase and Wen had been living as fugitives, pursued across the globe by numerous enemies. Their dangerous lifestyle grew more complicated after suddenly finding themselves as parents once they'd snatched Tu from his communist captors. Wen, a former Chinese spy, had escaped the same corrupt and brutal government that had "created" Tu. For a while, she had successfully disappeared, having secretly erased her existence, and was free—or was at least some form of that undervalued and overused word.

Now the MSS was hunting all three of them.

They'd safely hidden Tu in America with Wen's grandmother. US officials had no idea the boy was there, but the Chinese knew, and they would not stop looking for Tu. Ever.

"I've lost track of how many people are after us," Chase told Wen that morning, each knowing he hadn't. Yet, it wasn't the MSS who worried him most. The ones who kept them both up at night, the ones they could not seem to evade, was a cabal known only as "the shadow people." The clandestine group had been pursuing them for years, and somehow always seemed to be able to locate them. During all that time, Chase and Wen hadn't been able to discover who was chasing them, or why they wanted them dead.

"Chase," Wen said, pulling him out of his worrying. She pointed at Tu, and gave him a look as if to say, "*Make our little boy smile.*" Suddenly, nothing seemed as important. They'd brought Tu to a carnival to celebrate his eighth birthday, hoping to help him find a piece of lost childhood magic. Chase looked around, deciding which ride to suggest while remaining always vigilant, looking for threats. Wen never took her eyes off "the field," as she called it, seeing the world as one infinite battlefield.

They were practiced at moving without detection, with a long protocol of precautions when traveling—non-traceable burner phones, decoys, and elaborate cyber tactics, as well as vIDs, a spray-on application Chase and The Astronaut had invented, used to defeat facial recognition systems. However, when Tu was with them, they also employed Sepio, an elite, private security force whose exorbitant fees matched their skill level, their clientele exclusively billionaires.

The three of them were anonymous, lost in the big carnival outside San Diego. Chase was determined to pack a chunk of childhood, which had been mostly denied to Tu up until that point, into the evening. With that in mind, the colorful lights, happy music and joyous shrieks, the constant hum of loud conversations, and the practiced pitches from the midway's hucksters all came into focus, and Chase welcomed it.

"What's that?" Tu asked, pointing to the Wave Swinger, a massive pillar of lights and murals supporting a tilting disc which resembled the garish ceiling of some futuristic cathedral. Suspended from the kaleidoscope of blinking colors were long chains, each ending in a seat carrying a single passenger who was being swung sixty feet above the ground at a dizzying angle and speed.

"I believe those are called the 'evil swings,'" Chase said, grimacing. He recalled making the mistake of getting on the ride as a twelve-year-old. "It's a vomit-inducing torture device."

Tu looked at him with the same expression he did whenever Chase was being sarcastic. "Why would they have something so horrible here?" he asked innocently. "I thought you said this was fun time."

Wen shot Chase a dirty look. "It is not called the evil swings. That is the Wave Swinger, and it's actually great fun."

Chase shook his head at Tu and pulled a finger across his throat as if to indicate it was a life-threatening proposition to get on. "Not this one," he insisted.

Wen scowled at Chase, quickly switching to a bright smile for Tu. "Which one do you like?" she asked Tu, while making eye contact with one of their security detail. The man indicated an all clear.

Wen tried to relax as she searched for any sign of trouble. She didn't *expect* any, as no one could have any idea where they were, yet she never trusted whatever illusion of safety they found themselves in, even as she attempted to have fun.

None of them knew that less than ninety feet from their precious boy, a clown with a gun was pushing toward them through the happy, excited crowd.

Chapter Two

Tu's face lit up as he gazed at the Ferris wheel, mesmerized by its colored lights and magical appearance which seemingly offered excitement and thrills. "That one looks beautiful!"

Chase thought the Ferris wheel was a good choice, but suggested they start with the merry-go-round. However, as soon as the vintage calliope music began and Chase saw Tu sitting on a lion, he realized that even though the boy had only just turned eight years old, his genetically modified adult mind wasn't going to enjoy such a boring ride.

"Why do people like to just go in circles?" Tu asked as they were getting off. "It does not seem a very good use of time."

"You'll like the Ferris wheel better," Wen said.

Chase was about to say something about it being the same thing except turned on its side, when Tu looked up with bright eyes and said, "I do like to go high."

Looking at the other children around them, Chase

suggested getting some cotton candy, which Tu had never had.

"It's sweet," he said, smiling. "Feels funny in my mouth."

The line to the Ferris wheel moved quickly, and soon they were secured in their seat, three across. For a moment, the look on Tu's face was like that of a normal boy. They slowly climbed, taking in the view as the carnival sprawled out below them with its crowds and varied noises.

Tu pointed to the sky ride. "Can we do that next? I'd like to float over the whole park."

"Sure," Chase said, enjoying Tu's excitement.

"Look, you can see the ocean from here," Tu said, as they reached the top. "I like this ride very much."

But Wen wasn't looking out toward the Pacific. She had seen something down below that concerned her, two men that seemed out of place. Although dressed casually—to most people the pair would've appeared as two guys out to enjoy the carnival—Wen could tell by the way they walked they were not interested in the rides, the Midway games, or the junk food. They were looking for someone.

As the Ferris wheel came around lower, she got a better look. They were definitely carrying concealed guns. One had a slip holster inside his pants, the other a shoulder holster hidden under his light parka. As their gondola passed the entry gate, completing their first rotation, the suspect closest made eye contact with her, and moved toward the Ferris wheel.

Wen tapped Chase on the shoulder and motioned with her eyes back to the ground. "Blue parka," she said casually, as if it were nothing, but he never would've picked the man from the crowd without her description.

"Blue parka?" Tu asked.

"I asked Chase if he brought his blue parka."

Tu was normally excellent at detecting lies. However, Wen had been trained to not only beat polygraph machines, but also the world's best interrogators. Tu let the comment go.

A second later, their gondola reached the top of the wheel's arc, and the ride abruptly ground to a halt. Wen tried to look down to see if blue parka had stopped it, or if the operator was giving them the obligatory thrill moment of letting them take in the view. Taking advantage to scour the area, Wen spotted two more figures approaching the Ferris wheel with an out of place determination.

Tu, unknowing, kept shifting in the seat, smiling, trying to take in as much of the whirling lights, streams of laughing people, and saturated rainbows of the carnival. It amused Chase, listening as Tu tried to hum the mix of multiple musical medleys which blended into a cartoonish chorus high above the flashy scene.

"I'm getting out," Wen said, slipping under the safety bar.

"What?" Tu asked, alarmed. "We're at the top!" He looked down, studied the wheel, and said to Chase, "We're approximately twenty meters above the ground. Since you're metrically challenged, that means around sixty feet. If she falls, gravity will pull down on her mass, and there isn't enough air resistance to push back in twenty meters, but enough to kill her. Terminal velocity . . . Wen is small and light . . . yet gravity accelerates all objects at the same rate, regardless of mass . . . I do not want her to fall."

"She'll be okay," Chase assured him.

Tu looked down nervously. "Is someone after us again?"

Chase glanced down at Wen, then back to the innocent face of a scared little boy, a boy who had almost been killed during their escape from China, a boy who had learned fast that the world was nothing like the sheltered existence of the protected "lab" he'd grown up in prior to meeting Chase and Wen. Chase wanted to pretend nothing bad was happening, that they were safe no matter what, but Tu deserved more than that.

"Yes. The killers have returned."

Chapter Three

Wen, trained to climb radio towers, high scaffolding, tall buildings, and cliffs, initially had no problem rapidly descending toward the ground. Then the giant wheel began turning again. Suspended above the oblivious crowds, Wen slid from the glowing rim of the Ferris wheel in towards its axis.

She hoped the pursuers were MSS, believing their orders would be to take the boy alive, but these men didn't *look* like MSS. That meant they were shadow people, the ruthless and mysterious outfit who'd been relentlessly tracking them. As often as they'd barely escaped with their lives from the shadow people, Chase and Wen still had no idea *why* the lethal group wanted them dead.

By the time she made it to the center of the wheel, Wen found herself upside down. She was unfazed though, her only concern that Chase and Tu wouldn't reach the ground before she did. After a sliding back roll put her right again, and in an effort to reach blue parka before he got to Chase and Tu, Wen made a dangerous leap through the crisscrossing steel supports. Falling the final fifteen feet, she managed to twist and land upright while Chase and Tu's gondola was still third from the bottom.

Obviously trained in martial arts, blue parka, a clown, and two other men attacked. *I guess they've decided guns would attract too much attention*, Wen thought, filing that clue away in her brain. *Maybe they believe four against one gives them enough advantage.* She moved rapidly toward them. *Apparently they haven't read my file.* Wen sprang into the air. *Four to one—I like those odds.*

She dropped the first two in seconds. During the sudden mayhem, the clown and blue parka fled. Seeing Chase and Tu get off the ride safely, Wen dashed after the men.

Why are they running? she wondered. *Leading me into a trap? Isolating me from Chase and Tu? Where is our security team?* Whenever they had Tu with them, Chase and Wen traveled with four trained officers. *What is going on?*

Then she spotted one of their detail, Brenda—tall, ex-military police, fierce, smart. She intercepted another shadow person, this one wearing a green jacket. Wen kept an eye on the confrontation as she followed the clown. It was too late when she saw the knife. Green jacket stabbed Brenda twice before she snapped his neck. A crowd gathered quickly around them as the two collapsed. Wen knew help would be on the way, but feared it would be too late for the woman she barely knew. The music seemed intensely garish as she continued to run.

Where are the others?

The clown dove into the crowd, crashing into a chubby boy, sending him into a trash can amidst an explosion of popcorn. Wen jumped over the kid, keeping the clown in her sights as he headed toward the Tilt-A-Whirl. The adjoining attractions, gates, and lines for food trailers left the clown no choice but to go across the quintessential carnival ride's seven free-spinning cars, each packed with screaming riders, revolving around the rotating platform as it raised and lowered. The clown, trying to anticipate the shifting floor, caught a glancing blow from an apple-red car as it blazed past. His purple hair askew, the clown stumbled, but caught himself just before a royal-blue car slammed against his back. He spun around, looking as if he'd been assaulted by a cartoon gone wild. Managing to avoid another blow, he leaped over the guardrail and disappeared.

Wen barely escaped a similar fate, but got through unscathed. The clown's celebration was short-lived, however, as he landed in a bumper-car corral. Sliding across the graphite-layered metal floor, he was once again dodging brightly-colored cars—these equipped with gas pedals and driven by sugar crazed teens.

Wen closed in on the clown as blue parka entered the car corral, attempting to stop her. He wove through the maze of thick rubber bumpers coming at him from every direction, their long contact poles scraping the electrified ceiling. Arcing sparks cascaded above, wisps of smoke carrying the smell of ozone.

Hemmed in by a jam up, the clown jumped on a hood, and ran along the tops of the little dodgem cars, stepping on protesting kids as he went. He nearly cracked a young girl's head as he tripped over a purple car, trying to avoid grabbing the pole carrying the current down. The booming music drowned out her screams.

A park attendant joined the pursuit, trying to prevent blue parka and the clown from disrupting the rides. *That's an unwelcome development,* Wen thought. *Next the police will be here.* She needed to get to the men before the officials did.

Why aren't they using weapons? After everything they've done to get to us in the past, it seems unlikely shadow people would suddenly be concerned about killing innocent bystanders.

Yet that was the precise reason Wen had chosen *not* to use her Glock. There were just too many people, the majority of them children.

Shadow people have always tried to kill us in the past. Why would they change tactics?

Do they really think they can take us alive?

Maybe these aren't shadow people...

Maybe it's about Tu...

There were too many questions without answers, and that bothered her far beyond the immediate threat. She could handle the physical aspect—stopping, restraining, killing, *that* was easy to control. Understanding the *psychological* motives behind their pursuers was more difficult. More *urgent.*

The cars suddenly and simultaneously halted. The colored lights fizzled off, and the ride's music went silent, replaced by a chaotic chorus of screams. Wen followed the terror stricken faces and saw blue parka's smoking body fall from the fence surrounding the corral. He'd touched the ceiling and the metal chain link at the same time, completing the circuit, the amps sufficient to stop his heart. His lifeless body hit the polished floor next to a terrified boy in a yellow car.

Wen lifted her eyes from the horror and saw the only person still moving among the grotesque scene as the clown escaped out the other side.

Chapter Four

The gridlock of smash-em cars made it difficult to move. Wen's leg momentarily got stuck between the bumpers of two blue cars driven by red-haired pre-teens, presumably siblings. Her delay allowed the clown to slip into the thick crowds lined up for other rides, their bodies forming natural barriers. Wen followed through the concourse and into the midway, with its games and hawkers.

A few more steps and I'll have him.

She'd closed to within ten feet when he disappeared between two tents. She scoured the area, but he was gone. Experience told Wen not to waste time checking in the tents, believing he wouldn't risk isolating himself in there. Nothing but a trap could be inside. Neither scenario seemed particularly appealing or likely, so she reverted to muscle memory, and went where she would go if it were *her* being hunted.

A moment later, rising from behind two trailer rigs containing large generators for the sky ride Tu had so badly wanted to go on, Wen saw the Ferris wheel, and wondered where Chase and Tu were.

What if there are more shadow people around? Chase can handle himself in most situations, but...

Something bothered her. The normally highly-trained shadow people suddenly seemed much less effective. Something had happened that had made them change their tactics, and she needed to know what that something was.

Trusting that Chase had moved Tu to safety, and counting on the growing darkness of late evening to ease their escape, Wen scanned the area again. Those same conditions would make it more difficult to find the clown.

In the brightly colored lights of the surrounding rides and blinking signs, Wen spotted the man boarding the sky ride. Knowing she'd already be three gondolas behind him, and having done enough high wire acts for the day, she gambled that the clown wouldn't risk getting off mid-ride if he didn't see her.

Careful to stay out of his line of sight, she ran toward where the ride ended on the other side of the carnival, working her way through the lines for the more popular attractions. She passed one called the "Top Gun," a dual-armed Kamikaze ride that appeared to use centrifugal force to propel two long curved cages, filled with passengers, high into the air, then inverting them, before plunging back down to immediately repeat the process.

By the time she reached the receiving platform of the sky ride, the clown was four gondolas away. She waited, Glock in hand. Unfortunately, the open section offered no hiding places, and he quickly spotted her. Still, there was nowhere for him to go, and barring him winning a shootout—not a likely scenario—the clown was trapped.

He jumped so fast, flying from the sky ride gondola in a

blur, Wen had no time to shoot. Forcing herself past the ticket-taker, she saw he had landed on one of the Top Gun's cages. With no time to get back to the ground, she'd lose him unless she repeated his stunt.

So much for no more high wire acts, she thought. Then, muttering one of her favorite mantras, "Hesitation kills," she jumped.

Wen landed on the other cage as the two independent arms swung them in opposite directions. She clung to the wiry mesh as the riders inside screamed. It took all her strength to hold on against the G forces, feeling as if she were on top of a five thousand pound pendulum that was swinging out of control. She counted, trying to get the rhythm of the ride, knowing as soon as it slowed near the ground, the clown would drop off.

She glanced up at the fixed tower and wished there was time to climb over it to reach the other side. It would be a tough move, but she could make it.

It's a long way down...

Surviving the forty foot fall wasn't a concern. Death ended the game, but her training had taught her to ignore that factor and just keep playing to win.

No time for fear.

Wen needed both hands to stay on the metal grid and couldn't get to her gun. Getting an accurate shot would've been impossible anyway. She'd *have* to jump the next time around.

Three more seconds . . . two . . . one . . . now!

Wen flew through the air, but her timing was off. She caught the edge of his sleeve, landing backwards on his cage. Twisting, she used the momentum of the ride's downward plunge to rocket herself up. Her move stunned the man, yet he recovered quickly, slamming his fist onto her hands as she clutched at the metal caging. Wen, anticipating his strike, swung her feet up, kicking him hard. She didn't want to knock him off, though. She needed him alive.

"Who sent you?" she shouted above the fluctuating carnival cacophony and the deafening buzzing of the Top Gun.

"Get off!" He pounded at her hand again.

She came back with another round of kicks, managing to move her sore hand down somewhat out of his range without slipping off. The ride, still in full swing, rotated fast. Its operators didn't seem to know what was going on atop the spinning cages.

Wen got to his neck. "You're going to tell me who sent you!"

His arms slipped and he fell backwards. She tried to hold on to him, tried to grab for his legs, but the force of all the opposing directions was too much.

The clown went down headfirst. There was no scream, just an ugly, broken, body on the muddy ground, a red nose ball, and purple wig sitting in pooling blood.

Chapter Five

When Brian Elliott lost his job with the insurance company, the only reason they'd given him was a reference to an obscure rating agency.

"Your score no longer qualifies you for this position."

Brian had been with them for six years and never missed a day. His supervisor had always given him glowing reviews. The thirty-something pot-bellied baseball fan sometimes appeared puzzled, especially when deciding which candy bar to choose from the vending machine, but this time, he left the office sincerely and extremely mystified. On his commute, he stopped for a twelve pack of beer. Once home, he called his best friend, Steve, to tell him the news.

Instead of the dial tone, a brief but loud siren wailed in his ear, followed by an announcement telling him that Steve Kornbluth was not a trustworthy person, and it was not wise to deal with him. Brian thought it was a joke, so he tried again. This time, the call went through. Brian told Steve about the message.

"I don't know what's going on," Steve said. "I lost my

job today, got evicted, and the banks cancelled my credit cards."

"I got fired, too," Brian said. "They told me something about how my 'score' no longer qualifies me."

"You're kidding. I got the same spiel. What score?"

"I don't know. Do you think they'll cancel *my* cards?"

Steve checked his emails and found one from the airline. "What is *this*!?"

"What?"

"The airline says I can no longer fly?"

"Like you're on a no-fly list?"

"No, they say my HaPPI Score is too low."

"What's a 'Happy score'?"

"Beats me. It's an acronym." Steve spelled out HaPPI. "This is so screwed up..."

"Can this be real?"

"Yeah it's freakin *real*! My life is a mess in one day."

"Do you think our firings are related?"

"Seems like it. They both mentioned our scores. Damn, wait until my wife finds out."

"Isn't she almost done with nursing school?"

"Yeah, a few more weeks. At least she'll start earning money."

"At least there's that, but we have to find out *why* this is happening."

"I think I know why..."

"What?" Brian asked.

"Hold on, Keri's texting me . . . oh, man, you won't believe this . . . she just got kicked out of nursing school."

"What. The. *Hell*. Is. Going. On?"

Mumford Grimes loved the yacht. If he couldn't live on an island, he'd want to live on a yacht—just a little *bigger* than this one. Fancy boats, first class flights, and unlimited expense money were just some of the perks of his job—which is what he called it, but really it was an *adventure*. Grimes preferred adventure to work, beaches to traffic, tropical air to air conditioning.

However, his current assignment, which was now creeping into its twenty-third month, had been unlike anything that had come before, and came with such lavish perks because the targets were a billionaire and an ex-Chinese agent. And not just *any* agent, but the best he'd ever seen—and he'd seen plenty. Grimes had a past that included all the biggest news stories that had never made the news. He was the guy they went to when all else failed, when it was do or die—and he *did* it.

Now he was part of a group that the billionaire and the spy called 'the shadow people', and his targets had so far managed to elude him and his associates for twenty-three months.

"They're not easy to find," he told his contact, a man called Belfort. Yet the people Belfort represented had somehow located Chase Malone more than fourteen times. On each occasion, and against all odds, he and the Chinese woman had slipped through their fingers, usually leaving one or more of Grimes' cohorts dead.

"The cartel is growing impatient with you," Belfort said.

Grimes squinted his gray eyes, looking through binoculars at the Oregon coast. He wanted to say this time would be different, but knew the danger of those loaded words. "None of your other operatives have fared any better."

"That sounds like an excuse."

"No, it doesn't," Grimes said, as he was known to never give excuses, only results.

"Do you recall when we hired you?" Belfort asked. "We offered twice your normal fee, you asked for triple."

"Yes." He scratched at the stubble of a week old mustache, a nagging reminder to keep his act clean.

"And I explained the *special* circumstances."

"Ye-es," Grimes said hesitantly, because Belfort had actually been extremely vague on that initial contact. "We know a lot more now."

"Yes we do. About the targets, and about you."

"If you no longer require my services . . . "

"Don't be silly. You know that's not an option."

And Grimes did know that. Very well. He'd stayed on the never-ending case because if he quit, he would be their next target.

Chapter Six

Wen spotted Chase and Tu, jumping off the Top Gun cage on the next pass. Police were closing in around the carnival and would no doubt be swarming the clown's corpse any minute.

Wen got to his body before anybody else did, *finding no pulse.* They'd been forty feet high when he'd gone off head first. *Did he slip?* she asked herself. *Or did he jump? It seemed more like he let go intentionally… a suicide rather than getting caught.* Wen moved his head, pulled off the clown nose, and snapped a fast photo. *His neck is broken… Dead men tell no tales.*

People were coming. "What happened?" someone yelled.

"He fell from the ride," Wen answered without looking up, adding, "It's okay, I'm an EMT." She checked for identification, but found none. She quickly pressed three of his fingers onto her phone and tapped the button on a special app Chase had developed to capture fingerprints. Men like this usually had history. Maybe they would get lucky.

"Is he dead?" another person shouted from the small crowd, now circling around her.

"Yes," she said. She could hear the crackling chatter of the police radios on the approaching officers.

I've got to get out of here.

With the number of bystanders growing, Wen made her move, standing up and slipping into the crowd. While instantly assessing the safest and quickest way out through the tangle of lines and gates, she noticed a woman taking in the scene differently than the other spectators. There was pain in her face, not of personal loss from the clown's death, but rather of professional disappointment that their job had been blown, four men dead. Wen knew the look of a pro at a mission gone wrong. She belonged with the shadow people.

She would've liked to question the woman, but police were filling the area. The woman, realizing Wen had seen her, instantly melted into the swarming crowd. Wen pursued, ready to take a photo with her phone, knowing she would only get one chance, and only if luck was with her. She advanced, pushing through the crowd. When people saw her rushing through, they jumped out of her way.

The woman sprang onto a vendor cart, then onto the roof of a food truck—the same one she had bought the cotton candy from for Tu earlier. The woman looked back and Wen snapped a photo. It felt like catching a picture of lightning, the next frame bringing darkness, and in that split second the woman jumped off the truck's roof and vanished. By the time Wen got to the other side, there was no trace of her in the sea of people, but now she had a face for the woman, and the fingerprints of the clown.

She caught up to Chase and Tu in the parking lot. "Security?" she asked, wondering if any of their team had made it.

He shook his head.

"Are you *sure*?"

"Yeah," he said shortly, not wanting to upset Tu. "We can't wait."

"You okay?" Tu asked Wen, obvious relief on his face and concern in his eyes.

"I barely slipped out before the cops started rounding up everyone for questioning," Wen answered honestly, knowing it was better to be as truthful as possible with the boy genius. "Are you okay?"

"Yes, but I wanted to go on the sky ride."

"I know," she said, touching his face like a loving mother. "Another time."

"Shadow people?" Tu asked, once they were all in their car.

"I think so, but . . . "

"What?" Tu asked.

"They didn't *act* like shadow people," Chase said as he pushed the ignition button.

"Meaning they did not try to kill you?" Tu asked from the back seat.

Chase and Wen exchanged a parental glance. Obviously Tu was a very unusual boy, but they still couldn't get used to speaking with him about violence—especially when it was aimed at them.

Neither replied while Chase navigated traffic and Wen searched for more shadow people.

"Perhaps they changed tactics," Tu began, as if their silence had been due to something else. "It is possible shadow people had a different mission this time. Maybe to get me."

"That would mean they're working with the MSS," Chase said, momentarily forgetting Tu was eight years old.

"No," Tu said. "Could be they discovered my secret." They always referred to the genetic engineering that had created Tu's super intelligence as his "secret."

"I hope not," Wen said, reaching behind her for Tu's hand. He took hers and they shared a quick squeeze. She silently tried to understand how that could have happened as she considered the ramifications of such an occurrence, and hurried to transmit the photos and prints.

"I've just sent everything to The Astronaut," she said, referring to Nash Graham—a math savant widely sought out by the world's intelligence agencies, including the CIA, NSA, MSS, Russian SVR, and others. He possessed a computer-like intelligence, and, like them, lived as a fugitive.

But, unlike Chase and Wen, Nash Graham *knew* who was after him.

Chapter Seven

During the drive back to the secret compound where Tu and Wen's grandmother were staying, Boone, Chase's only sibling, called. He spoke cryptically of a problem that couldn't be discussed on the phone, so Chase arranged a morning flight. Chase's older brother had given him his first job in high school, climbing skyscrapers for his window washing business. The crazy vocation provided the brainy billionaire with an early taste of adventure. After their father died, the two already close brothers had grown even closer.

Although Chase was distracted by what trouble Boone could be facing, after Tu was tucked in bed and asleep, he and Wen continued to explore possibilities for why the shadow people hadn't just killed them. The mystery deepened after they confirmed that all four of their security team's members had been killed at the carnival. Their tragic loss brought more urgency to the quest to learn who the shadow people were.

"Why can't you stay?" Tu asked the following morning as Chase and Wen were getting ready to leave.

"We've been through this," Chase told him warmly. "It's safer if we're not here. I've tripled the security team. You'll be safe, and we'll be back to check on you in a few days."

"You know we'll have fun," Zǔ mǔ, Wen's grandmother, told Tu in Mandarin.

"This is not fair. I should go with you," Tu said, hugging Wen. He knew the rules, and accepted them with a kind of sweet dignity, yet they could easily see the deep pain and worry in the boy's eyes.

The private plane, leased by one of Chase's shell corporations, flew them to the Crescent City, California airport, about twenty miles south of Brookings, Oregon. Forty-five minutes later, they arrived at Boone's vacation home, perched on a high cliff just north of Whaleshead Beach, situated between the coastal towns of Brookings and Gold Beach. Boone, a successful businessman, had made his multi-million-dollar fortune in west coast building maintenance—specifically in the window washing of Bay Area skyscrapers. Chase recalled his time of climbing high rises and the other daredevil jobs he and Boone had done together, dangerous work their parents never would have condoned.

"Beautiful view," Wen said, staring out over the Pacific as if searching for her homeland on the other side of the vast ocean.

"Thanks," Boone said, handing her a bubbly water

infused with fresh lemons and limes. He had recently purchased the luxurious getaway as an escape from the pressures of San Francisco. At Chase's insistence, Boone had structured the ownership so it could not be traced to him, since Chase's family had become targets of some of his enemies.

They sat on plush chairs arranged in an arc near the windows so the ocean dominated the view, yet they could still see each other. Chase filled his brother in on the carnival scare.

"Is Tu okay?" Boone asked.

Chase nodded. "Tough kid."

"I'm sorry to drag you away from him after such a horrible experience," Boone said, "but this may all be connected."

"What?" Wen asked, trying not to sound impatient.

"I've lost a series of contracts lately. I mean a *lot* of them."

"For your cleaning company?" Wen asked.

"Yeah. The losses are starting to jeopardize my business."

"I'm sorry about that," Wen said. "But how does it involve us?"

"I did a lot of digging into the clients who stopped using me. Some are corporate clients, others are municipalities," Boone said. A slight breeze tousled the curly brown locks that fell thickly around his boyish face. "It turns out all of them have been using a special service—something called HaPPI Score."

"What's a HaPPI Score?" Chase asked.

"It's an acronym for Historical and Predictive Profile Indicator. It's a risk assessment algorithm that does a lot of other things, but they know everything about me and my company. I'm told that HaPPI knows so much, they can almost predict what I'm going to do in the future."

"Sounds like SEER," Chase said, referring to Balance Engineering's secret Search Entire Existence Result advanced photonic quantum information processing, deep learning, AI, quantum algorithm system that Chase had developed, and that his business partner, Desmond "Dez" Jefferson, operated.

"Sounds like the Chinese social credit system," Wen said.

"Tell me about that," Boone said. "I've already had to lay-off a lot of good workers. People who are more than employees, they're friends."

"The Chinese Communist Party calls it a 'national reputation system.' Individuals and businesses are tracked and reviewed, and a trustworthiness score is determined. It involves everything. Even a small infraction, like playing too many video games or failing to sort recycling properly, can result in big penalties. Smoking in a non-smoking zone, not showing up for dinner reservations, being overweight, spending too much . . . it goes on and on. They watch *every* aspect of their citizens' lives."

"It sounds like what I've heard about HaPPI," Boone said. "But HaPPI is secret."

"Where'd you get your information?" Wen asked.

"I hired Flint's firm."

Chase nodded. Flint had been an ex-CIA officer who, before being killed, had become Chase's head of security.

"What if the Chinese are connected to this?" Chase said.

Wen was already worrying about the same thing. She hadn't touched the refreshing drink Boone had offered her, and even though Chase didn't show it, he worried about her. Wen barely ate, existing on adrenaline, and when they weren't being chased, she looked drained.

Chase raised his glass and eyebrows at Wen to take a sip.

"They're fresh lemons from my tree out back," Boone offered.

"What risk do *you* pose to anyone?" Chase asked, knowing his brother treated his employees like family, spent many hours each week doing charity work, and was incapable of hurting anyone.

"Apparently," Boone said, looking directly at Chase, "the biggest risk factor in my profile is my affiliation with you."

Chapter Eight

Boone had to rush back to San Francisco to try to salvage a long-time customer from pulling their business. "Now it's not just new contracts," Boone muttered as he left. "*Un*HaPPi would be a more fitting name for this nightmare."

"We'll put The Astronaut on it," Chase said. The term "Astronaut" had been coined to describe a small group of high performing savants used by the world's governments for covert purposes. Their Astronaut, Nash Graham, was perhaps the most impressive of them all.

Chase worried about Boone. He'd always said his big brother was the nicest guy in the world. Their mother had leaned heavily on Boone since their father had been murdered, and it infuriated him when his enemies went after his family.

"Boone is a sweetie," Wen said, as if knowing his thoughts. "And he's also strong."

"But he may lose his company. He doesn't deserve this."

"I know, but we're on it now."

After checking in with Zǔ mǔ and Tu, Chase and Wen decided to stay at the beach house until the following day. They kept a stash of postcards with them, and put one in Boone's mailbox to send off to Tu. It took The Astronaut only a few hours to report his initial findings, his brooding face and deep-set eyes appearing on Wen's tablet. She recalled when they'd first met in Edmonton, Canada. He'd explained that his brain was wired differently than normal people's. That was before she and Chase had found Tu, a boy not unlike The Astronaut, although Tu's "wiring" had been tampered with.

Both of them could tell the day of the week on any date for the past two thousand years, and had a magical ability with numbers. The Astronaut knew the number Pi carried out to nearly a million digits by memory. Tu, however, couldn't do that, or answer 'twenty-six to the eighth power,' as The Astronaut had done at their initial meeting, just before he'd saved her life for the first time.

"Two hundred eight billion, eight hundred twenty-seven million, sixty-four thousand, five-hundred and seventy-six," he'd said instantly, explaining that his mind was constantly filled with digits and equations, and that they were all different colors—extraordinary colors. His tone had been almost desperate when he'd told Wen that if he didn't continually use the equations, push the mysteries to be solved—problems *needed* solutions, things *wanted* to be created—he would go to a place where the numbers stopped making sense. "A dark and random world where I would be lost . . . where I would go mad."

She looked at The Astronaut's face on the screen, his thick, silver hair a perfect example of being windblown and disheveled, yet amazingly neat. It framed a distinguished, close-cut mustache and beard, giving him a clean, yet rustic look. He was a series of planned contradictions, others accidental. The Astronaut, a man who had difficulty showing emotion, or even being touched, loved her completely.

"HaPPI, it turns out," The Astronaut began, "is a nasty little thing right out of Orwell's 1984, but is definitely real."

"A massive social credit system?" Chase asked.

"Yes, much in the same way that the internet is a big computer network."

"So more complicated?"

"Who's behind it?" Wen asked.

"It's owned by Bargo, a little-known tech company," The Astronaut replied.

"I'm not familiar with them," Chase said.

"Hence my comment, 'little-known tech company,'" The Astronaut repeated, annoyed. "Bargo is secretly and extensively obtaining every shred of data there is on everybody, and putting it into algorithms to assess an individual's risk of everything. Will they kill themselves? Will they kill someone else? Will they lose their job? Will they quit their job? Will they excel in their job? Are they drug addicts, or, might they become one? Do they have the potential to be depressed? Are they likely to get hooked on opioids, to steal, cheat, gain weight, get sick? Are they—"

"I get the idea," Chase said, praying The Astronaut would not continue to list off thousands of combinations of possible queries, something he was prone to do.

"Vote Democrat or Republican, or not at all? Likely to gamble? To commit a crime? Domestic abuse?" The Astronaut hissed like a cat impatient with regular humans who didn't understand the brilliance and intricacies of explanations and how important his point was.

"*Okay*," Chase said, rolling his eyes at Wen, hoping she could get the math savant to stop citing examples.

"Do they complain about the government? Did they complain about the pasta? Do they steal from their boss?"

"*Thanks*, I got it."

"Did they cheat on their time sheets? Expense reports? Exams? On and on and on . . . everything is factored into a nearly infinite artificial intelligence algorithm that builds a comprehensive and predictive behavioral profile."

"How are they getting all this data, and what are they doing with it?" Wen asked.

"Bargo keeps feeding HaPPI data from everywhere. They get a lot from illegal sources, substantial quantities from government agencies. There seems to be a loop of sorts."

"A loop?" Chase echoed.

"A pattern," The Astronaut responded, with perhaps his favorite word. He had a special talent for seeing patterns in everything, and claimed nothing existed without making a pattern or being part of a larger one. "Every answer can be found if one can discover the correct pattern," he often said, giddy with excitement, yet never outwardly revealing it. If you were in front of him while he talked, though, his eyes literally sparkled.

"What's it tell you?"

"There is somebody within the government that is utilizing this company illegally, and potentially also feeding them much of the data, making it accessible."

"Any idea who?" Wen asked.

"Yes, someone we all know quite well." He paused, as if giving them time to figure it out themselves. However, if they thought they knew who it was, neither voiced it. Chase had a fleeting thought, but was afraid to say it out loud. "No guesses?" The Astronaut continued. "I would have imagined that after everything, you would have no trouble identifying the villain in this plot."

"Who is it?" Chase demanded, convinced and bothered that he already knew.

"All of the evidence points to Tess Federgreen and CISS."

Chapter Nine

Tess Federgreen, head of the ultra-secret Corporate Intelligence Security Section—or CISS—had been both a savior and an adversary to Chase and Wen ever since Wen had first escaped China and the MSS. CISS, arguably the least known and most powerful clandestine agency in the world, had been formed as a joint operation of the CIA, NSA, and FBI, with an unusual mandate to prevent war between corporations.

After they finished with The Astronaut, Wen suggested they clear their minds by going for a hike on the narrow trail within the coastal forest.

"If Tess is behind HaPPI, then this can't be a coincidence that they've targeted Boone," Wen said as they walked.

The cliffs, hills, and occasionally exposed bluffs, combined with the lush vegetation along the southern Oregon coast, created an enchanted land filled with countless varieties of mushrooms, giant pine trees, and a thick green understory that seemed a Tolkien realm where one could imagine fairies thrived.

"Tess knows everything about us," Chase reasoned while they navigated a carpet of giant ferns. "She couldn't have *accidentally* gone after Boone. This is about me."

"To argue the other side, The Astronaut *did* say that HaPPI has done the same thing that it did to Boone to thousands of others."

"I'm sure that's true, but you know this is a set-up. Tess is trying to flush us out."

"Tess has always been able to find us," Wen said. The trail descended down toward the beach. "It doesn't make sense to go through all this trouble just to destroy his business."

"Well, it's working," Chase said. "She's got my attention."

"You know I'm no fan of Tess's, but what if it's *not* her? The Astronaut only said that all indications pointed to her."

"It's her."

"But it doesn't make sense."

"Nothing with Tess *ever* makes sense."

The winding trail snaked in and out of the densely wooded areas up to a cliff top, looming hundreds of feet above the surf.

"That's not true," Wen said as they stared out across the stunning view of giant rock monoliths, one with a tunnel through it. Waves crashed on the rocks as if shattering giant champagne bottles. "One thing about Tess, she only does things that make sense. She's one of the most calculating women I've ever known."

"Right . . . Well, she doesn't make sense to me. Of course, no women *really* makes sense to me."

"Let's see what The Astronaut comes up with."

"I'm not going to wait until he verifies it," Chase said. "I'm going to call her. Tell her to stop."

"And if she won't? Or denies it altogether?"

"I don't know," Chase admitted in a perplexed tone as they started walking again.

The path eventually dropped back down to the sand, revealing a secret entrance to a breathtaking beach. Chase and Wen cherished rare moments like these, absorbed in the beauty and tranquility of the private scene, lost from the world of killing, spies, assassins, and the latest crisis. Then, oddly, the peace of the moment brought Wen back to reality.

"It's been almost twenty-four hours since the carnival," she said, thinking of Tu. "The Astronaut has not found any new information. Even photos of the clown and the woman yielded nothing." A shell drew her hand down to the sand. Its odd shape and smooth, pearly interior reminded her of Tu, the little boy's simpleness wrapped in complications. She pocketed the treasure. Chase saw this and winked, then began his search for something, too.

"It wasn't like any other shadow people encounter," Chase said, stating what had been bothering them since the Ferris wheel.

"We have to figure out why."

"The clown's fingerprints are still the biggest mystery."

"Why he jumped is the bigger question," Wen said. "Details like that haunt me."

"Because he chose to jump rather than get captured?"

"It was not even a certainty that I was going to catch him. At least not that he knew."

"Who was he dying to protect?" Chase asked, finding a perfectly round, smooth rock filled with repeating lines. "What fate worse than death awaited him if he talked?" He showed the stone to Wen, who nodded in approval.

"And why do the fingerprints show up as 'restricted' in the government database? Even The Astronaut is unable to get past any of the different databases. What or who is protecting them?"

"Why don't we ask Tess?" Chase said.

"For all we know, that woman and the clown worked for her. I don't want her involved."

They walked silently through the warm sand for a minute. The late-October temperatures were only in the fifties, but on the sunny beach, it felt closer to seventy. A heavy mist, one might even call it fog, moved in erratically across the water.

"Looks like a bank coming off the ocean," Chase said. In Oregon, the coastal weather could change every few hundred feet. One cove could have sun and blue sky, the next could be in fog and clouds, others might even be in rain.

"Let's get back up to the high ground," Wen said, searching the tree line for any sign of trouble. "We should head back to the house."

Chase inhaled a deep breath of the moist sea air before pulling her into a tight hug and long, sensuous kiss. Their eyes met and held. The intense care and love they felt for each other was never forgotten amidst their crazy life of danger.

They left the beach hand in hand.

"I love the fog," Wen said as they climbed the trail,

emerging back into the sun. They went a different way out onto a jutting cliff that rose above a thundering cove. Walking to the edge, they paused to absorb the three hundred-sixty degree view before heading back into the trees.

That's when they saw the men following them.

Chapter Ten

Chase crouched as Wen moved behind a tree to conceal herself while she got a better look.

"Shadow people," she said.

"Have they spotted us?" Chase asked in a beleaguered tone, wondering if *anywhere* on the planet would ever be safe.

"They're following us. They know right where we are."

"Then why haven't they taken a shot?"

"Same as the carnival. They want something else." Wen checked her pack. She only had a Glock 19 and a hunting knife.

"I've got my multitool," Chase said in a helpful tone.

She looked at him, annoyed.

"No one knows where we are, and we were only going for a walk on the beach," Chase said defensively. "Tu *did* warn me to always carry a lightsaber."

She gave him a '*not-funny, why do you always joke when we're in danger?*' look. "It's never *just* a walk with us. And they never know where we are until they start shooting at us."

Chasing Risk

She knew Chase didn't like guns, but long ago she'd taught him not to go anywhere without a weapon. "The multi-tool doesn't count," she'd told him many times.

Wen led them half-walking, half-crouching down a gully that broke off from the trail, some of it well-worn, appearing to have been cut through to a lower switchback by lazy hikers.

"What else would they want other than to kill us?" Chase asked.

"This time we're going to find out," Wen said, taking out her pistol, checking that she had two backup high capacity thirty-three round magazines. She also had a ten-mag plus one in the gun. *Seventy-seven shots*, she thought as she accelerated their pace down the hill.

"Do we *really* want to be giving up the high ground?" Chase asked, panting. He rarely questioned her on such matters, yet Wen, the logistics and strategizing leader between them, had trained him on the importance of maintaining the high ground whenever possible.

"We're not playing defense," she said, tossing Chase her knife. "We're going offense. This time, we're going to catch one of the shadow people and end this once and for all."

"Do I really need *two* knives? I think the multi-tool is the big player here, thanks hon." He tossed the knife to her. She glared at him, then tossed it back. He caught it expertly, smiled winningly, sheepishly, and held it tight, knowing she was right.

After reaching a small clearing between the trees and an edgy part of the lower trail above the beach, Wen used a set of binoculars to scan the area. "There's a sniper, high powered rifle," she reported. "Reminds me of the set-up when we were backpacking in California and thought we were safe, thought we were alone in such a remote area, and yet the shadow people still found us. Remember that sniper waiting in the tree?"

"Of course," Chase said.

"Why do they send them?" she asked, a little too much anger in her voice. "Then I have to keep killing them."

Wen, a trained and talented assassin, despised killing—a paradox. Raised and made loyal to the Chinese Communist government, that she wanted to destroy, had been taught the ways of espionage and weapons. Peace and tranquility were not to be hers in this lifetime.

"Maybe they're going to kill us. Maybe it's not like the carnival, or maybe at the carnival they were just waiting until we were out of the crowds *before* they killed us," Chase said. "This doesn't have to be something different this time. It could be all about lining up the perfect moment to take us out."

Wen thought about that. She knew better than Chase how much was required to train, outfit, and transport assassins; to obtain the intelligence necessary to complete a mission against high valued targets such as them. Whoever the shadow people were, they were no small group. They were either a nation-state, some branch of a US intelligence agency, the Russians, or some other intel or terror network. Or, in direct correlation with Tess Federgreen's mission at CISS, they could be working at the behest of a billion-dollar multinational corporation. Wen could think of dozens of reasons why someone on that list would want them dead, but none of them were really good enough for all the trouble, time, and expense. The people who'd been sent were top professionals—it just so happened that, so far, Wen had been better. Yet, at some point, somebody was going to come along with superior skills. Wen often said, "On any given day, even the best can lose."

"And what do you think?" Wen asked as they circled back around off the trail, bushwhacking through the dense ferns, damp foliage, and exposed roots.

A large banana slug oozed under Chase's foot. "Well that's disgusting," he said. "I think that playing offense may not be such a good idea today. We don't know how many there are and how to find where they are." He walked into a giant spiderweb. "It's like being back in the South American jungle," he added, pulling the sticky silk from his face and hair.

"Running isn't a great idea either, for those very same reasons," she said.

"I think if we follow this ravine, it will take us right back up to the road. We can either hitch a ride, or stay in the tree line and jog back to Boone's place."

"You don't think they have somebody up there in a vehicle?" Wen asked. "I can tell you they're not going to just kill the two of us and then walk out of here. There's a vehicle somewhere."

"Let's chance the road."

"No. I want to know who the shadow people are. Don't you?"

"Of course, but I'm not willing to *die* to get that answer."

"Sooner or later, they're going to get us in a situation we can't get out of, and then we'll die without ever having tried. We can't stop them unless we *know*."

Chapter Eleven

Dag Kirrem, the boyish, forty-something CEO of Bargo, looked across his large desk to his two most trusted lieutenants—Executive Vice Presidents Marta LaMontange and Reggie Hansard. They were all in a celebratory mood. Bargo had just received another contract from a Fortune 50 company.

"We're growing into a monopoly," Reggie said. He was two years younger than Dag, yet the African-American felt at least a decade older, even though he didn't look it, only because Dag appeared perpetually twenty-nine.

Dag smiled. "We're already there," he said. "There's no one outside of China who has so much data, and the ability to take the aggregate and use it so many ways."

"We slice and dice and monetize," Reggie said, smiling for a moment before his expression turned sour. "But the media is going to get us sooner or later. With all the uproar about China's social credit system, they're starting to look at how such a thing might be possible in the United States."

"We're covered there," Dag said.

The two aides had heard his arguments before. In fact, considerable time had been devoted to that very topic at the last board meeting. It was not something Dag was blind to, nor was it something he was worried about. "HaPPI protects itself. And there's the committee."

Marta, the youngest in the room at thirty-six, sat quietly, her poker face revealing nothing, yet the body language of her lean, triathlete form and tight ponytail projected an intimidating aura of stinging judgment.

"I know," Reggie replied. "But the committee brings up its own problems."

The 'committee' had been formed specifically to handle scrutiny from the media, consumer groups, and politicians.

Dag waved them off. Even though he had some reservations, his confidence in what he'd created was absolute.

"The committee uses HaPPI, so, in principle, it's just as exposed," Reggie argued, his white teeth flashing.

"It'll never get that far," Marta said, finally speaking up. Both men knew that her long silences were not to be taken as weakness or uncertainty. Marta listened and surveyed like a lioness on the hunt, ready to attack and kill her prey. Both men respected her immensely. One of them even feared her. "We have so much data . . . on everyone . . . and everyone has a weakness . . . *anyone* can be convinced."

They all knew that the word 'convinced' meant 'destroyed', or at least *threatened* about being destroyed. There wasn't one without the other.

"Bargo now has the power to shatter anyone's credit rating, their social reputation, a person's *everything*," she added.

Reggie didn't really have any *moral* problems with that.

He just didn't want to get caught, didn't want his stock options in Bargo to become worthless, so he pushed, wanting to test the strength of the committee's abilities. "What happens if a politician, or a reporter digging deep into HaPPI, gets too close?"

"We tell them to stop, and if they don't, we take their credit, and incremental steps to make them feel our power," Marta said stoically, eyes penetrating through Reggie, making him feel naked.

"And if they keep coming?" Reggie asked.

Dag eyed him suspiciously.

"Just playing the devil's advocate, here," Reggie said defensively.

"We take their job," Marta said coolly.

"And if they *keep* coming?" Reggie asked, shooting Dag a sheepish smile.

Marta's gaze was like ice. "Then we take their marriage, their friendships, whatever."

"Whatever?" Reggie echoed.

"Whatever," Marta said firmly. "You know what that means. We do what we have to do."

Chase knew Wen was right. They had to face the shadow people every time they popped into their lives because with each encounter, their odds of survival diminished. "You know that I'd follow you into the fires of hell—and *have* many times," Chase said. "I think the fact they came after us when we had Tu at the carnival, and now *Boone's* been targeted . . . they've really spooked me." He gripped the multitool in his pocket.

"Yes, but think of this—the carnival showed us that the

shadow people now know about Tu. And that woman got away, so they probably have photos of Tu. Next time, they'll go after *him*. We have to do this *now*."

"Let's go," he said.

After forty feet, they backtracked in a wide sweep.

"Since they've lost us, they'll probably be tipped that we saw them," Wen said. "Meaning we've lost the element of surprise."

"Who cares," Chase said. "We wouldn't want it to be too easy."

"Remember the Shackelford trail in California? We did the same thing. The sniper thought he had us, even after seeing us break off the trail. And we still got him, because most snipers are good at long-distance shooting and not much else. The shadow people employ specialists."

As they came out of the thick undergrowth, Wen spotted one of the men.

"Still waiting for his shot."

"Where's the other one?" Chase asked,

"I don't know, but as soon as we get this one, we'll have his phone, and we might be able to find out. Feel like playing decoy?"

It had become a running joke between them. Chase would draw fire or move to distract Wen's target. Even though they laughed about it, both understood the serious stakes at play. He could see the pain it caused her. One day they would push their luck too far and he might not come back.

"If that's the plan," he said.

"Stay low for as long as you can. Once you get near that giant beech tree, make a move into the ferns, then back up. *Don't* go forward. The sniper will take the shot, but it'll take him half a second to get lined up. They don't like to waste bullets."

"You're going to get him in half a second?" Chase asked, concerned that couldn't possibly be enough time.

Her rare smile in these circumstances gave him confidence. "It won't take that long."

Chapter Twelve

Wen found the sniper not nearly as well concealed as he should have been. Professional, yes, but prepared to move with his targets.

Why are you still waiting here? Wen silently asked him as she approached, but she already knew the answer. There were definitely more. There would have to be at least four to cover the quadrant. The sections of fog would complicate their mission, and definitely made the situation more lethal for everyone involved.

There was no time to ask the question that invaded her every waking moment: *How do they keep finding us?*

Wen hit the sniper's legs before he heard anything, buckling his knees and bringing him down onto the verdant carpet of ferns.

In his practiced movements as he tried to fight back, Wen could tell he'd had extensive training, most likely military. Yet with her skill and having the element of surprise, it only took a couple of seconds to put his face into the dirt, giving him a mouthful of bark and pine needles. Holding her gun to his head, Wen pressed the full weight of her body into him, knowing he could easily throw her off, but he'd obviously decided she'd use the gun if he twitched a muscle the wrong way.

Finally, Wen hissed her desperate question. "Who sent you?"

He only grunted.

She shoved his head harder into the black soil and leaves, looking around for any of his friends. Seeing no immediate threats, she grabbed a handful of hair and yanked his head back.

"One more time. *Who. Sent. You.*"

Knowing his eyes were far enough out of the dirt that they would be darting wildly, searching for any advantage, Wen scanned around them for the same, trying to anticipate his actions.

"Talk!" She shoved his head down again.

His response came in German. "*Ich spreche kein Englisch, Schwein!*" He spit mulch.

She repeated the question in German. "*Wer hat dich geschickt?*"

He still refused to provide any information. She told him in German that he only had seconds to live.

"*Du auch!*"

His response translated to, "So do you!" The warning wasn't news to her. She knew that he was not alone, that somebody else would be coming. Maybe he was playing decoy.

She asked him again.

He repeated his refusal, laced with profanity, adding that he wished her to die in a violent rape.

Threats and insults meant nothing to her, but she needed the information. Wen pulled back on his long sleeve black T-shirt so forcefully it ripped around his neck. Simultaneously, she struck his head with the barrel of her Glock.

He jerked back, but she buried his face deeper into the damp dirt. His torn shirt revealed a tattoo of an insignia at the base of his neck. She memorized it in case there wasn't time to photograph it before the others found them.

Chase suddenly screamed her name. Without hesitation, she put a bullet into the German's head and spun around, aiming her gun where she knew the next person would be, because that's where *she* would've been. Training told her in a situation like this to fire without looking. However, Wen knew that families and children used these trails, and she'd rather die herself than shoot a child. The extra instant it would take to identify the assailant could mean that difference between life and death.

She pulled the German's body up as she dove down. The move brought with it the glint of another scope, the same one Chase had seen. Wen sent two shots toward it, the first to where the sniper was, the second to where he was going.

Dead.

She knew there were at least two more opponents out there, and that she shouldn't risk photographing the tattoo and searching the German, but she believed the other two snipers would lay in wait, since that was their advantage, their expertise. Coming out into the open had no upside for them, only risks. She took a quick photo, found no ID, left his rifle, but grabbed his Beretta 92FS 9mm semi-automatic pistol.

Chase, unwittingly still playing decoy, started coming toward her. She held up two fingers and pointed them in a fan motion around the trees, silently telling him it wasn't over.

Chapter Thirteen

As Wen moved toward Chase, she silently vowed to never again be without a full arsenal. It had been foolish to assume they were safe at the beach—or anywhere—especially after the carnival. Once she reached him, they both crouched in the foliage.

"Trade weapons," she whispered, handing him one of the pistols, knowing she was better with a knife, and Chase needed a gun to be lethal at all.

"Why?" he asked. "Do you want the multi tool?"

She looked at him as if the answer should be obvious.

"Yep, good call," he whispered back.

"The other two should be . . . there and there." She pointed ahead of them, having deduced that professional assassins, rather than hunting from behind, would be lying in wait, completely camouflaged. "It's also possible that after hearing the shots, they might have already fled in different directions."

"Let's go."

"Wait." Wen touched his arm. "If the snipers are still

out there and they get a shot, they aren't going to miss." She paused and stared through the forest, trying to see someone.

"Then let's get them first," Chase said.

Wen noticed several broad leaves moving in an unnatural way and immediately went lower, convinced she'd found the second sniper.

"You see one?" Chase whispered.

"Yes." The mist had cleared briefly as sun found its way through.

"The woods could be *full* of them," Chase said quietly, clearly frustrated.

"This is a serious operation," she said in a tone mirroring his. "Someone is paying these pros big money—a multi-million-dollar payday for the hit."

"Yeah, people don't risk their lives for minimum wage."

"Not in this business," she said, fighting back a nagging thought. "*Why* did the clown on the Top Gun sacrifice himself?"

"Do we really have time to go into that now?"

"Money can't answer that question. Only two things could produce a suicidal effect like that—fanatical devotion to a cause, or intense fear."

"How do either of those connect to you or me? Who would we scare that much?"

"I don't know." She looked back toward where the movement had been. "I need to go get that one. You work around the other way, up near that big-leafed tree. The sniper will be up there. You'll have to kill him before I get to mine, or else he'll shoot me."

"At least there's no pressure," he whispered, smiling.

She said "*I love you*" with her eyes, and quickly moved away.

Ninety seconds later, Wen determined that since the sniper had not broken concealment or killed her, at least for the moment, she was safe, even this close to his lair. She assumed the sniper was watching the trail, which was why she and Chase had stuck to the rough and moved perpendicular to it.

Time to meet death yet again, she thought to herself. The mournful echo in her head reverberated so loudly that, for an instant, she believed someone had actually uttered the words. The distraction brought a rare mistake—she moved too loudly and inadvertently announced her presence.

The sniper hadn't known where she was, but knew she'd be coming. The earlier shots had made him hyper-vigilant. Three rapid shots pierced through the patchy fog.

Only the rotting stump in front of her, in the process of being reclaimed by an active army of ants, saved her, the soft wood and remaining bark blowing apart with the first two shots.

Now able to estimate the sniper's exact location based on the shot's trajectory and the loudness of the report, she returned fire. Wen kept shooting until she heard him fall.

He had been low on the ground, not where she would've been. She almost always preferred the high ground. From his position, it was impossible to tell the contour of the forest floor through the lush greenery. She scanned the area swiftly and went to collect evidence, needing something to identify the man later.

It turned out to be a woman. Someone like her, trained to kill, out on a mission. It made her sad.

"Who sent you?" she whispered.

Someone moved in her peripheral vision. She couldn't

tell if it was Chase or another sniper. She would've pursued, except a steep canyon opened between her and the blur of movement. Absent the ability to fly, it would be impossible to get there in time, and attempting to cross would only expose her to their hunters. Instead, she finished checking her latest victim for identification or a phone. There were neither. She had been hoping for another tattoo, something tying these to a military unit, cult, something targetable, but there was nothing.

Wen snapped a picture of the woman's face—mid-thirties, crewcut, a familiar sight in her business, muscled, determined look, angry even in death. The weapons gave her nothing, but she took the woman's fingerprints anyway. She left the sniper's rifle behind—it wouldn't help her—but took the Beretta 92FS 9mm semi-automatic pistol.

Wen quickly backtracked the way she came, cautiously trying to decide if it was Chase or another sniper she'd seen. With each step, she became a little more reckless in her movements, convinced now that it had been the last sniper fleeing.

Three down, one to go.

The odds told the story. The sniper was smart to leave. If it had been Chase, and a sniper was still in the area, Chase, and maybe Wen, too, would already be dead.

A few minutes later she found her answer when she spotted Chase up ahead, moving toward her. He held up two fingers.

She shook her head as she held up one finger and made an X sign over her mouth, letting him know she'd gotten no information.

Chapter Fourteen

Bargo had already done "whatever it takes" to one person who had tried to pursue a wrongful dismissal case against the company. They'd decided to use him as an experiment, secretly turning his own social media profile against him and outing him as being gay and dating transgender people. A devout Christian, the man had suddenly found himself ostracized by his family, friends, and community. It absolutely wasn't true, everything had been planted and manipulated, but it *was* convincing.

"That was an unusual case," Marta said, clearly knowing where Reggie's thoughts were. "Disgruntled employee. We've taken steps. It won't happen again."

"But it *is* an example of what the committee will do to someone."

"We take it as far as we have to," Dag said. "The world's out of control."

"Social media, the Internet . . . technology has unleashed the demons of humanity. And we're the ones that are bringing that back in check," Marta said, her tone and inflection always making her words sound indisputable, facts set in stone. "Sure, there will be some innocent victims along the way, and I'm sorry about that, I really am. But we have the opportunity to stop crime, to level the playing field, maybe even end war."

Reggie wanted to say, 'Who are we to decide?' or 'Are we wise enough for such a role?' Instead, he simply nodded.

Marta wasn't convinced. She'd always thought Reggie too soft, usually skirting the mission. "We're not some evil, greedy corporation trying to dominate an industry," she said calmly, yet with daggers in her eyes, tired of having to explain, knowing Reggie would call her explanations 'justifying.'

"She's right," Dag chimed in. "We're trying to save the world here, folks. Anyway, if I was going to abuse the system, I would punish Red Sox fans. But I'm not going to, because they have almost as many rights as a Yankees fan."

"Yeah?" Reggie said in a lighter tone. "What about New England Patriots fans?"

"Well," Dag said, scowling as if the thought of them made him queasy, "they are a separate matter entirely, and the committee can do what they like with them. I can't stand here with a straight face and tell you the world wouldn't be better off with less Patriots fans."

He paused for a minute as if he'd just said something deadly serious, then kicked in a laugh with the timing of a practiced comedian. Even Reggie joined Marta in sharing Dag's infectious laugh.

"Seriously though, Reggie," Dag continued, "I get your concerns. We've got so many safeguards in place. However, we need to keep the train moving. There are going to be privacy advocates, fourth amendment people, and maybe even some Patriots fans, who will try to get in the way, thinking we're doing something wrong. But just because it's different, doesn't mean it's not right. Just because it's never been done before, doesn't mean it's not how we should do it going forward." He stood and paced in front of the windows, as he liked to do when pontificating. "The world never had seven and a half billion people connected with the Internet, full of conspiracy theories and plots, haves and have-nots, income inequality exploding . . . we need a new way to deal with that. HaPPI is the way. Bargo can handle it. We can't count on governments to do this. Politicians, as we know from our own data and research, are not the highest quality people in the database. We don't want to leave our future in their hands."

"But we *are* for-profit," Reggie said.

"It's the only way to keep the train moving ahead. Someone's gotta pay for all that coal, pay someone else to shovel it in. Layin' track is expensive work, don't you agree?"

"Seems our motives are good," Reggie said.

"*Seems?*" Marta asked.

"No, I mean, they *are* good," Reggie corrected. "Poor choice of words."

"Enough of this," Dag said, waving his arm dismissively. "I appreciate you keeping us honest, Reggie, but we've been through this. *We're* the good guys."

"But what happens when we're gone?"

Dag took a deep breath, trying to keep his patience. "Where are you going?"

"No, really. Twenty years from now, we'll all be rich and retired somewhere, hopefully with a good HaPPI score," Reggie said, smiling like a salesman pushing his luck. "And there will be other people sitting in these chairs, a new, *different* board . . . What are *they* going to do? Can we count on them to make the same decisions as us?"

"I think we can."

"Why?"

"I can't tell you why. The world will be different in twenty years. The HaPPI Scores will have changed society. It'll be a better place, and people will know that HaPPI might even be arbitrating a world government by then— that's entirely possible. The point is, those people, the ones you're referring to, who'll inherit our roles and responsibilities, will have an *easier* world to operate in. Everyone will have seen and know the results of HaPPI. Bargo will be revered, and our successors will be operating in a more tranquil world; one hopefully devoid of crime, where equality *really is* equal."

Reggie nodded. Dag was a persuasive man. When he spoke at all-hands closed-door corporate events, it was like listening to one of the greatest motivational speakers of all time—an inspired combination of Martin Luther King, Jr. and Steve Jobs. "Okay," Reggie said.

"Just remember we're in the dark ages right now," Marta added. "*These* are the difficult times. We have to weed out a lot of bad apples, and a lot of pain comes with that. It's regrettable. You know we go to great lengths to avoid damage, but there will be some. We'll make mistakes, but we have incredibly powerful tools to correct those mistakes. If we break it, we can fix it. Don't worry, Reggie, the committee knows what they're doing. They've been carefully chosen."

"Of course they have," Dag said, checking his phone. "This is not a vindictive board of Orwellian overlords seeking revenge and totalitarianism. This is good people doing hard work."

"I know," Reggie said, trying to appear relaxed. "And you've seen the most recent committee report?"

Dag squinted back at him, appearing annoyed for an instant before recovering. "Yes. Yes, I have."

"It could be dangerous."

"Reggie, will you *relax*," Marta said. "Changing the world is dangerous business."

Chapter Fifteen

As they jogged back to Boone's cottage, Wen kept her gun ready. "I want to get these prints and photos to The Astronaut as soon as possible," she said excitedly. "We may finally have something."

Chase, although also optimistic, recalled the prints they had gotten off the clown at the carnival. "We may get more restricted profiles."

"Having links to the US intelligence community makes sense for the shadow people," she said as they climbed over a fallen tree. "Who else could move in and out of our world so easily?"

Chase checked to make sure they were maintaining a safe distance from the trail. "Maybe we'll get lucky." He wanted to get back to Boone's quickly for a different reason than she did. Wen's warning about the shadow people going after Tu had him extremely worried.

Wen suddenly hit Chase's back and he knew immediately to get down. As they both fell into a defensive position among the leaves, she pointed.

"Over there, another sniper."

"So he didn't go up to the road," Chase muttered, wondering how many more shadow people could be waiting to strike.

"It's actually another woman," Wen corrected, recognizing how trained women carried themselves like sleek hunters. In the animal kingdom, she would've called them jaguars. "We've got to catch this one."

"It could be a trap," Chase said very quietly.

"Of course it's a trap. It's *all* one big trap. We've got to go in anyway. When someone is trapping you, it's the best time to fight them." Wen surveyed the upper reaches of the trees, searching for the slightest movement. "They believe they have the upper hand, that they've surprised you. That's why they're weaker, their false strength exposed. They'll take more chances."

"So they're really falling into *our* trap . . . the fools," Chase said sarcastically. "She's heading down the coast that way."

"Perfect. Can you scale down that cliff?"

He looked ahead at the cliff jutting out into the ocean. "Yeah, I think I can handle that," Chase replied casually, with the confidence of an experienced climber, which he was—skyscrapers, cliffs, towers, mountains. It was all about just getting to the top. The methods of *doing so* changed, but those challenges brought him out like fights did Wen. There was no dread in surmounting those heights. He could do any of them. "Do you think I can intercept her?"

"You'll be waiting for her on the beach, but I'll get her long before she reaches you."

"If not?"

"Then you're the failsafe."

"Better than being the decoy," Chase said.

She blew him a kiss and was off. A second later, she had become invisible in the undergrowth. Her camouflage abilities would've been legendary had her existence not been so secret.

Chase had to run fast if he was going to beat the sniper to the base of the cliff. From their vantage point, it had looked like an easy descent, but he knew looks could be very deceiving. Once he reached the cliff, what he thought were solid angles, footholds, and handholds in the rock, could instead be variations of color and yield nothing. The trail to the top of the cliff from where he'd left Wen was also more winding, with many hills. He cut through and straightened wherever he could, but sometimes those choices only slowed him more. Finally, he came to an edge of a cliff and was able to look over.

Chase was astonished to see the sniper below, moving at a steady jog. It would be close, but he could still beat her if he went down the cliff faster than he wanted, faster than was safe. Even more surprising was that he could also see Wen, and she was not nearly as close as he was.

He looked up and down the beach. *Where's the sniper heading? Why lead us to a beach where she'd have no advantage?* he wondered as he bolted up the trail as fast as he could. Breathlessly, he reached what he called "the point," an incredible monolith surrounded on three sides by turquoise surf.

Quickly surveying the area, Chase looked for any marks from previous climbers, finding none. Continuing his automatic reflex assessments of the most expedient way to descend, he decided he couldn't take the most desirable route, which would leave him too exposed to the sniper.

No sense getting shot off the cliff . . . it would be far easier just to fall off.

He dropped down the first twelve feet until he reached a loose, cracking shelf with scattered vegetation. From there, although it got a bit more dicey, he found a foothold and went down. While still on top of the cliff, he had mentally charted his course, as he had done so times before. Some climbs required more adapting along the way than others, and this one was turning out to be more challenging than it looked.

Due to the curve of the cliff as it narrowed below, he hadn't been able to see the wet rock face halfway down, covered by a curtain of thick foliage. This close to the ocean, he should've been expecting it. Fog now shrouded the area. Any weight put on the vines would easily separate them from the rock and send him into a free fall. Even sturdy-appearing trees were only clinging on to the rock face with shallow roots, and could not be trusted. The rocks were also dubious in places.

Chase continued to carefully ease down, but, needing to go faster, he reached for a small outcropping that didn't look quite solid enough, but there was nothing else to grab on to.

It shattered in his hand. His feet kicked against the rock face, hoping to find traction, his hands fighting for purchase on anything as they scraped down the loose, jagged cliff.

Chapter Sixteen

Chase dropped nearly ten feet, landing in a weak little pine tree, which held just long enough for him to grab onto another outcropping. *Close call*, he thought, looking down as his muscles strained, seeing how much farther he needed to go. A fall would be fatal, but with each foot closer to the ground, the risks would diminish.

He grabbed onto a viney branch to get him to the next hand hold. The spindly vine pulled away from the stone it had been clinging to for so many seasons, and he plunged more than twenty feet.

Crashing onto a narrow shelf, Chase absorbed the blow and kept moving. Working his way through a tight gap, he followed the contours of the wall as it sloped at a gentler rate. From there, he scrambled down a slight trail until he found the sheerest and wettest part of the cliff. He should've been exposed for the rest of his descent, but a patch of the same fog that was dampening the cliff also protected him from view.

He went lower fast, sliding, dropping, clinging, desperate

for a handhold, descending so rapidly that even if he'd found something to grab onto, his fingers would not have been strong enough to hold on. The cliff completely fell out from under him as he slid forty, then fifty feet more. The wall abruptly thickened in a seam just wide enough that his foot caught. His ankle felt as if it had exploded while his femur took such a jolt he thought it might snap. The excruciating pain screamed an injury, but there was no time to figure out how serious the damage was while he continued to move. Everything below the knee of his right leg alternated pin-prick numbness or pulsing torture. Slamming into the slab, which had just inflicted its toll, he rolled and grabbed the rock, but it wasn't enough.

He went over the edge.

While dangling in the air, flexing every muscle in his upper body, he held on, momentarily thinking he'd actually stopped the free fall. However, Chase had enough climbing experience to know he was in trouble. His strength drained, he couldn't pull himself back up, and there were only seconds left before his straining muscles released.

When his fingers sprang open, it was as if a pilot had pulled the ejection seat lever while the plane was upside down, sending Chase back into a dive.

At least the pause had slowed his descent, allowing him enough presence of mind that he managed to get hold of another seam and landed on something solid with his good leg. The impact brutalized his left knee, but he continued to reach out blindly, madly, breaking every climber's rule, clawing for anything as his body buckled. Finding some notch in the rock, he held. His shoulders, still suffering from the last impact, somehow absorbed the shock.

Chase gasped for air as if coming up from the depths of the ocean with faulty scuba gear. He hadn't realized he'd stopped breathing somewhere up above. He gulped oxygen. Using every ounce of concentration to maintain his grip, Chase steadied his breathing.

Finally able to look around, grateful to be enveloped in fog, he felt like he'd just been dropped from a plane into a storm cloud roiling with thunder, exploding with lightning. Now low enough to know he'd survive the drop to the ground below, Chase was gripping the slick rock, picking a fast, safe route to the sand, when he heard the female sniper utter three terrifying words.

"I see you."

Chapter Seventeen

Chase frantically attempted to peer through the mist, but he couldn't find the sniper. *How can she see me, but I can't see her?*

He'd *heard* her. She was close. Close enough that she wouldn't need a sniper's rifle or scope to shoot him off the cliff. He knew her bullet would surely come any second.

Why hasn't she shot me yet? Will Wen hear the shot?

He looked back up the long way he'd come.

I must have been exposed during the slide.

Realizing that if she hadn't said something, he wouldn't have known she'd spotted him, Chase didn't want to waste his best last chance.

I've got to get off this rock, now!

He looked around, the fog still clinging to the cliff preventing him from seeing what was below.

I can't be far from the ground . . .

But twenty feet was a long way to drop into the blind. That unknown climber's nightmare—the void—could swallow him.

No choice. Talk about a leap of faith.

Almost instantaneously, in the 1.6 seconds since she'd told him she knew he was there, his thoughts blurred in a moment of decision.

I'm not as fast as a bullet, he thought, even while all his experience and instinct told him to hold on, to *never* drop into nothingness. Even with his muscles burning, his grip was still sure. He wasn't positive that his still-on-fire-knee or his other possibly-broken-leg could support what he was about to force them to do, yet a bullet was coming. She knew where he was. She would shoot him maybe before his next breath. His *last* breath.

No choice, he thought again.

Chase opened his hands and embraced the fall.

He plunged into a blind nightmare, his senses lost to the fast and terrifying drop into nothingness.

A bullet might have been better.

He heard the sniper's voice again. "Come and get me. Hurry," she said. The invisible, loudly whispered words sounded eerie as the fog took him.

Why is she talking to me? It makes no sense—

Before he could complete the thought, his feet slammed into the rocky ground. Agony violently awakened his numbed senses. Bouncing sideways, his shoulder crashed into the sand before he rolled into a saltwater tide pool.

I'm down . . . I'm alive.

He felt his leg. There was a chance it wasn't broken, but now the bullet seemed assured. The fog had lifted by the ground, enough so he could see the water lapping against the shore. Bracing in a defensive position, Chase scoured the beach, but couldn't find the sniper.

He suddenly realized she might not have been talking to *him*.

What did she say? 'I can see you. Come and get me. Hurry.'

He looked out at the water, and through the parting mist, Chase spotted a boat.

"There isn't a getaway car," Chase whispered. "There's a damned getaway *boat!*"

He looked back up the beach, trying to find Wen.

She's still too far away...

But he recalled seeing her from the clifftop. Testing his leg, Chase was surprised by its strength. Although his ankle was tender, his knee would be the problem. He could probably walk on it, but it wouldn't be easy, and running was out of the question.

He stayed quiet, hoping the sniper would say something again, and give away her exact location. It now seemed obvious that she hadn't been talking to him, but was instead in radio communication with the boat, which was really a small yacht. His partner, Dez, was a boating enthusiast, and had taught Chase a lot about the luxurious watercraft. He studied its lines and thought it looked like a Sunseeker Predator.

Appropriate name, he thought, but that was just a guess. *They must be sending a dinghy for her.*

Crouching behind a rock, alternating between watching the Predator and the shore, he saw the yacht's crew lowering a small dinghy into the water.

She's probably too smart to talk again, but she's still somewhere on this beach, waiting to rush into the water. Waiting to put a bullet in my head.

Chapter Eighteen

The most recent report from the Bargo defense committee showed an audit for a subcontractor which Bargo was in the process of acquiring. They had purposely been privately funded from the beginning in order to avoid regulatory scrutiny from the SEC, FTC, and the financial market gauntlets. However, they *did* utilize acquisitions to build a vertical integration whereas they would not rely on subcontractors.

"The Donnelley case very much proved that using outside contractors leaves Bargo exposed," Dag said, trying to deflect where Reggie wanted to go.

"Sure, but I'm talking about Leon Franken."

"We hit a wall, so he lost his job," Dag said, looking beyond Reggie at the monitors showing the statuses of various aspects of HaPPI's implementation, a million private bits of data. Much of it he didn't understand, but the rest of it he did.

"And we handled the situation," Marta said.

"But the man who was making $150,000 a year, and living in a million-dollar home, is now homeless."

"So?"

"His car was repossessed. He's unable to even rent the shabbiest apartment. He's locked out of using Airbnb, Facebook, twitter, a hundred other online sites—"

"Your *point*?" Dag said, no longer able to mask his impatience.

"Franken's last known address . . . he was staying with an old college friend. We took his retirement fund, all his credit cards . . . the guy can't even get a *job*. Don't you find that a *little* extreme?"

Dag flashed the forced smile he used when he was tense or annoyed. In this case, it was both. "Franken was coming at us. He wasn't stopping."

"Is he stopping now?"

"He will," Marta answered.

"He seems more determined than ever. Now he wants revenge, and now we're dealing with a man who has nothing left to lose. What arrows do we have left in our quiver once we've taken so much?"

"You *know* the answer to that," Dag snapped.

The two men stared at each other until Reggie threw up his hands. "Someone needs to bring this stuff up. How many more Franken's are out there? Who else are we underestimating?"

"Look, Reggie, I *appreciate* you asking hard questions, and I don't doubt your loyalty, but this is the committee's purview."

"But we're the executives with oversight *on* the committee." Reggie had always been a fighter and an athlete. His muscled frame held no contempt of intimidation, but he unconsciously used his stature to appear foreboding when his words lacked the strength. He often sensed negative reactions without understanding them.

"That's why you get the reports. But the committee knows what they're doing." Dag stood, facing him. "They have the systems and the training. You don't."

Reggie's muscles tensed. "But this is all new territory."

"We have the final step," Marta said, her words as effective at puncturing their egos as a referee's whistle.

"With all due respect," Reggie began, "the final step has *never* been implemented."

"That's right."

"But the committee will *have* to implement it in this case," Reggie said. "Isn't that obvious?"

"Yes. I think that is all but a certainty," Dag replied.

"And you're going to *allow* that?"

"I don't see where we have a choice. Franken is still coming at us."

Marta cleared her throat, wanting to end the tense conversation between them. "There is no other choice, Reggie. The committee will do what they have to do. That's why they're there. Think of the greater good. To win a war, some soldiers have to die."

Reggie nodded, knowing he was outnumbered. It wasn't surprising to him; it *always* happened. All the words his mother had taught him about being a black man in a "white world" floated to the surface of his mind with ever increasing clarity. He was playing his role to make sure everyone was fully aware of the risks and the options—or the lack thereof.

"Erasure," he said quietly.

When neither of them responded, he repeated it again,

loudly, wanting to make sure they both knew what the committee was about to do to Leon Franken.

"Erasure."

They were going to erase a person. The first, but surely not the last.

Chapter Nineteen

The fog continued to dissipate in spots while building in others. Chase could now see that he was in a large cove.

This must be Thunder Cove...

The monoliths which protected the beach took a constant pounding from the waves. Caves and etched openings in the cliffs created thundering echoes as the tide came in. He had studied Boone's coastal map, or rather, watched Wen study it. She considered maps to be another weapon, needing to know every escape route, all the exposed places, hiding spots, and a hundred other strategic bits of data available to her.

Thunder Cove was a perfect rendezvous point, protected and hidden by the steep cliff he had climbed down and the massive stone monoliths in the water. The beach inside the cove could not be reached on foot except during very low tide. Chase scanned the surf, trying to gauge the tide, but couldn't tell for sure if it might be low enough for Wen to make it from the adjoining beach. There was still too much drifting mist to see, yet somewhere to the north, a wave-battered rock tunnel separated Secret Beach and Thunder Cove. Wen would have to come through the treacherous opening.

The sniper must've come through it too, unless she used a rope to climb down.

He stayed low, frantically searching for the sniper. She'd been so close to where he'd come off the cliff.

Where did she go?

He knew Wen wasn't going to get there in time. He took binoculars from his pack, careful to keep them pointed away from the occasional moments of sunlight so a stray glint off the glass wouldn't give away his location.

I guess she didn't see me come down—or rather fall down—the cliff, or she would have already killed me.

He watched the dinghy get closer to the shore.

One man inside . . . likely armed and trained far better than me.

Chase, keeping behind large, slick, black boulders, moved toward the surf. Finally, he spotted the sniper pacing on the beach about fifty yards away.

I've got to get her before the dinghy lands.

He was glad he had the pistol from Wen, because he sure didn't want to try to sneak up and stab the woman. *That would be an awful experience, and one I'd most likely lose. . .*

He watched her move, then rechecked the distance of the dinghy and started counting. Wen had taught him the importance of every instant, of knowing what would happen in the next few moments. He knew he'd have to go in two seconds.

One-one-thousand . . .

He glanced up the beach one last time for Wen, but knew she wouldn't be there yet. He was too far away to get a decent shot. He'd have to go closer, which meant revealing himself *without knowing what other weapons the sniper had.*

Two-one-thousand . . .

He ran.

When he'd gone only five feet of the fifteen he needed, as if sensing his presence, the sniper turned and looked right at him. In that same instant, Chase tripped and fell into the sand. The tangle of seaweed that brought him down had saved his life, the bullet she'd fired sailing over his head.

Without aiming, he came off the beach and fired, but she was already running toward the water, abandoning her rifle as she dove into the surf. Watching her swimming toward the dinghy, Chase ran to the waves. The sniper was already out beyond the break when he waded in, getting off three more shots. None hit. He went for her rifle, figuring it might be more accurate, but by the time he found her in the scope and fired, she was halfway between the shore and the dinghy.

The rifle kicked back harder than he expected, and his aim had not been steady. As he was lining up for a second shot, Wen ran past him and dove into the surf like an Olympic swimmer. She swam twice as fast as the sniper. Chase remembered she had once told him about how the MSS put her through rigorous swimming trials—diving, underwater demolition, SCUBA, and a series of other in-water defensive and countermeasure training. She was closing the distance, but he wasn't sure she would be fast enough.

Then, to his horror, he saw the man on the dinghy aiming a machine gun at her.

Chapter Twenty

Wen swam hard. The man in the dinghy fired at her, and Chase quicky realized his strategic error—he should not have been shooting at the sniper when the man in the dinghy was the bigger threat. He turned the gun and aimed, having now mastered the weapon to the extent of his abilities, and fired. Anticipating the kickback, this shot went much better, blasting a chunk out of the side of the little boat.

The man immediately returned fire at Chase.

"Mission accomplished," Chase said, happy to have so easily drawn fire from Wen. "I'm the decoy *yet again*."

A large piece of driftwood, at least twenty feet from Chase, took the bullet. Coming from the unsteady platform of the dinghy, while choppy seas tossed him about, the man was having a difficult time hitting his target.

Chase fired another round at the dinghy and quickly searched the beach to make sure there were no additional adversaries in the area, another lesson he'd learned from Wen and hard-fought experience. The fog continued to give way, allowing Chase a clear view of the tunnel Wen had come through. Waves crashed in and around the stone passage. He couldn't believe she had made it. Wen would have had to time it perfectly to avoid getting smashed into the rocks or sucked into a whirlpool.

A bullet tore a spray of sand ten feet in front of Chase, reminding him that the man on the dinghy should not be taken lightly. Chase moved to the other side of the boulder and fired back. This time his shot went wide.

The sniper was now less than twenty feet from the dinghy. Wen was still at least that distance from the woman. It was going to be close but Chase could be of no more help. The rifle's detachable magazine had run out of ammo.

He fired the Glock toward the dinghy, but knew it didn't have the range to hit. "Let's see if you take the bait," Chase said out loud. "And leave Wen alone." Either way, he knew it was going to be two against one, and Wen would be a sitting duck in the water.

The man fired toward Chase, then immediately shot at Wen, who disappeared under the water's surface.

"Come on, Wen," Chase said, scared she'd been hit.

Helpless to do anything, Chase watched through the binoculars as the sniper reached the dinghy and began climbing in. Suddenly, Wen emerged from the depths and pulled on the woman's leg, trying to get her back in the water. The woman kicked at Wen. The man was yelling something Chase couldn't hear, but was not shooting. Chase assumed he was trying to get the woman out of the way so he could get a clear shot at Wen.

The women's struggling rocked the dinghy and knocked the man down. Wen got both hands on the woman's belt while pushing her legs against the side of the boat. The position provided enough leverage that both of them went tumbling back into the ocean.

The man reached the side of the dinghy and looked for a shot as Wen and the sniper vanished. Seconds later, they came back up, swinging and pushing. Chase had no idea what skills the sniper possessed, but he knew she was going to lose this fight.

The two women went down again, this time for much longer. The man looked overboard searching. After a while, not sure what to do, he took another shot at Chase, but just as he fired, the dinghy capsized, and he went in. Wen had come up on his blind side, rolled the boat, and, using its forward momentum, rocked it over.

Once he went in, she got on top of the boat's underside and, with some sort of super mariner maneuver or Navy SEAL tactic that Chase couldn't see or understand, righted the dinghy.

The man surfaced and began swimming to the Predator. Wen tried to get the outboard motor started to pursue him, but didn't seem to be having much luck. From the shore, Chase knew she was about to dive in and swim after him, a reckless move.

"Don't!" he yelled. "Who knows what's waiting on the Predator!"

But she couldn't hear him. Instead, she threw her hunting knife. Incredibly, it hit its target. The man struggled a moment before sinking.

Chase saw something on the Predator that terrified him, and he began waving his arms and screaming at Wen. She wasn't watching the shore, so she missed his warnings, but saw the same thing an instant later, diving into the water just as a man wielding a grenade launcher fired from the deck of the Predator.

Wen was in midair when the dinghy exploded in a fireball.

Chase slipped out of his shoes, dove in the water, and swam frantically toward her, desperately hoping he'd reach her in time.

What if she's unconscious from the explosion, has a concussion . . .

Is already dead?

Chapter Twenty-One

Convened around the room were people from the highest echelons of the intelligence community; a brain trust, known as the Elevation group, the powerful members rarely gathered in one place at the same time. Although their shared goals often had them working together, they occasionally had opposing missions, which made up the paradox of the US intelligence agencies. They often competed for talent and budget dollars, which resulted in clashes that sometimes undermined their efforts and countered US national interest.

Seated at the table, the director of the CIA, ostensibly in charge, conducted the meeting. The others, arranged in order around the large, open-center round table, collectively held enough clout to shake the very foundations of the world. To the right of the CIA director sat Susan Shields, an officer at the agency so high up, that only the director actually knew *what* she did. Beside her were two other top CIA officials. Tess Federgreen, the head of CISS, was in the next chair, knowing she should be in charge, that she would do the best job, that all the smart people and egos in the room *still* didn't grasp the inherent danger to the United States and the world—but she did.

The Director of National Intelligence officially had seniority. However, everyone in attendance knew that behind closed doors, he was actually three rungs down on the ladder. Still, he was the liaison to the White House, and, as such, he opened the meeting.

"People," he began in a pinched voice that annoyed Tess more than his constantly blinking eyes, "we've got to lock this up. We're *this* close to integrating HaPPI into the everyday routine." Ignored, he continued. "Has final initiation been authorized?"

"Yes," the CIA director said.

No one was surprised that the final decision was not coming from the White House, but rather the head of the CIA. In the real hierarchy of the intelligence circle, the president was viewed simply as a temporary, even honorary, position. The real power was held by those who transcended the changing terms and differing political parties from one election to the next. Continuity trumped the change.

"There are some potential issues," Susan said. Locking her arms over a tightly contained voluptuous chest, the svelte, hot rod, brain machine of a woman leaned back in her leather chair, totally at ease in her body, her position, her finger-tip retrieval of any information she could possibly need.

Tess, knowing what was coming, tensed.

"I don't see anything in the report," one of the men stated.

"It wasn't in the report. Too fluid. I chose to add it in person."

"Then give it to us," the man said tersely. None of them liked surprises.

"Chase Malone, who has become known to us over the course of several operations, has injected himself into the Bargo essence."

"For what purpose?" an impatient sounding woman from the NSA asked.

"It seems his brother was struck."

"Struck?"

"Struck by HaPPI."

"*That's* what it's called?"

"Yes. Whenever HaPPI targets an individual or company, Bargo refers to it as being *struck*."

"I thought it was hung," another man from a different agency asked.

"No, that's something different. More of a mistake."

"And wiped?" someone else asked.

"That's digital death."

The person who'd said "wiped" seemed to shiver as he nodded his understanding.

"Was Malone's brother inadvertently caught up in the system, or did someone *do* this?" the NSA woman asked, looking around the room as if an idiot should come forward to claim the error.

"We're not sure," Susan said, shifting her toned body. "HaPPI may have erroneously blacklisted him and lowered his rating."

"Oh for God's sake—I thought Bargo's computers were infallible?" a man said. "People make mistakes, but the algorithms are always correct."

"Dag's team is still working out some final bugs, but apparently it was triggered by Malone's brother's affiliation with him, and his best friend being a federal inmate. There are some other smaller, looser infractions as well, somehow compiled and multiplied."

"Well. . . Chase Malone. I thought he was off-grid to begin with. How many problems can he create?"

Several people turned to look at Tess. "Conceivably, quite a *lot* of problems," Tess began. "As was mentioned, he's been a useful asset in several operations." Tess knew she knew more than any of these cronies, even Susan, but Tess's one weakness, her relationship with Chase, debilitated her confidence. The bad timing ostensibly made her cheeks go red. Susan noticed immediately and smirked back at her.

"And yet he's rogue," somebody interrupted.

"Not exactly," Tess corrected in a tone that made it sound as if she might reflexively kill the next person to question her. "It's not that he's *gone rogue*. He's *never* been fully cooperative. I've simply managed to create circumstances in which he played along."

"So you've manipulated him before. Good. Do it again."

Tess thought of Chase and Wen. She knew it would be impossible to make her colleagues understand the complexities, the priorities, the stakes, and the *unlikelihood* of the HaPPI ending they all desired.

An inch away from all-out corporate war, she thought, *and they all think what they think matters.*

Chapter Twenty-Two

In mid-stroke, Chase saw the man on the Predator now aiming a rifle. *Can I get to Wen in time.* He had nearly reached the burning wreckage when Wen suddenly emerged from the churning waters.

"Back to the shore—hurry!" she panted breathlessly.

Chase, stunned she had been underwater for so long, yelled, "Are you okay?"

"We're no match for those weapons!"

Chase looked back at the Predator one more time, fearing the big boat might come after them, before realizing it was too large to come in any closer to the shore, and their only dinghy was sunk.

But what weapons do they have that might still reach us?

Wen had already lapped him and was pushing her way through the surf. He soon found her collapsed on the beach and pulled her behind the same boulder he'd been shooting from minutes before. She fought for control of her breath while trying to see around the black rock. She threw up a mouthful of water, heaving for air. Chase thought she might pass out.

"We're safe," he said, not sure it was true as he tried to get her to rest a minute.

"I thought I had her," Wen gasped. "We *need* to know."

The furious anguish in her voice surprised Chase, yet he understood completely. Their growing frustration of being pursued by unknown assailants had frayed their already brittle nerves.

"She had no tattoo," Wen said, and in her tone, Chase heard the unspoken regret of killing another person, especially a woman. Under the salt water dripping from her hair, she had tears in her eyes. "A second tattoo would have meant another connection."

"I know," he said, also upset to not have the solid lead they desperately needed. "There's still a chance the German's tattoo will mean something."

Wen crawled around the edge of the boulder, doing reconnaissance on the Predator. Chase stood behind her, looking through the binoculars. "The sniper!"

Wen's attention snapped his way. "What?"

"She made it!"

Wen grabbed the binoculars. After staring for a second, she ran to the surf.

"No!" Chase yelled.

She stopped. There was no way she could make it back out to the yacht alive. "How did she survive?" Wen asked, knowing the answer from her own training. The sniper, realizing she was beat, had played dead.

"It looks like they're leaving," Chase said.

"Once again without killing us."

"Well, we did kind of decimate them," Chase said, trying to read the name of the Predator. "The boat is called

'The Release'. That might be a good clue. A Predator called The Release—how many could there be?"

"Maybe we'll get lucky," Wen said. "But first we have to get out of this cove."

"We're already drenched." Chase looked back at the tunnel, now filled with violently churning water. "Guess we'll have to swim around."

"Okay," she said, uncharacteristically resigned from the defeat. Chase pulled her into a tight hug, held her face, steadied himself in her eyes for a penetrating two seconds where they both gained the energy and vitality to go on.

The swim was cold and hard, and they needed to rest several times while making their way up to the trail and eventually back to Boone's. They approached the cottage cautiously, as if it might be another trap, instinctively wary of a waiting ambush.

Tess looked around the table, knowing this time she would not just be working against corrupt corporations, criminals, and foreign agents, but would be fighting people who were in the room with her.

"In this case," the NSA woman said, "I assume we've restored his brother's status?"

"Bargo is reviewing the situation," Susan said, tapping a pen slowly, steadily, on the arm of the chair.

"What do you mean 'reviewing the situation'?" the DNI said. "They made a *mistake*, jeopardizing the program. Fix it."

"It's complicated."

"How hard can this stuff be? Just have HaPPI give him some glowing reports."

"Chase Malone's brother was a highly successful man. He's lost a series of contracts to competitors that should have gone to him. They can't just unravel those. And there were other reasons that the competitors got those contracts to begin with."

"What reasons?"

"We don't exactly know."

"This is a cluster," the man said. "How can we *not* know?"

"Is Bargo withholding information?" someone else asked.

"Bargo doesn't even know, once the commands are put in, the machine learning takes over. It's all about the algorithms."

"That's the way *all* AI works. The initial program is set, and then the machine learning kicks in and creates a new program, written by the machines."

"I *understand* that, but there must be a safeguard, a way in . . . can they write a damn program to tell us how the other program did it?"

"Not that simple."

"Of *course* not."

"Still, we need to unravel this mess," the DNI head said. "If we've initiated, this thing could implode."

"Not likely," the CIA director corrected. "HaPPI is proven. We've seen it, and verified it in all the simulations."

"What?" the NSA woman asked.

"It's all already played out. Any opposition can be suppressed almost immediately. If an opponent suggests something is amiss, they're history. We can quell that opposition by utilizing the core capabilities of the program. There's a clear path . . . HaPPI is a self-fulfilling and self-correcting format."

"Meaning it destroys anyone that gets in its way?" Tess clarified, in a tone that made it unclear if she was criticizing, or praising the program.

"Exactly," Susan agreed, adjusting her glasses. "What are we supposed to do about Chase Malone?"

"I'd like a little more time," Tess said.

"Risky," Susan said. "What are you going to do with the additional time?"

"I've turned him before. I can bring him in again."

"What advantage does that give us?"

"Rather than him fighting us on the outside, he can be an asset from the inside."

"I ask *again*, what *kind* of an asset is Chase Malone?"

"A safeguard against something going wrong with HaPPI," Tess said, trying to make her weak case stronger. "As powerful as this system is, I think we all know that HaPPI is like playing with matches in a dynamite factory."

Chapter Twenty-Three

Mumford Grimes watched as the dinghy exploded from the RPG he'd just fired. And he watched as Wen swam back to shore. Then, to his astonishment, he saw Lena Shelby surface and begin to swim toward the Predator. Shelby was the best on his team. He wasn't surprised she had been the lone survivor, but he was surprised that she hadn't completed the mission.

Grimes worked for a powerful cartel, although he didn't know exactly *who* they were. Only that his contact was a man called Belfort, and even then he doubted that was his real name. The Cartel had a seemingly bottomless source of money and power, and most important was their intel; the Cartel knew *everything*.

He helped Shelby onto The Release, the yacht an ultra-modern, sleek, Predator class luxury cruiser that belonged to the Cartel. "You okay?" he asked, admiring her toned, wet body.

"No!" she snapped, gasping for breath, shaking off his grip. "I almost *died* out there."

"But you didn't."

Shelby looked over her shoulder, as if worried that Wen might be coming for her.

"They're on the beach," Grimes said, handing her a set of digital binoculars.

She waved him off. "I don't care."

"What happened? How did they get away?"

She glared at him.

"I thought you were the best."

"I *am*," Shelby spat saltwater. "She's *better*."

Grimes smiled. "I don't think so. She just had the wind today." He believed that the wind could change directions at any time, and give or take the critical edge needed in his line of work.

"She had something," Shelby muttered.

"Come on, I'll buy you a drink," he said as a crew member handed her a big, warm beach towel.

"Something strong," she said.

Grimes frowned. He didn't drink while engaged against a target. It had been twenty-three months, seventeen days, and nine hours since he'd touched alcohol. "Belfort is expecting a call."

"I'm sure he is. Let me get out of this wet suit and have that drink first."

"Seems reasonable, but he's not going to be happy."

"Then I'll have another drink *after* the call."

"Maybe the others will have better luck."

She looked at him questioningly."

"We've got Trigger and Lou heading back to the brother's cottage. Maybe we'll still have some good news for Belfort.

"No," she said. "Trigger and Lou are about to die."

Chasing Risk

Chase and Wen swept the entire house and determined the place was empty.

"We need to leave," Wen said, lowering her gun.

Chase gripped his aching knee as it twisted slightly. "You think they'll come here?"

"It doesn't matter. We need to sleep, and we can't do it here." She ran her hands down both sides of his leg. He winced. "It's seriously bruised, maybe sprained, but not badly."

He looked at her tired frown through the haze of his own exhaustion. There hadn't been much sleep the night before, and after everything they'd just been through, rest was definitely required.

A thudding sound came from somewhere outside while they were still in the front hall.

"I heard it," she hissed, before Chase could warn her. Wen, having her weapons bag ready to load into their car, quickly unzipped it and pulled out a submachine gun. Tossing it to Chase, she grabbed another for herself. Both weapons were fitted with suppressors, however, the noise in the little cottage would still be loud, and could bring the neighbors, whose house was only a couple hundred yards away.

Wen pointed to a loft that extended part way over the living room. Chase took her cue and quietly climbed the narrow wooden ladder, then carefully detached the hooks and pulled it up behind him.

Wen looked at the little closet by the door, but decided against it, since it would be a good place to get trapped. Instead, she went into the first bedroom and crouched under a window. Her position allowed her a view to the door while being partially concealed behind the bed.

As expected, one gunman came in the front door and another through the back door simultaneously. Wen scolded herself for not getting out of the cottage faster. While they were searching the inside, these two—and who knew how many more—had had time to get into position. *Chase will have the first shot*, she thought. *If he takes it.* Wen visualized the scene. *The front door man would get hit, and then back door man would immediately run past the bedroom toward the noise.*

A split-second later, she heard a single shot that she recognized as the report from a Heckler & Koch MP7. The body dropped. *Good job, Chase.* Then, as predicted, footsteps came from the back of the house. She counted, anticipating when the person would pass her door. She fired an instant before the man crossed into view.

Her bullets cut him down. She was already moving, and reached him just after he landed on the floor. The blood streaked wall showed his slow descent, but he was still breathing.

Chapter Twenty-Four

Wen shoved the bloody man with her foot, kicking his gun away. "Good, you're still alive," she said, squatting next to him, submachine gun dangling at her waist, pistol in hand.

He rolled in pain. There had to be at least four or five bullets in his legs, more in his arm.

"Any tattoos?" she asked, pushing his sleeves up as he screamed. "How many others?"

The man moaned.

"*How. Many. Others?*" she repeated firmly.

He still didn't answer.

"Clear?" Chase yelled.

"Not yet," Wen shouted back as she squeezed one of the man's legs.

He cried out in agony.

Wen released her grip, fearing he might pass out. "How many others?"

"No others."

She believed him. "Who sent you?"

"I don't know," he said in a breathy voice.

"You're lying," she said, pressing her Glock against his head. "Last time. *Who* do you work for?"

"Gronzinski."

"Who is that?"

"I don't know. I don't know if he's even real."

She saw Chase cross the end of the hall. "Check the windows."

"Call an ambulance," the man said weakly. "Please."

"How much are you getting paid?" It seemed like an unimportant question, but it would give her a lot of information—the caliber of agents they were using, how deep their pockets were, even the currency would be important.

"Three hundred US."

She was not surprised. $300,000 was similar to the amount from the man she'd killed in the California mountains. "And if you kill us?"

"The same."

Wen smiled. The man had just confirmed there were two missions—capture, or kill. "Tell me why I shouldn't kill you then."

"Do it, I don't care," he said, sounding as if his vocal chords were on fire. "I may not survive this, may never walk again."

She checked his legs. "You'll walk, you'll be fine. But I'm going to kill you unless . . . " She held up her phone, teasing him about an ambulance. "You haven't told me enough. I'll let you live, but you have to tell me more."

"What?"

"About the arrangement of who you're working for."

"It's not like that. You know we don't know."

"The money, the down payment, you can keep it. I just want the account number. Where it went."

He was silent.

"Should I squeeze your leg again?"

He gave her the number. "Call the ambulance."

She stared at him as if that was never going to happen anyway. "How's it look?" she called to Chase

"Good," he responded, appearing at the end of the hall.

"*Call*," the man moaned, sounding weaker.

"Check this," she said to Chase, giving him the number and bank info.

"I know about HaPPI."

Wen suppressed a gasp as she tried to maintain her cool. "*What* do you know about HaPPI?"

"Call the ambulance. I'll tell you while we're waiting."

"Tell me *now*."

"No."

"You're not in a position to argue. You're going to bleed out." She searched him roughly and took his phone.

"If you let me die, you'll lose your best chance to know what you need to know."

"How do you know we're interested in HaPPI?"

"It's in your file."

"Where's the file?"

He glanced at the phone.

"What's your passcode?"

"Call."

"The only reason I need the code is to get in it *now*. I can get in it later *without* the code."

"But you want to see it now."

She glanced at the finger on his left hand. No ring, but a trace of a tan line where one used to be. She stared into his pained eyes. "You have children."

A strange, scared sound escaped his lips, before he stopped and tried to deny it.

"Wrong line of work for a family man," she said.

"It pays well."

"Not today, it doesn't."

"Please, call the ambulance." His voice was fading.

"Give me the code."

"18-34-60."

Wen tapped the numbers in. The screen unlocked. She called the ambulance.

"Thank you."

She scrolled through the contents of his phone. "Tell me what's not in the file."

He hesitated.

"I can still kill you before they come."

"HaPPI. The CIA is involved."

"Do you know a name?"

"We should go," Chase said, appearing again.

"I don't know," the man wheezed. "But it is a secret division inside the CIA."

Wen couldn't help but think of Tess and CISS. "Did you have direct contact?"

"Of course not. That's not how it works."

"Did you ever hear a name?"

"No. The man your friend just killed, *he* knew. Told me once it was an unusual sounding name."

Wen looked at the man, thought about reminding him that his friend had been trying to kill Chase and her. "How is HaPPI connected to the people who sent you?"

"I don't know."

"But you believe it is?"

"Yes."

"We *have* to go," Chase said, now standing next to her.

"Look, I told you," the man began. "I was hired to kill you, and you just shot me all up. We're not friends, but I can tell you this." He paused and grimaced as pain flooded through him. "The people after you, they're not playing, and it *is* complicated. Take whatever information you think you've gathered, then multiply that by a million, and you won't even have a *glimpse* of what you're up against." He gave her a woozy stare, and then added, "They're going to keep coming. I may have failed, but there is so much arrayed against you, more money than you can imagine. And they'll find you. They're going to find you, and Chase Malone, and kill you both. You cannot win."

Chapter Twenty-Five

Dag, Marta, and Reggie walked the corridor, a long room on a secure floor of Bargo's San Francisco building. At exactly one hundred forty-four feet long and eighteen feet wide, the windowless corridor would have been a stark and hollow chamber were it not for the ten-foot-high 5K monitors that lined the entire length of the place on both sides.

Jim Bradly's image filled one of the sections. His smiling face caused Dag to furrow his brow and clench the fist of his swinging hand.

Jim Bradly had been the first fatality of HaPPI, but he would not be the last. Dag frowned when he saw the report. He didn't like the dirty side of this business, yet, with Bradly, he considered his hands clean. His job—his *duty*—was to protect Bargo at all cost.

"A guy like Bradly didn't understand how important our work is," Dag snapped, as if the whole episode was occurring again. "I'm not going to let some low-level, white-collar, *loser* bring everything crashing down because *he* didn't understand how the world works."

Dag recalled the unfortunate drama. HaPPI had been implemented. Bargo had used it in an attempt to muzzle Bradly. They just kept pushing and taking from him.

"Clearly, Bradly wasn't stable to begin with," Marta said, as if discussing a machine. "Or he never would've killed himself."

Reggie was upset with the report, and Marta thought it was inconvenient in its timing, but pointed out how many coal miners had died the prior year, how many lumberjacks, trash men. "Every business has its risks and liabilities," she spouted. "Thirty thousand people died in auto accidents last year, yet I can't stop General Motors from making vehicles, or Exxon from selling gas. That option would never even occur to anyone. It's a dangerous world, and remember, gentlemen, we're trying to make it *better*."

"Sure, but with Bradly, our tactics were too heavy-handed."

"How many people died last year at the hands of violent criminals?" Marta shot back. "Isn't Jim Bradly's life a small price to pay in order to spare all those other potential victims?"

"It should have been *his* choice, not ours," Reggie said.

"It *was* his choice," Dag said.

Reggie nodded. He knew the debate was over, and he had two reasons for not pressing further. One, he agreed with Marta. He knew in the end HaPPI was going to improve the world and save countless lives. There was a chance to correct all the mistakes humanity had allowed. And two, he knew he was in it too deep. If he even thought about leaving, he would be the next Jim Bradly, until he didn't exist anymore either.

Belfort's face appeared on the tablet. "Another failure?"

"They escaped."

Belfort nodded, as if he'd been expecting this.

"But Trigger and Lou—"

"Are *dead*," Belfort barked.

"They were due to check in," Grimes said, looking at Shelby, who was off camera.

"Well they aren't going to."

"We should have sent more . . . " Grimes said, unnerved about Belfort knowing that two men under his command had been killed before he did.

"Do you know that they call us the 'shadow people'?"

"Yeah," Grimes said. He'd been paid well by the Cartel, even before the hunt for Chase and Wen began nearly two years earlier. He didn't understand why they kept him. They'd lost at least twenty operatives that he knew of, but he suspected that the real number was closer to twice that.

"Yet even in broad daylight, we have not been able to accomplish anything."

"In fairness, once you changed the mission to taking them alive, that made our job more difficult. They're *extremely* dangerous."

"That's why we use professionals like you."

"And now the boy?"

"We *need* the boy."

"And the program?"

"That's why we need Malone *alive*."

"But why do we have to take the woman alive?"

"That's not your concern."

Grimes wanted to argue. He understood about Malone and the boy, but there seemed to be no similar reason for capturing Wen. Killing her would still be a challenge—they had tried *many* times before the objectives changed—but if they could take her out, everything else would be simpler.

"Then I need more people."

"Not until I see something," Belfort said. "Put together a plan. Be imaginative. I don't care if you need a tank, a submarine, and a thousand men. You come up with a way to get me Malone, the woman, and the boy, alive. I don't care about the cost. I'll get you everything you need. Chase Malone is out of time. He may not know it yet, but this has to end."

Chapter Twenty-Six

Making sure they weren't being followed, Chase drove back toward Brookings. Moments after they left, the ambulance passed them en route to pick up the injured man. Chase phoned Boone to make sure he had a solid alibi in San Francisco. The police would be investigating.

"Poor Boone . . . that's all he needs, trying to explain a shootout at his vacation home that left one man dead and another injured," Chase said after the call.

"Two men dead," Wen corrected.

"You don't think the guy we left is going to make it?"

She shook her head. "He'll be DOA at the hospital."

Chase got a room at the Brookings Beachfront Inn, registered under one of their many aliases. They *had* to sleep.

Wen, ready to collapse, started up her laptop and sent the prints, tattoo, and other information she'd collected to

The Astronaut. After a long series of encrypted routers connected a voiceover Internet call to Zǔ mǔ, they both talked with Tu while Chase iced his knee before rinsing off in a quick shower.

Then, *finally*, Chase and Wen fell into bed together, locked lovers in an instant, blissful sleep.

The blue digital clock glowed three thirty-two a.m. when they resurfaced from deep sleep. As the sound of the waves loudly breaking on the rocky sand kept rhythm, the two fugitives made love.

Just after five a.m., they emailed The Astronaut, hoping for anything to ID their pursuers. Nothing yet. Chase checked in with Boone to make sure he was okay, and then went through the encryption protocols to phone Zǔ mǔ. She always woke before the sun, and often stayed up late. Sometimes Chase wasn't sure she *ever* slept. He affectionately referred to her as "the old witch woman."

"Tu sleeping good. It's good here," she told them in her broken English.

While they were talking, Chase logged into an app that allowed him to follow the security around Tu in real time. He gave a thumbs up to Wen.

"Are you ready to leave?" Wen asked her grandmother.

"I stay ready," Zǔ mǔ said in a sad, resigned voice.

"We'll find a place where you can stay longer this time."

Zǔ mǔ knew this wasn't true, but allowed herself a soft smile. "That will be good."

An encrypted text hit Wen's phone while they were still on with her grandmother. She quickly typed a response.

"What was that?" Chase asked once they'd finished with Zŭ mŭ.

"Astaria."

Chase knew they were in trouble. Whenever Astaria, a former Mossad agent, contacted Wen, things went from deadly to even worse. "How bad?"

"Bad enough that she's going to meet us at the Crescent City airport."

"She's *here*?" he asked suspiciously.

"I just told her where we were. She's flying from LA as we speak."

"So it's bad?"

"We'll find out soon."

As they were readying to leave the hotel, Dez and Bull called with more information on Bargo and HaPPI. Desmond "Dez" Jefferson, a renowned African American engineer, had been with Chase since the beginning. The two had developed a breakthrough AI program, and in the intervening years, had secretly been working on several other advanced technologies.

Chase and Wen had rescued Bull, a superstar hacker nicknamed for her energy drink addiction, from the Russian mob. She'd worked with them ever since. After losing the use of her legs in an attack meant as a message to Chase, she'd hooked up with Dez, who had lost a leg during the bombing of his boat—also by enemies of Chase.

"It's a very hush-hush company. There's almost nothing out there on HaPPI," Dez said. "But we've managed to link several corporate clients back, and discovered that they operate HaPPI through at least two dozen subsidiaries."

"Why?" Chase asked.

"It seems a way to keep control," Bull said. "Bargo has created different companies to serve specific classes of clientele—local governments, police, key industries."

"Interesting."

"But based on what we can tell, Bargo is collecting *everything* on *everyone*," Dez said.

"When Dez says 'everything,' he *means* everything," Bull said. "They're storing biographies, employment records, medical reports, credit profiles, service records, social media presences and the online data of the *entire* US population. Imagine how valuable that kind of information would be on, say, an aircraft carrier captain, or any military commanders. They seem to like targeting rising officers in all branches of the military."

"China has been doing the same thing for at least ten years," Wen said. "Another connection between Bargo and the Chinese Communist Party."

"It's total," Bull said. "Tweets, dating sites, porn, every internet post and comment, like, and click—both domestic and those originating from overseas U.S. military installations."

"What's the agenda?" Chase asked.

"Like Bull said," Dez replied. "Control. Bargo maintains a massive data center in Nevada—"

"Bigger than even the NSA's Utah facility," Bull added.

"You wouldn't believe what they have," Dez said. "Their profiles are more sophisticated—"

"—than *anything* the NSA or CIA—" Bull interrupted again.

"—is doing," Dez interrupted back, both in hyper chatter back and forth. "Bargo builds incredible matrixes out of this stuff."

"*Way* beyond family trees of friends and associates. It's predictive." Bull finished with a big swallow, obviously still chugging the energy drinks.

"How accurate is it?" Chase asked.

"Looks a lot like SEER percentages," Dez replied. "Except it's not targeting trends and flow. They look at the individual *so* precisely."

"It's like having big brother implanted in your brain," Dez and Bull said simultaneously, and then laughed together.

"We know, it's not funny," Dez said seriously.

Chapter Twenty-Seven

On their way out of town, Chase convinced Wen to stop at the Hungry Clam, a little seafood joint on the waterfront at Brookings Harbor. Boone had told him that they served the best fish and chips in Oregon, and since it was his favorite food, his request seemed perfectly reasonable.

"Do I have to remind you that there are people trying to kill us?" Wen asked.

"We *have* to eat," Chase replied, giving her what he considered to be his special smile.

Wen checked the rearview mirror. She hadn't seen any trace of trouble since Boone's place. "I guess we can canvass the harbor for the Predator while we're there."

"Yeah," Chase said, smiling. "We can ask around. Maybe someone knows something about The Release. A yacht like that would stand out in a small marina."

While waiting for their order, Chase talked to an employee at the Marina refueling facility who remembered the Predator.

"Yeah, The Release," the scruffy man said. "Beautiful."

Chase slipped the man a twenty. "Recall anything about the people onboard?"

"A beautiful woman, a boat guy, crew, four or five toughs."

"What do you mean by 'boat guy'?"

"Guy was in charge. Totally at home on a yacht like a Predator. Dude looked like he lived on a boat, or an island, full time. Like, *years* in the tropics, know what I mean?" His stubble and weathered face made him look older than he probably was, but Chase figured the guy had been working at the marina long enough to know.

"Yeah, I think so," Chase said. "And the toughs?"

"Intense group. Even the hot chick looked like she could kill you a couple ways. The whole scene kinda freaked me out," he said, looking over his shoulder. "Hey, you a cop or something?"

"Something. Did you hear anything I might want to know—where they were from, where they were heading, any names?"

"Maybe," the man said, eying Chase suspiciously. "But I already gave you a hundred's worth for only twenty."

Chase pulled out a hundred dollar bill. "Give me something solid, and I'll trade you *this* for the twenty."

"I'll give you a name, but I keep *both*," the man said, smiling, snatching the hundred and winking again.

"Okay."

"The hot chick called the boat guy Mumford."

"That's not worth a hundred, let alone one-twenty."

"Yeah, but one of the toughs called the same guy Grimes. So Mumford Grimes. Although, I guess it could be Grimes Mumford, but for one-twenty, I can't be expected to be a phone book. Try Google or Facebook."

"Probably not the type of guy to leave a digital trail,"

Chase said, mostly to himself. "But a name is worth one-twenty. Anything else?"

"Nah, but that babe . . . "

"I know, she was hot."

"Yeah. Kind of stood out among the toughs."

Chase knew he was talking about the sniper. "Didn't get a name on her, did you?"

"I wish. And a phone number."

Chase thanked him and jogged back to report to Wen, and eat the best fish and chips in Oregon.

"I just uploaded the content of the cell phone to The Astronaut," Wen said, handing him his order. "Apparently our friend was careful. No identifying name on his phone, but there are files about us, and he was telling the truth. There *is* CIA information, and marks that could be HaPPI. Maybe The Astronaut can get lucky and piece it together."

"I have something even better," Chase said, sticking two thick fries leftover from her plate in his mouth.

She forked his coleslaw that he didn't touch. "The Predator is here?"

"No," he said, swallowing. "But the man in charge of that fancy boat has a name: Mumford Grimes."

Wen stared at him as if he'd just proved Bigfoot existed. "We have the name of a real live shadow person," she said. "And I've heard of him."

Chapter Twenty-Eight

Wen and Astaria had worked together on several occasions back when they were both still with their respective intelligence agencies. Astaria, who still took assignments from the Mossad, was now freelance. In a way, so was Wen.

"Remember, I trust Astaria, but she is not trustworthy," Wen reminded Chase.

"Those kinds of statements always confuse me," he admitted.

"It's the nature of this business. Things like trust, loyalty, betrayal, and honesty are subjective. They shift like sands blowing in the wind."

He kissed her. "I love it when you talk philosophically."

"I've always been able to rely on Astaria, and as far as I know, she has never betrayed me. But even she would admit that, one day, she might."

"I remember," Chase said. "If what she's pursuing is in conflict with what you need, then you're expendable to her."

"As long as our objectives align, there will be no problem."

"Would she risk your relationship?"

"Absolutely. Because even if she betrays me, it doesn't mean I would not trust her again, as long as we're pursuing the same goals."

"The spy game sounds a lot like the corporate world," Chase said. "But how do you know if you're truly working toward the same goal?"

"Ah, that is the tricky part."

"And?"

"We figure it out as we go."

"Oh, well, that's reassuring."

Chase and Wen got out of their car. "We were lucky she was nearby," Wen said.

They watched as the private plane landed. Astaria jogged to meet them in front of the small terminal. When she reached them, she embraced Wen, finally releasing her after a passionate kiss. Chase, recalling a similar scene from when he'd first met the former Mossad agent, was fascinated by this side of Wen.

Astaria looked at Chase, her icy blue eyes flashing a combination of heated flirting and keen, killer awareness. "It's good to see you still alive."

"Is that meant with affection?"

"Of course. I love Wen, therefore, I love you." She kissed him sensually on the lips. "I love you both." Her embrace lingered a little longer than he was comfortable with.

"Okay, Astaria, we need information," Wen began. "You said you knew something about HaPPI."

"HaPPI isn't just a simple case of Bargo trying to corner

the market on big data," Astaria said. "It's a product of the US intelligence community."

The three of them walked toward the rental car.

"How do you know this?" Chase asked, opening the door for Wen and then the back passenger for Astaria.

"HaPPI is the crisis of the day within the clandestine world," Astaria said. "You and Wen are arriving late to the party."

"Then catch us up," Wen said.

"There's some dispute whether Bargo was started by the CIA, or approached by the CIA *after* they began getting traction in the data assembly arbitration and aggregate field."

"Why does it matter which happened first?" Chase asked, pulling out of the airport and heading up the coastal highway.

"*Everything* matters in our business, silly." She winked at Wen. "However, it may be of little consequence with your recent interest in Bargo."

"What does that mean?" Chase asked.

Astaria pulled a slim bottle from her bag and took a sip. From the rearview mirror, Chase noticed a couple of guns in there as well. "I caught you peeking," Astaria said, lightly brushing her fingers over his shoulder. "Those are the twins."

"Twins?" Chase echoed, embarrassed, but not sure why.

"Micro Uzis," she purred like a proud mother. "A little wild, can be tough to handle, but *so* cute, and real killers."

"Nice," Wen said.

Astaria opened her bag to let Wen see the guns, then casually said, "So . . . what exactly is your interest in Bargo?"

Chase looked at Wen, wondering how much to say. Wen replied with an imperceptible nod.

"Go ahead, Chase," Astaria said, giggling. "She just gave you permission." Astaria winked at Wen.

"Bargo mistakenly targeted my brother, and it's ruining his life." He pulled off onto a narrow dirt road that led to the ocean.

"That's your first mistake," Astaria said. "Bargo doesn't *make* mistakes, so they must've had a reason for going after him. What have they done?"

"They've taken his rating and credibility down, so he's losing lots of contracts on his window washing business," Chase said. "*Big* contracts. San Francisco skyscrapers and others in LA, Seattle, Portland."

"If that's what you're trying to figure out, I would follow the money. Who's getting those contracts, and what advantage does that give to somebody else? It's like a giant jigsaw puzzle. But you need your Astronaut and fancy AI programs to figure it all out, because it's beyond simple human understanding."

He parked the car. They got out and headed for the sand. Astaria and Wen took off their shoes and ran on the beach, then rolled up their pants, and splashed in the waves for a while before retreating reluctantly back to the car and returning to the airport. Chase parked and they all stood on the tarmac near Astaria's plane.

As two men in suits approached, Astaria slipped a hand into her bag. At the same time, Wen casually moved to the other side of a concrete post, where Chase could see she now had her Glock in hand, aimed at the men.

Chapter Twenty-Nine

Bull and Dez had been working all night—her hyped up on Red Bull energy drinks, him buzzing on green tea.

They had been connecting with The Astronaut across the web through their encrypted portals. He'd been awake the whole time as well, but nobody knew how he stayed up, since he abstained completely from caffeine and other stimulants.

On an all-nighter months earlier, Bull had seen him do some sort of zonal meditation and tonal chants every few hours. Each time, he came back seemingly good as new. Wen claimed she had once seen him stay up for three days straight without any signs of fatigue or diminished capacity.

Bull took the assignment with her typical sardonic attitude. "Oh, we have to save the world again? Wait, let me guess, this time it's really, really, *really* important."

She sat in her wheelchair, surrounded by the best computer technology and massive curved 360° 5K monitors.

"I take this little problem a bit more personally," she

said, while trying for the hundredth time to pierce Bargo's firewalls.

"Why?" Dez asked, amused by her perspective on things.

"Bargo is like a giant mechanized hacker. They collect data by whatever means necessary, in every way possible—legal or illegal—from the internet, the darknet, and even from old analog systems."

"True. And that bothers you?"

"They use it in a way to control and manipulate people, and therefore society as a whole. Screw them," she said. "*I* do stuff like that, and I get arrested. *They* do it, and they get another few billion dollars."

The Astronaut heard her rant. "I think you are onto something," he said. "Although it won't be simple to get into their systems—"

"When we do, I'm building a catch system to reverse engineer it," Dez interrupted. "It's the only way we can bring them down."

"You destroy a company built on data with data," Bull said. The Astronaut had explained that to her.

"And thinking of them as a hacker is a better angle to go with," The Astronaut added. "Although, it is considerably more complicated than that." His initial probes into Bargo's algorithms had frightened him, but he didn't want to discourage Bull and Dez, so had only given them a partial warning. "Their machine learning has advanced to such a stage that there is a real possibility that Bargo has already lost the role of the genie."

Bull had worked with The Astronaut enough to pick up on the hidden meaning in his words. She stared at the code in front of her as if it might leap from the screen and attempt to strangle her.

"And if they still have some control," The Astronaut continued, "AI anarchy could happen soon."

"Have you run this by Chase?" Dez asked, since both knew he was one of the world's leading experts on artificial intelligence.

"Yes," The Astronaut replied. "He thinks there's a chance Bargo can maintain control of HaPPI."

"That's good," Bull said.

"But only because Chase believes Bargo is running something like a modified version of RAI." Rapid Artificial Intelligence, the invention that had made Chase and Dez super wealthy.

"Then it's possible that Bargo is infringing on our patent," Dez said. He offered a tray of expertly rolled sushi in a rainbow of colors to Bull. She enthusiastically accepted.

"Sue the bastards," Bull said. "We'll beat them in court." And then to Dez in a whisper, "Delish!"

"That would be a no-win battle, even if it were true," The Astronaut said. "Still, RAI gave Chase great insight and understanding as to what Bargo is doing. He speculated that Bargo installed a layer of AI in the HaPPI programs that made sure they maintained ultimate control, while still allowing the program and machine learning to run free range, wild west style. It's not good to combine food and work Bull, digestion is impaired."

"Regardless, we now have the tedious task of figuring out how to break it apart while avoiding detection," Dez said.

"Sounds like long hours ahead," Bull said, reluctantly putting the sushi aside and cracking open another energy drink. Because Chase and Wen had saved Bull's life, she did their dangerous work not only because she loved them, but because she also loved the game. She never forgot how dangerous it was, though. She had almost died going up against another lethal and technologically advanced foe. Bull made it out alive, but hadn't walked since.

Both Chase and Dez had promised her she would walk again one day, in spite of what the doctors said. And she believed them. Instead of deterring her from this risky line of work, it had made her more determined to fight those seeking to oppress and control others using technology.

"I've got two cases of Red Bull and a carton of cigarettes," Bull said. "I'm ready for whatever the night brings."

Chapter Thirty

Chase readied for the attack by quickly scanning for cover. *Why don't I have a gun?* he wondered, but the men passed by without incident. Wen told him later that they had fit a profile, and the fact they had no luggage added to their suspicion.

"Sometimes, we are too careful," Wen had said. "But we live."

"Bargo may be trashing your brother to elevate someone else," Astaria continued as if the men had never appeared. "That shifts the power into another place, so they need to weaken a different party. To force a merger here, do something else there, nothing to do with washing windows whatsoever. By the time it gets to the end goal, they don't know they've done it because all they entered into their machine was that they wanted the price of oil to raise by thirty dollars a barrel. So the machine starts doing it, and the steps necessary to make that happen may begin with your brother losing all his contracts, nothing to do with oil, and yet," she touched Wen's cheek, "*everything* to do with oil. You follow?"

"Sure," Chase said, and his engineering mind did, although he was still spooked by Astaria's mysterious and commanding confidence. He had worked with his programs RAI and SEER long enough to understand how one thing affects the other, and that a seemingly unrelated event could change the outcome of an original equation.

"Good." Astaria smiled, licking her lips as if she might kiss him again. "So then you just need to figure out what the objective is."

"I'm not sure it even matters," Chase said. "What we *need* to do is shut them down. A single corporation cannot be allowed to wield this kind of power."

Astaria laughed and looked at Wen. "It's always amusing how the smartest people can also be the stupidest."

"And fools can be so ingenious," Chase said, quoting someone, but he couldn't recall who.

"He understands computers, artificial intelligence, algorithms, and finance technology, and yet is unable to grasp the espionage and power that controls the world," Astaria said, retying her thick, frizzy black ponytail and turning back to Chase. "I would think that spending so much time with Wen would give you an idea, but no matter. Lessons will come . . . and be learned."

"What division of the CIA?" Wen asked.

Astaria's face went hard, as if the question were a personal insult. Wen had seen the look before, and knew it meant that she didn't know. Astaria suffered greatly when there was a puzzle piece missing that she could not identify.

"You need someone from Bargo to give you that information," Astaria said, as if giving the punchline to a dirty joke.

"It seems unlikely anyone from inside is going to talk," Chase said.

"There's someone no longer inside, but recently enough, and high enough, that she knows enough to be dangerous."

"Who is she?" Chase asked.

"Where is she?" Wen asked.

"Cristina Crawford. Bargo is looking for her, too, and they're about to find her. I can give you an address, but you may already be hours too late. But if you do find her in time, know that by speaking with her, you will be telling Bargo that you're a threat," Astaria said, her seductive expression suddenly turning into one of serious concern, as if an Academy Award performance had just been given.

"I'm immune to Bargo's games," Chase said. "I hardly exist anymore."

"So naïve," she said, shaking her head and looking from Chase to Wen as if she might start laughing. "*No one* is immune to Bargo. They're already more powerful than you can imagine, and I assure you, they are *not* playing games."

Chapter Thirty-One

Dag picked up the phone, looked at the number, and sighed. He never enjoyed these calls, but dealing with "the company", as he referred to the Central Intelligence Agency, was a necessary evil.

If we're able to continue the progress we've made with HaPPI, perhaps one day they will be obsolete. Maybe not one day soon, he thought, *but those twenty years that Reggie spoke of when I'm retired. Certainly by then the CIA will be retired, too.*

He pressed accept, smiled so he'd sound friendly, and said, "Hello?"

"We have a problem," the female voice on the other end of the line said.

He'd been expecting one. Dozens, really. Dag held his smile a little longer. "What is it this time?"

"It seems one of your algorithms tripped over the wrong person."

That made him smile genuinely. There were no wrong people for the algorithm to trip over. The algorithm was created to trip over wrong people. "Who?"

"Boone Malone."

He typed the name into his computer. It was an unusual enough name that there were only four matches in the United States. "Which one?"

She gave him the address—San Francisco.

"He grew up and remained close friends with a federal convict, his brother is also a fugitive . . . oh, his brother is the infamous Chase Malone. Creator of RAI. We actually run a version of that technology ourselves. Why does this concern you?"

"We've worked with him in the past," she said.

"All the more reason," he joked.

"That's not amusing."

He decided to spar a little longer. "Maybe it wasn't meant to be."

"That's *equally* not amusing."

"Okay, okay. So then what's the problem?"

"The *problem* is you've riled up Chase Malone. He is not a simple man."

"Nor am I." He stirred his glass of grapefruit/cranberry juice and swigged it after a shot of pure lemon juice. His face puckered for an instant before he shook it off.

The woman grew frustrated. She thought of Chase and his partner Wen Sung, and Nash Graham The Astronaut, along with a hundred other details that Dag was not going to be able to comprehend. She knew that he considered himself a spy, and yet he was anything but. "You don't appreciate the gravity of—"

"Can't *you* just handle that problem?" Dag asked. "I mean, you're the *CIA*. You have people who can handle that, right?" He rinsed out the glass and set it on the counter.

"If it were that easy, we wouldn't need people like *you*."

"Then what do you want me to do?" he asked. "Reinstate Boone Malone's HaPPI Score, because I'm not sure . . . " He looked around the shared kitchen, obviously searching for a snack.

"I'm afraid it's too late for that. Chase is already looking for answers. I don't expect he'll stop until he gets them."

"Chase Malone is not exactly in our system," he said, back at his keyboard, an open box of gluten-free crackers, a can of sardines, and a block of cheese now next to him. "His wealth and tech knowledge has left him somewhat exempt. He's removed himself from the very framework of the society that we're solidifying."

"You need to think of something," the woman said sternly.

"Why? I think this is *your* problem."

"I assure you, this problem belongs to *both* of us. Don't take this threat lightly. As you just stated, his wealth, the fact that he's outside the system, and the incredible resources at his disposal means—"

"Means what?" He popped a cracker in his mouth.

"He could destroy everything you've worked for."

Dag laughed and swallowed. "One man. You're vastly underestimating HaPPI. We're well beyond the tipping point. It's not *us* who's too late. Chase Malone is too late." He cut a piece of cheese and paired it with another cracker.

"I think you're feeling too secure—years before you should."

"Fine, fine. I'll show you how insulated we are. I'll clean up your mess," Dag said, turning the morsel in his fingers as if assessing a rare stone.

"*You* made the mess," she shot back.

"Do you have any suggestions as to how we should deal with it?"

"Use your imagination, all that power you *think* you have."

"I have to ask again. If this threat is *so big*, why can't you just *remove* it?"

"I have my reasons."

"I'll bet." Dag could imagine a number of scenarios where the CIA had screwed itself because of all its double dealings and shady operations. He decided right then to turn HaPPI on the woman he was speaking with.

Whatever it takes, he thought as he chewed, wiping his fingers on faded jeans. *Someone has to make a choice. Someone has to fix this—who's right, who's wrong, who lives, who dies. Data is the way to decide.*

Chapter Thirty-Two

Dag felt agitated after the call. *It makes no sense that Chase Malone can do so much damage, and yet not warrant some kind of hit from the CIA.*

He pulled up everything they had in their system on Chase, and was surprised by how little there was.

What is this guy, a ghost?

Even his known associates were scarce.

It's like Chase Malone no longer exists.

Chase's wealth, and the tools The Astronaut had given him, not only allowed him to disappear himself, but he'd also been able to move his mother far enough off the grid that she was untouchable.

"But your brother had too much of a life to be protected," Dag said out loud. "Your brother is still your weakness. If damaging Boone's reputation upset you so much, what if we erase him completely? Maybe *that* will stop you." He pulled a plastic toothpick out of his pocket and cleaned his teeth.

Dag summoned only Marta to his office, not in the

mood for a debate with Reggie about the ethics and ramifications of what needed to be done. Marta was always so practical.

After explaining the situation to her, he asked what she suggested, and was not surprised when she came to a similar conclusion that he did.

"We find Chase Malone, we cut a deal," she said. "Reinstate his brother all the way up the ladder, and if that isn't good enough, we threaten him with erasure."

"And what if that just pushes him further?" Dag asked.

"I don't know."

"Neither do I." He showed her the synopsis on Chase Malone. "I actually fed the scenario you suggested into our system, and this is what the predictive algorithms gave back."

"That he's not going to go for it," Marta finished before he could tell her. She sniffed the air and turned up her nose. She hated fish.

"Right." He knew that about her, and sunk his hand in his pocket.

"Okay, so we have all the big data at our disposal. Give it to the committee. See what they come up with."

"We may be obliged to give it to the full board."

"You think the board will have a problem with this?" she asked.

"Not if we can handle it with normal actions. However, if we have to proceed to unconventional methods…"

She nodded. "I understand. I'll pull Blanco and Carlyle and see if we can come up with something as a kind of subcommittee."

Dag smiled. That was exactly why he liked Marta. There was nothing she wasn't willing to do. She was totally devoted to HaPPI and Bargo.

"We found a solution to the problem," Marta said when she returned to Dag's office a few hours later.

"I'm listening," he said.

"We have Boone Malone arrested."

"On what charges?" Dag asked, already liking the idea.

"We have a list," she said, handing a slip of paper to the Bargo CEO.

He skimmed it, raising an eyebrow. "To spend the rest of his life in prison?" he said almost hesitantly.

"Yes," she said, like a child pleased with herself who knew she shouldn't be.

"Are you *sure* we can get this done?" he asked, knowing that they could, but using the question to buy time for his thoughts to catch up with the plan.

"Of course. He can be picked up today." She checked her smartwatch. "Within the next hour, if you approve."

"And then Chase will have to come to us, because we're the only ones who can free his brother," Dag said.

"Exactly."

"Do it."

Within hours, Marta's subcommittee—experts on extortion, intimidation, and forceful intent—came up with a two-part plan. First, they would track Chase's digital fortune and attack it. Second, they would arrange for Boone to be charged with a crime.

"Once Boone Malone gets arrested and is in custody," Blanco explained, "the only way those charges are going to disappear is with a few mouse clicks from us. We make that abundantly clear, and *require* Chase to come onboard if Boone is to get his life back."

"If not?"

"Then Boone is going to prison for a *long* time, and Chase is going to be broke."

"Perfect."

Chapter Thirty-Three

As Chase and Wen's chartered plane took off from Crescent City, heading to Breckenridge, Colorado, Chase read a message. "Bull's using her best darkness-hacking channels on finding information on Grimes."

"I'll be impressed if she finds anything," Wen said. "I sent the same data to The Astronaut. We'll do a video call with him as soon as we level off."

"I still can't believe you've heard of him," Chase said, continuing a conversation they'd had on the drive from Brookings to the airport.

"He's got a reputation. Discreet, efficient, resourceful."

"We got interrupted before you told me the rest."

"Not much to tell. He was on a list the MSS kept."

"Meaning they would hire him?"

"No. They rarely used freelancers, but liked to keep tabs. Grimes allegedly did work for the CIA, but was mostly doing private jobs."

"What else?" Chase asked, knowing Wen had an encyclopedic mind for details.

"He was elusive. No known permanent address. Spent most of his time between jobs in the Caribbean, or sailing around the world to warm, exotic ports."

"Brookings Harbor is *not* warm."

"He's not between jobs."

"The tattoo belongs to an elite special forces unit known as 'Finale,'" The Astronaut said. "It's a kind of French Foreign Legion run out of Morocco."

"Wow," Chase said.

"That's not to say we have found the shadow people, though. Particularly since none of the others you have found so far have had the tattoo."

"But I haven't checked them all."

"If you checked enough, including the two on the coastal trail, maybe . . . "

"The German may have belonged to that unit once, but no longer works for them," Chase theorized.

"Or they don't all get tattoos," Wen said.

"You can't wish this into being," The Astronaut cautioned her, knowing how much she would've liked closure on who the shadow people were. "Even if every shadow person you've ever killed belonged to Finale, it doesn't tell us *who* hired them."

"It gives us a place to start," Chase said. "There has to be a record somewhere."

"Says the man who made his fortune in the digital realm," The Astronaut said. "People like this, as I'm sure Wen will agree, do *not* conduct business across the digital sleeves."

"He's right," Wen said. "They meet in dark alleys in

eastern Europe, in hidden rooms in Asia, shadowy locations in the Middle East, where they make arrangements, slice up deals as if mercenary merchants."

"The situations they create collapse and roll with the winds of assured secrecy," The Astronaut added.

"They don't leave a trace," Wen agreed.

"But if it *was* them, someone knows," Chase said.

"Somebody in *your* world, perhaps," The Astronaut suggested.

Wen was already thinking. "Astaria will know if Finale is pursuing us, or if a few members are working for the shadow people."

"Can she tell us who hired them?" Chase asked.

"I've already asked her for help with the shadow people, and she had nothing," Wen said. "But we didn't have this information then. You know in intelligence it's all about information—any scrap, any thread, something as small as one grain of sand can change an entire hourglass or coastal flow."

"What about Grimes?" Chase asked.

"Recognize him?" The Astronaut asked as a photo appeared on their screen.

"Not really," Chase replied.

Wen nodded. "I recall a blurry file photo of him. This one is much better. Where did you get it?"

"I took it," The Astronaut said, as if it should have been obvious.

"*You?*" Wen asked. "How?"

"I worked with him once."

Chapter Thirty-Four

Dag didn't like the idea of sending an innocent man to prison for the rest of his life, but he had studied Chase Malone's profile, and knew he would not allow his brother to rot in prison.

"It will only be a matter of time and a few hard days," he'd said. "Chase will cave."

"It's necessary," Marta said, reading his face. "In the end, it's a better solution than the CIA killing him."

"Maybe," he said. "But a man like Chase Malone is not easily put off. We could be asking for more trouble than we had to begin with."

"It doesn't matter how tough or rich Chase and his friends are," Marta began. "I read his profile as well. He won't take on a fight he can't win. As Henry Kissinger once said: *'The absence of alternatives clears the mind marvelously.'* Chase will have no choice but to cooperate and move on."

"And if he doesn't?" Dag asked, realizing he sounded like his other executive vice president, Reggie.

"If he doesn't, then there are other ways to deal with

him. And do you *really* think the CIA is going to let him screw this all up?"

"I don't like to depend on the CIA," Dag said. "They're dinosaurs facing extinction, obsolete in a new digital world that they foolishly think they understand . . . but they're years behind. *We're* years ahead."

"Exactly. They helped to create this problem. Much of Chase Malone's profile has been redacted, highly classified. Our systems still aren't able to get in."

"Soon, maybe." Dag had been trying to hire an Astronaut to help with such problems. "Keep me up-to-date, and let me know when the brother is in custody. Have you figured out a way to get word to Chase?"

"We won't have to," Marta said. "His brother certainly has a way to contact him. I'm sure it won't take him long."

"We still need to have a discussion with him."

"You've read the profile," Marta said. "Malone will find us."

Chase and Wen drove from Breckenridge to Crested Butte and found the address that Astaria had given them. Chase knocked on the cabin door while Wen kept ready for any trouble.

A young man with three days of stubble answered the door. "Yes?"

"Hi, is Cristina around?"

"Cristina? No one named Cristina here."

Chase eyed the man suspiciously.

"Really?" Wen asked, studying him closely. "Are you sure? We were given this address."

"Yeah, I'm sure. It's just me and Poncho . . . he's my

dog." He pointed over his shoulder to a golden retriever who looked less like an attack dog, and more like a big puppy ready to play.

"I understand she doesn't live here. We were mistaken," Wen said, utilizing her sweet and friendly skills. "Someone gave us bad information, but she's an old friend who we need to see urgently, and I think you know where she lives."

It was the man's turn to study her. "I don't know," he said. But the slight shake in his voice and the fact that he tried to stare in her eyes, but at the last minute looked down to the left, told her that he did know.

"I'm trying to help her," Wen said softly, making him meet her eyes again. Chase did his best to try and look nonthreatening and non-interested.

The young man glanced back at Poncho, as if seeking advice. The dog perked up as if it might be time for a walk, or a game of fetch.

"Poncho, do you have any ideas?" Chase asked, petting the pooch's head when he wandered closer.

Poncho just licked Chase's hand.

"Please," Wen said. "Cristina *needs* our help." The expression on her face and the pleading softness in her tone exuded so much trust that, despite knowing the truth, even Chase believed her.

Apparently, so did the man. "She lives just up the road," he said, pointing back the direction they had come. "It's number forty-three."

"Thank you," Wen said, touching his hand as if to reassure him she was the good person she was pretending to be.

And they left.

"That was good back there," Chase said as they were getting in the car. "I almost believed you."

Wen looked at him as if hurt. "I told him the truth. We

are trying to help her. She's in great danger, but not from us."

Chase nodded and started the car. "What are you doing?" he asked as she punched buttons on an attachment to her phone.

"It's a jammer," she said. "The Astronaut built it for me. It'll jam all cell signals within about a hundred yards. We have to hurry."

"Why are you jamming cell signals?"

"Because he's trying to call her right now to warn her that we're coming, just in case he was wrong about us."

"But as soon as we pull away, he'll get a call through?"

"Yes, but she won't have time to get away, and anyway, now I've got her number. The device also pulls the number he's calling."

"There it is," Chase said a minute later, slowing the car and pointing. "Forty-three."

"And there she goes," Wen said, jumping out of the still-moving vehicle.

Chapter Thirty-Five

Wen grabbed Cristina as she tried to flee. Cristina kicked wildly and scratched Wen's arms.

"Let me go!"

"We are your friends," Wen said softly, trying to calm her. "We just need your help."

"Who sent you?" Cristina screamed, her voice filled with fear. Her words echoed Wen's own desperate plea each time she encountered a shadow person—*Who sent you? Who sent you?*

"No one sent us," Wen said, locking her body around Cristina's as the two women fell to the ground. "We came ourselves. We're trying to stop Bargo."

"Bargo! I *knew* it. They sent you. They know where I am."

"No, we are not *from* Bargo. We want to *stop* Bargo."

"How did you find me?" Cristina tried to wrestle out of Wen's grasp. "They sent you!"

Wen continued holding her. Chase thought it would be best if he intervened, believing she might trust him more since he had not restrained her. "We know about HaPPI," Chase said. "They've destroyed my brother's life with it. We want to stop them."

"You idiot, you *can't* stop them! They're too powerful."

"We're powerful, too," Chase said, trying to be reassuring, yet realizing his words probably sounded empty and naive to her. "We have lots of connections."

"How can you stop them? Do you have any idea how *big* this is?" She glared at Chase while trying to claw at Wen's face. "You know nothing!"

"That's why we need your help. *Please*, if you tell us what you know, it will help us stop them."

"No!"

Somehow, she bit Wen's wrist. Wen shook Cristina, shoved an elbow in her gut, then rolled so she was on top of her.

"We're not here to hurt you!"

"You don't understand." Her eyes darted, desperate, panicked. "If I tell you anything, they'll *know*."

"They won't," Wen insisted. "We aren't going to tell them anything."

"You don't *have* to. They *know* everything!"

"*Please*," Chase said. "They'll keep getting more powerful and destroy more lives. We can stop them."

Cristina began to cry. "You're wrong. They're already too powerful."

"We can get you to a safe place," Chase said quietly. "We can keep you safe."

"No," she said between sobs. "No you can't."

Wen continued holding her, but now it was more like a hug. Soon, Wen felt Cristina's demeanor soften. "I'm going to let you go," Wen said. "Please do not run, because I will just catch you again."

Cristina nodded. She looked at Chase as Wen slowly released her arms. Chase gave her his best friendly *trust me* expression, hoping it didn't look as goofy as it felt. He knew what it was like to be scared. He understood the pressure and weight of having a massive Corporation against you. To his surprise, she did not run when she got back to her feet. Instead, Cristina stayed and turned to face Wen.

"I don't know who you are, but you're wrong to try to stop them. They'll use erasure."

"Erasure?" Chase asked. "What's that?"

"See, you don't know anything," she muttered, wiping her nose on her sleeve. "Bargo can make your *entire* existence disappear. There's nothing left to prove your life except the scared, shaking, empty shell of your body, roaming the streets. Do you understand? They *destroy* people who get in their way."

"They won't find us," Chase said.

"They can find anyone!" she raged, then looked over her shoulder frantically as if they might've heard her outburst. "I've seen what they do to people. They leave them like . . . like *zombies*."

"We *can* stop them," Chase said again. "Just trust us."

"You've already put me in danger by coming here. I'll have to move now. I'll have to go this morning."

"We can help you get to a safe place."

"There's nowhere safe," she said, staring at them as if greatly insulted, then repeated, "There is *nowhere* safe."

"We have places," Wen told her.

Cristina shook her head. Her eyes filled again before her rigid strength returned. "Dag Kirrem is an evil man."

Wen nodded, hoping Cristina would continue, and she did.

"He must be stopped. If you two think you can try, then

you're crazier than me. I ran as far and as fast as I could. I thought I got away, but if you found me . . . "

She walked back inside. Wen and Chase followed her, watching as she started throwing clothes into a couple of suitcases.

"We need to know where they get all the information," Chase pressed. "What they want to do with it, and if you can help us get into the system."

She scoffed an angry, betrayed kind of laugh. "They get the information from everywhere, that's their trick. They have lines into every tech organization, have hacked into government databases. They have algorithms, programs which *devour* social media, Google, and all the other search engines, shopping sites, *everything*. They either have reciprocating agreements, or they steal it, but they get everything."

She stopped and stared at a silk blouse, as if deciding if it was necessary to take. She flung it on the bed, apparently rejecting it.

"And then there's this incredible program that uses some super advanced, deep learning, artificial intelligence that takes the aggregate and puts it into new forms so they can know what a person is *thinking*. What they're going to do *before* they even do it. It's frightening to see."

Chapter Thirty-Six

Chase wanted to ask Cristina why she was packing, where she was going to go, but thought it better to keep her talking about Bargo. "Where's the main HaPPI facility based?"

"I've watched them feed a name in, click a few buttons, and in minutes they can tell where the person was going to eat dinner that night, and HaPPI got it right. They even predicted how much of a tip he'd leave . . . nailed that to the penny."

Chase thought of SEER again. "*Where* is their data center?" he repeated.

"I don't think you get it," she said, still ignoring his question. "Once they have the nation, *they* have the control."

"Tell us how they erase someone," Wen said.

"First they destroy their credit rating, they close their bank accounts, move the money. They delete all their social media profiles, on and on it goes. And it's all done simultaneously, instantly. Then their car is repossessed, they're evicted or their home is foreclosed on. Job gone, medical, dental records gone. It's a rapid spiral. Suddenly you're left on the street with nothing but the clothes on your back."

"And that's a complete erasure?"

"Yeah, but there are other ways, too. Ones where they destroy a person little by little. They change your posts on social media, send your browser to child pornography sites, change your political preferences. Maybe have you supporting hate groups, visiting gambling sites, charge heavy amounts to your credit card at bars, liquor stores—there are a *thousand* ways to destroy a person in the digital age. With nothing real to touch anymore, a new reality can easily be created by your enemies."

"But why do they do this?" Wen asked.

"They do it to anyone who opposes them, or tries to expose them. Anyone who questions them."

"But what is the *ultimate* goal?"

"That's the scary thing. Dag believes he's creating a better world. He thinks they can root out all the undesirables. They aren't using the tools to destroy people because they don't like them, they're using everything to protect *themselves*."

Chase and Wen shared a glance.

"The rest of the time, HaPPI scrapes little bits of data from everywhere, rewarding a person for doing good things —paying bills on time, staying out of trouble, recycling, whatever. But if you do 'wrong' things, like gamble, pay late, talk against a specific authority, get a speeding ticket . . . then they keep lowering your scores until your life gets very difficult. If you don't change, you'll eventually be forced into a dark place. Often it will lead to crime, prison, or suicide."

"And Dag decides?"

She nodded. "The best way is for people to do the right

thing, but it takes all privacy and freedom of choice away from us. And as he has already shown, the system is ripe for abuse." She grabbed a tiny jewelry box and put it in one of the suitcases. "When I first worked with them, I believed in the vision of creating a better world by rewarding people for good behavior and punishing them for bad behavior. But soon I saw that it happens outside of the legal system. Worse, if the machines interpret things wrong, a victim has no way to argue against them once they start coming at him. It can easily become a self-fulfilling prophecy. They come at you again, and the more things you have against you, the more likely you are to get hit, which causes *more* action. It's a vicious circle, and there's no way to appeal."

"But you said he's trying to improve things."

"He does . . . but there are so many issues. The first thing they showed me was a company that keeps track of troublemakers in bars. They share with all the other bars. If one person in one bar accuses you of something, suddenly you can't go into any bars that use the service anywhere in the country. It gets worse. Bargo then takes *that* information and feeds it into HaPPI, so now our poor bar customer can't go into restaurants or stores or movie theaters, and it *keeps* going. The same guy who had one too many on a Friday night now can't buy airline tickets, rent a hotel room, and a hundred other things."

"That's why you left?"

She heard a noise and looked frantically out the window. After realizing it was just a passing truck, continued, "I saw it was getting out of control. I didn't want to be a part of it."

"So why are you so afraid?"

"Because I made a mistake. I . . . I knew just leaving wouldn't matter. They didn't *need* me. There are a thousand Cristinas. But if I could show people what they're doing, perhaps there could be some oversight or regulations. Privacy advocates would take over. If there are enough people going against them, then they cannot destroy them all."

"So you took data?" Chase asked.

She nodded.

"And they *know* you have it?"

She nodded again, more tentatively.

"Do you *still* have it?"

The absolute fear in her eyes told him the answer was yes.

"Will you show it to us?"

"I . . . I . . . umm . . . *who* are you?" she stuttered, then shook her head. "How can I trust you? I've just told you everything, why do I feel like that's okay? Who *are* you?" She stopped moving and stared at them. "You said there was somewhere safe?"

Chapter Thirty-Seven

Reggie found Dag in the corridor, staring at screens. "We have another issue," the executive VP said.

"CIA or Malone?" Dag asked, keeping his eyes on the data darting across the monitors.

"China."

Dag turned to Reggie and took a deep breath. He viewed Chase Malone and the CIA as ugly inconveniences, but China was a threat.

"They're closing in," Reggie said, knowing his boss would understand he meant Groson, Inc., the lead Chinese company behind the construction of the social credit system. Bargo had long been ahead, but Chinese firms, such as Groson, had many advantages, and were getting closer.

"Groson?"

Reggie nodded. Both men had read numerous reports about China's Communist government backing Groson, utilizing their country's massive population to "feed" the database.

"In China, you're always being controlled by the list,"

Dag said. "The list knows, the list will see you . . . the list is public."

"And the list makes mistakes," Reggie said.

Dag frowned, thinking of Boone Malone. "Mistakes are built in," he said. "With billions of profiles and trillions of data points, there *will* be errors. Everything is correctable."

Reggie thought of bringing up the suicides HaPPI had caused, but didn't. Yet his cheeks tightened involuntarily. Dag noticed. "In China, expressing any facts or opinions that the government doesn't like will cost a person big time on the list."

Dag gave his VP a puzzled look. HaPPI could do the same thing, but only if the US government was a client. "And?"

"Groson has a cache of insights into foreign political, military, and business figures. It's part of a program called Overseas Key Information Database, or OKIDB."

"Damn it."

"Yeah, they have infrastructure, military, demos, and information on millions of people in at least twenty-nine countries, including at least eighteen million Americans. Their focus has apparently been on government workers, military, and politicians."

"We have to stop them," Dag said. "Have you briefed Marta?"

"Not yet."

"Do it now, and tell her we need the CIA to fix this."

"Risky."

The comment didn't surprise Dag, but annoyed him nonetheless. "You may think we're wading into increasingly dangerous waters with HaPPI, but I assure you it's the Chinese Communist Party that's the danger here. The Chinese leadership sees truth as an existential threat to its continued rule, to its very existence. If we don't beat them to information dominance, we'll fall to their force, and we'll *never* catch up."

Chase and Wen helped Cristina pack up. She'd been moving a lot since leaving Bargo, so it wasn't a major ordeal. "Bargo took everything from me. I've lost my job, my savings, my home," Cristina said, her voice filled with emotion. "HaPPI blew apart my credit rating."

"Don't worry," Chase said while loading the car. "You'll stay at the safe house until—"

"Until *what*? Bargo gets more powerful by the minute."

"You can stay there as long as it takes. After that, we'll help you get back on your feet."

"If they don't get *you* first."

"They aren't getting us," Wen said, strongly enough that Cristina stopped and nodded.

"But we need to know everything. We need the evidence you have."

Cristina had explained earlier that she had a flash drive filled with incriminating information on Bargo and specifics about HaPPI. "I don't keep it here," she said. "It's in Paonia, a town on the other side of the mountain where no one is related to me, so Bargo can't trace me there."

"Then who has it?" Chase asked.

"It's concealed in a hardware store."

"We don't have time for this," Chase said, frustrated. "Bargo . . . my brother . . . "

"You need to go over the pass. It's a gravel road through the aspens. Off the grid. It's your best chance to avoid Bargo."

"You really think Bargo has any idea where you are?" Chase asked.

"If *you* found me, they're already on their way." She looked out the window. "Do what you want, but I'm leaving."

They agreed to trade cars. Cristina would return the rental car to the Breckenridge airport and fly to Florida, where Bull had arranged a safe house for her in the Florida Keys. Chase took the keys to her pickup truck and transferred their gear and luggage.

"Last question," Wen said. "Do you know anything about the US government's involvement with HaPPI?"

"You mean the CIA?" Cristina asked, getting into the driver's seat.

Chase and Wen exchanged a glance. "Yes."

"There's a woman. I don't know her name, but apparently she's a big shot. Part of the CIA's most secret division, or something. She's driving the whole thing, or at least she thinks she is. Dag has other ideas."

"Like what?" Wen asked.

"That as soon as HaPPI is fully sourced—having the entire population's data rolling—governments are going to be obsolete."

Chapter Thirty-Eight

They drove the pickup down the road. "It's hard to imagine this way is shorter," Chase said as he rounded a switchback, climbing a steep grade. The entire area was filled with a million quaking aspens, drenched in yellow leaves.

"But you can't deny the beauty," Wen said. "It's like we've entered some glorious world."

It was a stunning display of autumn magic—bright golden hues floating against the sunlight, mixed with stubborn remnants of clinging green. In the distance, they saw occasional veins of orange or a rare burst of bright red. The rolling colors, alive and fluttering, opened to vistas backed by craggy mountains, as if mythical old women danced and twirled in dresses of yellow lace.

"I never knew there were so many aspen trees in the entire world," she said. "We're surrounded by nothing but yellow."

As they came around another turn, they saw a tall, narrow pine tree, speckled in fallen aspen leaves that could have been golden Christmas lights. To Chase it looked more like a wizard standing defiantly in an enchanted forest. And that's just what they needed, he thought.

"What if Cristina lied and told us the hard drive was in Paonia just to get rid of us?" Chase asked.

"She's telling the truth."

Chase had long ago stopped asking Wen how she knew whether somebody was lying or not. "She's really scared," he said. "There must be something she's not telling us."

"There's a lot she is not saying, but she told us enough."

"Hopefully the remaining answers will come in Paonia."

"We haven't seen any other cars," Wen remarked after a couple minutes of quiet.

"Incredible scenery. I would think there'd be a long line of traffic wanting to take all this in."

"It is a weekday, and I think the trees are a week or so past peak."

"If this is *past* peak," Chase said, "next year let's come back for peak."

They both went quiet again, knowing it would never happen. They couldn't do normal things. Their lives were no longer any version of normal.

"Do you think Cristina will make it to the safe house?" Chase asked.

"If Bargo is as dangerous as she says . . . "

"Yeah," Chase said, letting his mind wander for a few moments. "We'll check with Bull as soon as we get back in range."

"I wonder how many more Cristinas there are . . . "

Rounding the next switchback, Wen noticed in the side view mirror that there was now a car behind them.

"Could be a problem," she said.

Chase checked the rearview. "They're not close enough for me to see the driver."

Wen spun in the seat to get a better view with her digital binoculars. "It looks like four people—men. And I see a gun barrel. It's trouble for sure."

"Shadow people, or Bargo?"

"It doesn't matter right now," she said.

Yet he knew that, of course, it *did* matter. She would change tactics based on all their previous encounters with shadow people, but until she was sure, they were just another threat.

Wen pulled out her MP7 submachine gun and handed Chase a Glock.

"I'm driving, what am I supposed to do with that?"

"You'll think of something."

Chase left the gun on his lap. The narrow gravel road wound through the trees with steep grades and edgy drop-offs. He couldn't imagine a scenario that meant he could take his hands off the wheel to shoot.

Wen put her pack on and immediately rolled down the window. "It's a Jeep Cherokee," Wen said. "And it's getting closer. Looks like they're ready to make a move."

The dense forest of aspens, with their endless silvery-gray trunks adorned with distinctive "eye" markings, seemed like an ancient fortress. The forest floor was carpeted in golden ferns and yellow aspen leaves inches deep. The Cherokee came up fast, spraying gravel and dirt as it flew through dust and swirling leaves. Chase wrenched the wheel of the old pickup as they fishtailed around another switchback, this time descending.

Wen pointed to a turnout. "Turn around!" she yelled.

But it was too late. They had already passed it. Chase flashed back to a previous mountain road pursuit in California and formed a strategy. They tore around another tight corner, the trees opening into a field with a panoramic vista of distant aspen trees too numerous to imagine. They were so far above them the trees appeared as rows of yellow flowers. It was an ethereal world, but one they might not escape.

Chase worked the brakes and accelerator back-and-forth in an impressive demonstration of his driving skills.

"They found us so quickly," Wen barked, trying to line up a shot at the driver.

Chase had been thinking the same thing. They were on an obscure back road in the middle of nowhere. "Cristina either told someone where we were going, or she may already be dead herself."

Chapter Thirty-Nine

The two women glared at each other. "You can't just do whatever you want," Susan said. "Don't you realize people's lives are at stake?"

Tess, who had been doing this more than twice as long as Susan, resisted the urge to explode. Her control was legendary—until those evenings at the shooting range. "I don't think you understand the complicated nature of the HaPPI program," Tess replied calmly. "And what the implications are for the future. This is by far the *most* complex and significant operation in the agency's history. We must be precise in how we deal with our corporate partners. The stakes couldn't be higher."

"It seems to me *you're* supposed to be the expert on dealing with corporations, so how did we get in such a precarious situation?" Susan spoke as if talking to a child. "If it's so complicated, perhaps you, with your *vast* experience, could enlighten us. There are those who question the need for CISS to even exist, and yet *somehow*, you have allowed this issue with Dag to get to the point where it could cause inestimable damage."

"HaPPI and Dag are not just *my* mess."

"Chase Malone *is* your mess, and he has endangered the entire HaPPI universe," Susan said, turning from Tess to the director of the CIA. "With all due respect, Director, I think we should ask if Tess is the proper person to be handling this."

Tess flashed her a deadly smile. She had clout that extended beyond the reach of the director, and with HaPPI any closer to full implementation, she would have even more to hold over the director. Threats from Susan were only a minor annoyance.

You have no idea what you're talking about, she thought silently at Susan.

Tess had been trying to uncover the origins of Susan's rise for *months*. Susan had an entirely different view on the role of the CIA than Tess did, but she wasn't about to let this misinformed novice jeopardize what Tess considered the most urgent matter she had dealt with in her career.

"Perhaps then you can explain your reluctance to remove Chase Malone. It seems completely at odds with ensuring the success of HaPPI."

Tess looked around the room and chose one person to direct her comments to—the woman sitting next to Susan, Mary Gladwell, head of the CIA's highly secretive and illegal domestic dark ops division, codenamed Alva.

"I don't think it has fully sunk in with some of you in this room," Tess began, staring at Mary. "HaPPI is here *regardless* of what happens with Chase Malone, or even to Dag Kirrem. The tech giants have been harnessing big data for twenty years, and with each passing month, their capabilities and power expand exponentially. This has led to unprecedented profits for these corporations, begetting even more power. Trillion. Dollar. Companies. *Trillions!*" Tess continued to exclusively hold Mary's gaze, yet she stood and paced dominantly, her cowboy boots clicking on the waxy floor. "That is what the public has seen, but the public is unaware of *so much* more."

"As you say, the money and data has led to unprecedented power for these corporations," Mary said. "Isn't that what CISS is supposed to be doing? Countering that?"

"Yes," Tess said curtly, masking her pleasure that Mary had taken the bait. "When this much power is concentrated in too few hands, it will consolidate further and be exercised to gain more power, more profits, more control. We have reached the tipping point. There is no going back. The corporations are in control, and HaPPI is the one thing that will act as an insurance policy. We *must* tread carefully here."

"Doesn't HaPPI give the corporations *more* control?" one of the men asked.

"Exactly why this partnership with Bargo is an incredible opportunity."

Susan smiled.

"What about Malone?" Mary asked.

"We must not act hastily in removing Chase Malone," Tess replied. "I'm not ruling out that tomorrow should be his last day on earth, I'm just saying it should not be *today*."

"What possible advantage does he give us?" the director asked. Although he held great respect for Tess, he also sensed the potential for disaster, and the concerns of the other divisional directors in the room.

"Chase is a problem," Susan said.

"Bargo's control must be checked," Tess replied, in answer to the director's question. "Chase is an extremely capable asset." She looked at Mary again. "Even now he's helping us without even knowing it."

Chapter Forty

Chase hit the gas, taking advantage of a straightaway. He steered into the next turn and flew around it, the Cherokee just feet behind. Wen fired, but the bullets went wide.

"Why aren't you hitting them?"

"It would help if you'd tell me *before* you accelerate or take a turn."

Two men from the Cherokee began returning fire, forcing Wen back into the truck.

By the time they got to the next hill, with a burst of speed, the Cherokee slammed into the back of them.

Wen used the collision, leaning back out of the window and sending a spray of rounds across the hood and front corner panel of the pursuing Jeep. It wasn't enough to stop them, but it allowed Chase to put some distance between the two vehicles.

Seeing another downhill escape, Chase accelerated. "Hold on!" he yelled, stomping the brakes. An instant later, the Cherokee crashed into them. At the moment of impact, he punched the accelerator and ripped through the loose road. Suddenly, they were sixty feet ahead, but the next obstacle was a series of switchbacks, and soon they were right on top of each other again. Wen and the men continued to exchange fire, but between the bouncing truck and the erratic swerving and dodging of bullets, she was unable to aim.

"What was that?" Chase yelled, hearing a *clang* in the bed of their pickup.

"Grenade!" Wen yelled. "Get out!" She opened her door and leaped, hitting the road hard and rolling, as she'd done plenty of times in other situations and hundreds more in training. She came up fast, simultaneously scanning for threats, looking for cover, and searching for Chase.

"Where's my gun?" she hissed.

Their pickup truck exploded, careening off the edge of the road.

The Cherokee screeched to a stop. The men jumped out and immediately began hunting her.

"We're on them now," Grimes reported to Belfort.

"Are you there personally?"

"Not yet, but our people—"

"Our people always seem to get killed by Malone and the woman—mostly by the woman."

"They're in Colorado, in the woods. I'll be there soon."

"Finish it this time," Belfort said firmly, masking his weariness. He'd given the bounty to six men, two women, and Grimes. Each had operated independently. Belfort coordinated and shared the intel, but they knew nothing of the others—only that they *might* exist. Each of the nine "leaders" had employed countless assassins and used numerous mercenaries, but only the two women and Grimes remained.

It was an impossible mission.

He'd have to recruit more bodies soon.

The Astronaut was happier than he'd been in years. He cared about Wen more than anyone else in his life. *She sees me,* he often thought. *Sees me completely*. It was a new sensation for a man who didn't like people and couldn't stand to be touched.

Great stress had filled his life once the shadow people began pursuing Chase and Wen. He'd built databases and programs to protect them and discover the identities of their enemies, but even with all the shreds of evidence and clues, the shadow people had remained stubbornly elusive. Until he finally identified Mumford Grimes, a man The Astronaut personally knew. The fact that he'd worked with Wen's great nemesis horrified him, and yet it also allowed him to be the hero, to penetrate the dark and secret world of the shadow people, and to stop them.

However, there were two problems.

The Astronaut actually *liked* Mumford Grimes, and he had no idea where he was.

Chapter Forty-One

Wen rolled down off the road. Through a tiny opening in the thick ferns, she saw the four men split up. She moved stealthily, as fast as she dared, to peer at the mangled pickup truck, now smoldering forty feet below, down an embankment.

"Come on, Chase," Wen whispered, praying he wasn't still inside. Bright yellow aspen leaves snowed down on the wreckage, like flower petals scattered over a dead body.

She strained, but it was impossible to see if Chase was down there. She knew if he was, the chances of him being alive were near zero. Even if there had been an easy way down, the four armed men would have made getting to Chase impossible. Instead, she decided to concentrate on taking the men out one by one, a task made much harder with the loss of her Glock and the submachine gun. Wen checked inside her pack, finding she was left with just a knife and a handful of throwing stars—thin blades of hammered steel custom-made by an old master in Japan.

That should be enough, she said to herself. *Now I need to double back and get behind them.*

Suddenly, the stillness and beauty of the forest erupted in a barrage of machine-gun fire. Yellow leaves took the form of confetti as pine needles, bark, and shredded organic matter created a furious dust storm. Wen slid down the mossy hillside half out of necessity and half accidentally, quickly going into commando mode. She waded back through the ferns and underbrush, her hair gathering leaves and bark while she fought her way closer to the men.

After the gunfire finally ceased, the ringing in her ears made it temporarily impossible to detect the movements of the men.

They must have seen me jump out on the passenger side. I need to get to higher ground on the other side of the road . . . less likely to find me there.

Finally she found a stand of aspens that had grown close enough together that she could get a view of the road while staying concealed. She came up out of the leaves, hugging three narrow trunks surrounded by eight or nine others. Peering through a tiny gap between the silvery bark, she spotted one of the men standing by the vehicle.

The other three are out there looking for me.

She tried to see around another trunk. It was risky being blind.

They can't be far. I've got to make a move.

Wen darted into the road without her normal preparation or counting, swiftly arcing wide behind the Cherokee. Catching the man by surprise, she had him pinned on the ground before he could turn and shoot. Even though she was desperate to ask who'd sent him, there was no time. She had to remove the threat and get his weapon.

In a split second, she'd efficiently ended his life by snapping his neck. Believing Chase might be dead, and knowing the men had been sent to kill them, she felt no remorse. If it could save Chase, Wen would've killed him again without hesitation.

Taking his gun, she ran to the Cherokee for cover.

Are the keys in it? Yes.

She took them, but, leaning into the front seat, changed her mind.

If I start the engine, I'll be riddled with machine gun fire.

As much as she wanted to drive away, her best chance was on foot—especially until she killed the other three men.

At least now I have a gun. She didn't even mind that it was an ultra-modern Sig Sauer 729 submachine-gun. She stabbed her knife into one of the tires and would have done another, but it made too much noise.

Wen moved into the opposite side of the forest, putting dozens of trees between her and the road. She wanted to escape, but she had to find out what had happened to Chase. Crouching behind the aspens, she checked the weapon, horrified to find that it was equipped with a digital safety, meaning there was no way she could fire the gun without entering a four digit code to unlock it. It was like having no weapon at all.

Why would they have such a thing? Maybe good for a bluff, but nothing more.

Wen retreated further back into the trees, a new plan formulating in her mind.

Then she heard a twig snap behind her.

Chapter Forty-Two

Lisa Hayes woke up to a strange noise. She checked the time. It was still half an hour before her alarm would normally chime.

Why am I up?

A grinding sound outside pulled at her attention. She pushed back the window drapes and discovered the source of the irritating intrusion.

"What the?" she yelled. "*Hey!*" She pounded on the window, but the men loading her 2020 Acura onto a flatbed couldn't hear her.

By the time Lisa got dressed and had run downstairs and out the front door, the truck, with her car riding on top, was well down the street. She found a repo notice hanging on the knob of her front door. It was too early to call her bank, but she knew there'd been a mistake. The payments for her car loan were set up on an automated service. She'd never missed a payment. Lisa had near perfect credit.

Then she checked her bank balance and at first thought

she'd been the victim of a hack. Her account was empty. Her credit cards were maxed out.

Lisa dialed the 800 number on the back of her card, frantic that she'd been hit by some kind of identity theft.

Why isn't the call going through?

She began to cry when she pulled the cell phone away from her ear and realized her service had been cut off.

Lisa had never heard of Bargo, and certainly not HaPPI, and yet she had just endured one of the side effects of the new digital age.

Later that day, Lisa found herself in the office of Carol Hill, a lawyer who specialized in consumer protection law.

"You've been targeted," Carol explained.

"By whom?"

"I don't know yet. It's a murky world. There are these firms," Carol began. "They excel at in tapping into digital realms, and siphoning and storing vast troves of data."

"*Why?*"

"The data is consumed and digested by complex algorithms. A kind of 'risk score' is generated, but it's not something you're used to, like a credit rating. These scores have been likened to digital mug shots. *Everything* goes into them —medical records, employment, financial, browsing histories—there are hundreds of thousands of inputs."

Lisa looked horrified.

"Every website you've visited, every 'like' you clicked on social media, every friend, post, search query—*all* of it is collected and analyzed."

"Is this *legal?*"

"Some of it is, some of it might not be, but there are

significant gray areas. These firms peddle your risk scores to landlords, retailers, insurers, potential employers—it's endless."

"Can't the government stop this?"

"The government might just be the biggest customer of all for these parasites."

Carol promised to get back in touch with Lisa in the morning. Brian Elliott, his friend Steve—who had also lost his job—and Steve's wife, Keri—who had been kicked out of nursing school—had also contacted Carol earlier in the day. She saw similar patterns in all their cases, and had several other clients who were going through the same situation as well.

"These are harsh and blatant attacks," she'd told them all. "I'm preparing a class action suit."

Unable to even use Uber, Lisa replayed Carol's words as she drove home in a car borrowed from a friend.

Carol had explained that these kinds of issues had grown worse recently, but had been increasing for the past year or two as the unregulated collection of data from thousands of sources—including smart appliances, phones, vehicles, traffic and surveillance cameras, with the recognition of facial characteristics, voice tone, speech patterns, sleep habits, *everything*—skyrocketed.

And we give it to them voluntarily, Lisa thought, growing angrier again.

"We aren't allowed to see or review the data they use against us," Lisa explained to her friend when she returned the car. "These machines, super AI, algorithm things just rate us, and we can't do anything about it."

"But why did they roast your life?"

"Don't know. Maybe I voted for the wrong guy, visited the wrong site . . . Maybe all my data put together makes me look like some kind of risk."

"A risk to who?"

"Whoever pays for all this . . . I don't know. The corrupt elites who want to control us?"

"He who has the gold makes the rules."

Carol worked for the rest of the day trying to trace the attacks back to one specific company. She had a list of firms collecting the data. Some were independent, others were in-house operations, such as wireless companies, who created massive amounts of records and used them to expand their businesses by taking advantage of their users.

So much of our lives lived through our smartphones, she thought. But for the first time, she was truly fearful about what was happening. These cases were different. A class action lawsuit would be a powerful signal to the tech industry, but first she had to find out *which* company was behind it all.

There seems to be one huge corporation pulling everything together . . . a control so great that it could act like a super-leach that could suck the lifeblood from society.

It was the last thought Carol had before she died.

Chapter Forty-Three

Wen instinctively pulled the trigger, which fortunately could not fire, as she looked into the eyes of her beloved Chase.

He held up his hands, regret in his eyes that he had startled her, fully expecting to die. When the gun didn't go off, they both fell instantly into each other's arms and dropped to the ground.

"The gun has a safety," she whispered.

"Good thing. Would have been damn ironic if after everything, *you'd* been the one to kill me."

"Can you bypass it?" she asked, handing him the Sig Sauer.

Chase looked at the gun. "How many are left?"

"Three," she told him, sounding ashamed.

"We need that vehicle."

She nodded, knowing they'd now have to change a tire.

Chase knew, as she did, that they were sitting ducks with three men still out there. "I need more time to figure out how to get this safety off, and tools," Chase said, handing the gun back to her.

"What about your multitool?"

He shook his head. "No, this needs precision screwdrivers, proprietary heads . . . "

"I don't suppose you have the Glock?"

"I think it's still in the truck . . . "

"Let's forget about the Cherokee and—"

"OVER HERE!" a man shouted as he discovered the body of the man she'd killed. The three men left fanned both sides of the road with machine gun fire. Chase and Wen were far enough back to be safe from the initial assault.

"Let's get out of here," Chase urged.

Once the gunfire stopped, it became obvious the men still didn't know where they were. Wen led, slithering her way up the hill, cloaked in aspen leaves as they went deeper into the thickening forest.

"Once we reach the ridgeline," Wen said, "we'll be safe."

"For how long? We don't have any guns."

"Our best weapon now is distance."

They trudged through the trees. More shouts drifted up to them from the men below.

"How come they aren't driving?" Chase asked, puzzled.

"Well, I have the keys," Wen said, smiling, "and they probably haven't had time to fix the tire."

Chase actually laughed.

As they climbed higher, Chase wished he had water. Still only halfway to the top, he suggested a break. "They don't know where we are."

"We can't see them either."

A few minutes later, they heard the Cherokee's engine start.

"Guess they hot-wired it," Chase said.

"I thought you were the only one who could do that."

"They don't do it as good as I do," Chase shot back.

"Where are they going?" Wen mused. "They can't drive up here."

"Got a sandwich in there?" Chase asked, pointing to her pack.

"Sorry. Let's get up to the ridge so we can see what's on the other side."

"I already know what's over there. More aspens. *Lots* more."

He was right. At the top, more aspens came into view than they thought possible to exist in one place.

"There must be millions," Wen said.

"We can walk the ridgeline," Chase said, after only allowing an instant to absorb the spectacle.

"Risky. Let's go down and follow that line out," Wen suggested, pointing to a sloping seam through the trees. "I bet we can pick up the road over that way, and we'll be closer to Paonia."

Chase looked up at the sky. "It's a long walk. We might be spending the night out here."

"Walking."

"Yeah . . . we still haven't seen any other cars."

"Let's worry about that when the time comes."

"Shadow people or Bargo?" Chase asked a little while later.

"Shadow people," she said. "The man I killed had a tattoo."

"Finale?" Chase asked, referring to the elite special forces unit.

"The same."

Almost two hours passed in near silence as they tried to put miles behind them. They were still far from anywhere when a vehicle appeared in the distance. Chase and Wen had been following the dusty road for the past hour, careful to stay twenty feet off into the trees.

"It's not the Cherokee," Wen said, using the binoculars from her pack.

"Are you sure?"

"No, but from what I can see of the silhouette, I really don't think it is."

"There's one way to find out," Chase said as the vehicle slipped below a hill.

"Right." She handed Chase her knife.

"You know, the only thing I like *less* than shooting someone is stabbing someone."

"I know exactly what you mean," she said as the vehicle surfaced again. "Our only other weapon is the throwing stars, and I don't think—"

"You're right." Chase sighed. "I liked it better when our best weapon was distance."

They ran toward the vehicle.

Chapter Forty-Four

Wen squinted into the sun. She couldn't be sure from that angle, but it was definitely some kind of SUV's profile.

"It looks like the Cherokee!" Chase yelled.

She positioned a star in each hand. "I don't think so."

Chase thought they might have just committed suicide. "This is crazy!"

The vehicle slowed.

"They see us!" Chase shouted, clutching the knife.

A battered Ford Bronco from another century, brakes squeaking, came to a stop. An old man leaned out the window. "Y'all need some help?"

Wen quickly profiled him. Long, deep, inset laugh lines around his gentle, pale blue eyes, a kind and permanently boyish grin—a good and easy man, she decided. The type who enjoyed helping people.

"We seem to have lost our pickup truck," Wen said.

"Not an easy thing to do," the man said, looking back as if it might be broken down on the side of the road. "Can I help you find it?"

"It's not really findable anymore," Wen told him. "But we could use a lift."

"Where you headed?"

"Paonia," Chase said, then added in his best country speak, "Be obliged if you could get us there. Happy to give you some gas money."

"Sure, hop on in." He patted the old vinyl bench seat. A scruffy dog glanced up at him. "Move over Misty."

The dog stayed still.

Chase opened the door to let Wen in first, but she shook her head and climbed in the back. Chase got in front. Misty gave him an annoyed look. Chase recalled a woman who'd once rescued them whose dog had drolled on him. He remembered her name, Alasie, but not the dog's.

How do I always end up with the dogs?

"My name's Dunbar," the old man said, holding out his hand. "My word . . . are you Chase Malone?"

Chase looked back at Wen before he answered, a little surprised to be recognized by an old man out in the sticks. Wen just widened her eyes, as if she wasn't sure how to respond. Chase figured that if the old codger had already guessed his name just from a quick look at his face, there would be no point in trying to dissuade him. "Yeah. Matter of fact, I am."

"*The* Chase Malone, in *my* pickup truck, net worth 1.3 billion, holder of eighty-seven patents, inventor of RAI . . . Well, well, well. What are you doing way out here?"

Chase, unnerved by hearing the highlights of his biography, struggled for words. "We're enjoying the fall colors," Wen supplied from the backseat.

"I guess it seems a little unusual to pick up a billionaire in the middle of nowhere," Chase finally said.

"You might be surprised," Dunbar said, slowly pulling

away from where he'd found them. "I've actually done it before."

Chase laughed as if it was a joke.

Dunbar smiled. "No. True story. I picked up Howard Hughes wandering through the desert in 1967. Course, he was in a little bit different shape than you are, and I was a fair bit younger then."

Chase nodded and looked back at Wen as if they'd just been picked up by a crazy person, or entered the Twilight Zone. Wen shrugged, not knowing who Howard Hughes was, and still convinced Dunbar was just a sweet old guy.

Misty put her head on Chase's lap. Wen continuously looked behind them.

"Yeah, I'm a bit of a corporate history hobbyist. Sort of collect entrepreneurs like baseball cards. You know, as I said, I was pretty young when I first encountered Howard Hughes, and it kinda changed me. Something like that has a pretty big impact and all. Guess ever since, I've been fascinated by business-driven people and the like." He rattled off a bunch of facts about Jeff Bezos, Steve Jobs, Elon Musk, and Ted Turner, before Chase finally stopped him.

"Well, I don't feel so creeped out now that I know there are others you're obsessed with."

Dunbar laughed. "I wouldn't call it an obsession. It's really just a hobby. I don't have a thousand pictures of you pinned up all over my wall or nothing. I used to keep notebooks. Back before computers. Facts, figures, things like that . . . Clippings . . . But now I got everything on my Apple MacBook Pro. Kinda like looking at the charts."

They rounded a turn, Chase and Wen both watching for the Cherokee—or others.

"What were you doing up here today, if you don't mind me asking?" Wen asked.

"Same as you. I'm an old man. When you get this close to eighty, the world looks different. The beauty seems brighter. I try to see as much of it as I can."

"You have a lot of time on your hands?"

"Yes and no, right?" Dunbar said with a chuckle. "But I read once, 'time is a funny thing.'"

"So you came for the colors?"

"I come up most every day. There may not be a more beautiful spot on earth than this, at least in October. Colorado in October, no place better." He laughed again. "Although, I got friends in Virginia and New England who disagree, but they're wrong."

Chapter Forty-Five

Chase had thought the enchanted forest was more beautiful *before* he had to leap from an exploding pickup truck. All he could think about now was how many times they had escaped death.

Who are the shadow people? Why are they after us?

No immediate answers came.

He'd tried to meditate back before Dunbar found them, when the sunlight still illuminated the aspens, making them glow as if they were plugged into some invisible power source. None of his Buddhist teachings came to comfort him, no great insights, no inner peace. Only the image of Tu, a lost little boy wise beyond his years, who Chase had grown to love dearly.

He thought of their last conversation, when Tu had asked him to promise to take him trick-or-treating on Halloween. The Astronaut had told the boy about the holiday. He'd never heard of it during his life in China, and it had intrigued him, just as the amusement park had. Tu's form of excitement, of wonderment, was in analyzing an experience.

I hope that truly gives him joy, Chase thought.

It wasn't just the MSS coming after Tu now, though. The shadow people had tried to get him at the carnival. He was sure of it.

I guess that's why James Bond, Jason Bourne, and guys like that don't have any kids . . .

Dunbar seemed content to ride in silence, but every so often, he would make a comment or ask a question as if awakened from a trance. Chase couldn't help but like the old man. He kind of reminded him of his grandfather, and somehow made him miss his father as well. Whenever he was with Tu, he missed his father even more.

Tu should be on his way to Iowa now . . . I miss him so much.

For the last few years, Chase felt like he and Wen were in a constant epic battle with evil, anger, and lies. But riding along with Wen, Misty half on his lap, and the old man through the magical forest, he absorbed a strange moment of peace.

"What's in Paonia?" Dunbar asked, looking in the rearview mirror, directing the question to Wen.

"We have to pick up something for a friend."

"It's a little town . . . where at?"

"Mountain Hardware. Will it still be open?"

"Oh yeah. I go *there* just about every day, too."

"You're a busy man," Chase said, joining the conversation.

"Well yeah, you gotta keep busy or ya die. And . . . I actually own that store."

Wen tried to hide her surprise. Normally it would've been an insignificant detail, but now it seemed just one of too many coincidences. "Really?" She almost asked him if he knew Cristina, but decided against it.

"What are you picking up? I know the inventory pretty well."

Chase jumped in, knowing Wen might not have a believable answer for that one. "We need a spanner flange."

"They didn't have that at Bucky's Hardware in Breckenridge?"

"We left early, before it was open," Chase said. "Do you have one?"

"Sure, $19.99. Normally for a friend of mine, like you are now, I'd give you a discount, but seeing how you could buy the item, along with the whole store, I think I'll let you pay full sticker."

"No, I insist on paying full price, and will still be happy to pay for gas."

"Forget it, I was heading that way anyway. We'll be there in a few minutes."

Ten minutes later, they pulled up to the store. Inside, customers and employees alike all seemed pleased to greet Dunbar and Misty.

Chase and Wen split off while Dunbar was in conversation with someone about a Kohler valve stem.

"She said it was in the bulk nail bin," Wen said.

"Over here." Chase motioned to two five foot high spinning steel fixtures filled with bulk nails and screws.

"One green, the other gray—just like Cristina said."

"That's a good sign."

Wen reached around on the bottom of the gray one, just under the center post and above the 16d galvanized finish nails. "I got it," she said, pulling out a small, black, magnetized, hide-a-key case. She slid the top open and, as promised, inside were six flash drives. "Let's go."

"How?" Chase said. "We've got no wheels."

"Let's find Dunbar. Maybe he'll sell you his truck, or knows someone who can sell us something."

As they walked past the big front window, Chase spotted the Jeep Cherokee slowly rolling up the street.

They quickly found Dunbar. "Is there a back door?" Chase asked.

Dunbar looked concerned. "Someone you don't want to see out front?"

"Not really."

"Cause it's a real friendly town, and there—"

"Back door?" Chase interrupted insistently.

"Yeah, sure." He pointed. "Did you get your spanner flange?"

"Later," Chase snapped.

They jogged to the back of the store. Dunbar caught up to them in the back parking area.

"We need a car," Chase said.

"How about that pretty Mercedes?" Dunbar said, laughing. "I have the keys."

"That's *your* Mercedes?" Chase said. "I guess the hardware business is good."

"Yeah, well."

"I'm sorry Dunbar, we're in a bit of trouble," Wen said emphatically.

"I guess so. People who aren't in trouble don't usually take the back door."

"We need to get out of town," she told him. "*Now*."

Chapter Forty-Six

Bull and The Astronaut exchanged greetings across their encrypted private video network. The Astronaut had co-opted a slice of bandwidth from the US intelligence network known as 'Heaven.'

"Progress," Bull said, reviewing the shadow people files they had maintained since the first attack on Chase and Wen nearly two years earlier. "How do you know him?"

"Mumford Grimes is one of the best there is," The Astronaut said.

"Best what?" Dez asked. He was working on a multi-screen setup next to Bull.

"Hit man," Bull answered.

"I think Grimes would prefer the term 'cleaner.' He isn't always hired to *kill*," The Astronaut specified. "He cleans up messes."

"But mostly he's an assassin," Bull said.

"So why did you work with a low-life like Grimes?" Dez asked.

"I would never call Mumford Grimes a low-life."

"He's trying to kill Chase and Wen," Dez said angrily.

"Grimes isn't the one who wants them dead," The Astronaut said. "He's just the tool, like the Glock 19 Wen uses. That pistol can't kill anyone without Wen pulling the trigger. Taking away the Glock doesn't stop Wen from ending a person's life."

"You're saying if we stop Grimes, there'll just be another," Bull said.

"Precisely. Just look at the list of shadow people that Wen and Chase have killed. And yet they keep coming."

"So your pal, Grimes, isn't a problem?" Dez asked. "You just told us he's one of the best."

"Yes, and that's why he can be *reasoned* with. Grimes is smart. Practical. He understands the nuances in the world. He has been trained to look for the patterns."

"You think he'll help us?" Bull said.

"Grimes is our best chance to find out who is trying to kill Chase and Wen. He likely doesn't know their names, but he has all the information we need to allow us to discover their identities."

Marta walked into the corridor as Dag was just finishing up a phone call. He motioned for her to check one of the data screens. She nodded, having just received a similar alert. As soon as his call ended, he joined her in front of the monitor.

"Apparently the glitch has been fixed," Dag said, pointing to a row of numbers.

"I hope so," Marta said. HaPPI had inadvertently pushed hundreds of consumers past the standard "rating" stage into a combination of dynamic intervention and erasure.

Reggie walked in, a smile on his face. "Did you see? They stopped the glitch."

"We were just discussing it," Marta said coolly.

"Then maybe we can settle the class action."

Dag and Marta exchanged a glance. Bargo had discovered Carol Hill's intention to file a suit against them before Carol had even met with Lisa Hayes. HaPPI had many uses; in addition to scoring the risk of consumers, it could also detect the risk to companies and governments.

"It's taken care of," Dag said.

"What?" Reggie asked. "How?"

"You don't want to know," Marta said.

"Oh my god," Reggie said, putting his face in his hand. "We fixed the glitch. The problem was *solved*."

"We can't have a class action," Marta said. "The publicity, the questions, the scrutiny would be endless, the damage irreversible."

"What if another attorney shows up?"

Marta stared at him as if the answer to that was obvious.

"How many people are we going to kill?" Reggie asked, obviously distressed.

"Keep your eye on the ball," Marta said. "We are saving lives."

"It doesn't seem like it."

"Remember, it's about the net gain. We are on the right side of this."

"Risk assessment is the new religion," Dag said. "We have the power to create a better world."

Marta smiled. "They can't stop us."

"What about Cristina?" Dag asked.

Marta frowned. "We have the biggest intrusion

surveillance system in the world, and we can't find one dumb woman."

"She knows too much."

"I'll take it," Reggie interrupted.

Marta and Dag shared a surprised look.

"She was in my department," he said defensively. "I have some leads."

"Then finish her."

"What if they escape again?" Shelby asked as their plane took off.

"There will be another chance," Grimes said, wishing he and Shelby were on a beach on St. Lucia or one of his other favorite Caribbean islands.

"Belfort might disagree. The Cartel must be running out of patience."

"That's their problem. No one else has closed the deal yet, and we're getting closer."

"We are?"

"Yeah," Grimes said, closing his eyes, hoping for some sleep. "That's why we're not going to Colorado."

"Where are we heading then?" she asked, surprised.

"Iowa."

Chapter Forty-Seven

Dunbar smiled. "I'm always happy to join an adventure." He pointed to the Mercedes. "Jump in."

"Thank you," Chase said sincerely, climbing into the back of the car.

"Should I know *why* there's people you want to avoid?"

"Probably better if you don't," Wen told him.

"Still, it might make it easier if I do," he said as he drove down the narrow alley behind the hardware store.

Wen and Chase, both in the backseat, ducked down as they exited onto the main street on the side of the building.

"Is it that Jeep Cherokee?"

"Yes," Wen said.

"You really don't like those people." Dunbar chuckled. "Seems strange, a billionaire wandering through the woods, running from people in a Jeep Cherokee. Sounds like a good plot for a thriller novel. Ever read Nick Thacker?"

"The truth is, we don't know who they are," Wen said. "But they've been after us for more than a year, and they're trying to kill us."

"*Kill* you?" Dunbar echoed, shocked.

"I'm sorry we've put you in danger," Wen told him.

"Oh, don't worry about me," Dunbar said thoughtfully. "I offered to help, so I have to help."

"Thank you."

"But how can you not know *why* someone wants you dead?" Dunbar asked.

"They've never told us," Chase said.

"I could stop and ask."

"I don't think that's a good idea," Chase said, still not sure how many cards Dunbar was playing with.

"Are these fellas gonna be shooting?"

"I really don't know what their capabilities are, but they do have guns," Chase said. "And, again, as Wen said, we definitely have to apologize for putting you in a tough spot."

"We'll get through all right. I'm not too impressed with their vehicle," Dunbar said, looking in the rearview. "You two can sit up now. They don't seem to be following us."

Wen popped up and looked around, seeing the Cherokee way back on the road just as Dunbar took a left onto a side street. "They may still find us."

"I've got an idea," Dunbar said. "Maybe you can tell me where you *really* want to go. I don't think you much needed that spanner flange."

"No, we just made that up."

"Wouldn't make sense to come all that way for a five dollar item."

Chase frowned at him. "You said it was twenty."

"Seems you aren't the only one who makes stuff up." Dunbar chuckled. "If they catch us, they'll maybe want to kill me, too?"

"Yeah, 'fraid so," Chase said almost timidly.

Dunbar was silent for a few moments. "What happened to your vehicle?"

"They blew up our pickup truck."

Dunbar whistled. "Boy . . . I guess that was the truth when you said you lost your truck." He swung a right onto a forested road. The trees weren't all aspens, and many displayed red and orange leaves.

"Beautiful trees," Wen commented.

"Oh, the leaves. I planted most of these trees. Got tired of everything just turning yellow here. Visited my brother back east in Vermont. Had so many colors on their trees, I wanted the same thing."

"When did you plant these?"

"Don't know. Gotta be forty, fifty years ago."

"Pretty nice."

"Yeah."

Wen continued checking behind them.

"I don't think they knew you were in my car."

"Can't count on it," Wen said. "These people have ways. Do you have any traffic cameras in town, security . . . ?"

"Sure, there's some."

"Then they'll figure it out. You've taken enough chances for us. We should get out before they—"

"Now, hold on," Dunbar interrupted. "I'm not afraid of this. Let's figure out a way to get you safely out of town." He pushed a button on his dash.

"Paonia Police," a woman's voice came through.

"Hi, Peg, it's Dunbar."

"Hey Dunbar. Everything okay?"

"I need a favor. Can you patch me through to Jack?"

"Sure thing. Problem at one of your stores?"

"Nah, just want to help Jack earn his pay today."

Peg laughed. A couple seconds later, he was talking to Jack Gilbar, Chief of Paonia Police.

"Hey, Jack, there's a maroon Jeep Cherokee in town. Any chance you could pull them over for me?"

"Any chance they're violating the law?"

"I think they've got some unlicensed weapons in their vehicle."

"You know we don't look too kindly on that."

"Maybe you could be really careful and give them a talking to. They were on main, 'bout three blocks past the hardware store last I saw them."

Chase had been shaking his head the whole time. "You're going to get Jack killed," Chase blurted out as Dunbar ended the call.

"I don't think so. Ol' Jack's ex-Green Beret."

"You should at least give him a heads up that they've got machine guns," Wen said.

"Jack was FBI *after* the Green Berets. He responds to just about every kinda dangerous thing there is, and what's more, he *knows* Paonia."

"Dunbar, that may be, but you *really* don't understand," Chase insisted. "These people are hired assassins."

"*Okay*, if it'll make you happy, I'll send him a text in a minute. But truthfully, I'd be more worried for the folks in the Cherokee."

Chapter Forty-Eight

Dunbar pulled the Mercedes onto a long paved driveway. The huge wrought iron gate at its end opened swiftly. "Where are we?" Chase asked.

"Home."

"Home?"

"This is my place."

A palatial log cabin came into view.

"Nice cabin," Wen said.

"More like a mansion," Chase said. "I guess hardware is a *really* good business."

"Oh, that's just my guest house. Well, one of them. If you need a place to stay, you're quite welcome to stay in one as long as you need."

"*Guesthouse?*" Chase echoed, looking again at the huge home.

"Yeah. My place is up here another half-mile or so."

"The hardware store paid for all this?"

"No, I actually lose money on that store, but it's good for the town."

"So, since you know so much about me, mind if I ask how you made all *your* money?"

Dunbar laughed. "Turns out, you know, when old Howard died, he mentioned me in his will."

"*Howard Hughes* left you money? You were telling the truth back there?"

"Yep. You're the only ones who lie in this car."

"Normally we don't," Wen said.

Dunbar cackled. "That's okay. You had a good reason. I've been spending Howard's money for decades, and I still don't believe it."

"You're a good man, Dunbar. We appreciate what you've done for us."

"Maybe you'll mention me in *your* will. Kind of a tradition with you billionaires." He laughed so hard he lapsed into a coughing fit. By the time he got it under control, they were in front of the main house.

"That's the biggest log mansion I've ever seen," Chase said. "Why such a big place?"

"Well, all the local people built it. Back in the seventies, the economy was sort of busted, and I just kept building on the place and all the guest houses so they'd have work around here. I suspect everyone in three or four counties worked for me at some point or another.

"You really should stay here," Dunbar said. "And I'll check on Jack."

"We need to get to the airport," Wen said.

"Don't you think the people trying to kill you will think of that?" Dunbar asked as a text came in on his phone. "Yikes, you were right. Jack didn't fare too well."

"Oh no," Chase said.

"No, he's not even injured. But they blew up his police car."

"I guess I'll have to replace that," Chase muttered.

"Well that's kind of you, but you may not be alive," Dunbar said, looking up from his phone, his characteristic smile gone. "Cherokee's headed this way, and the other police are too far out to stop them."

"Great . . . " Wen looked around. "We can defend from here."

"You're forgetting we don't have any guns," Chase said.

"You have any weapons?" she asked as Dunbar led them inside the massive home. A vaulted ceiling with tree sized beams, balconies, and an Escher-like series of staircases greeted them.

"I might have a few." A minute later, after quickly taking them down several crisscrossing hallways, he stopped and opened a locked metal door behind a sliding wood panel.

"Wow," Wen said.

"It looks like an armory for a SWAT division," Chase said. "Do you get a lot of Cherokees up here?"

"Sort of a hobby."

"Like collecting billionaires?" Chase asked.

"Yeah, I guess they're somehow related. Comes in handy."

"MP7," Wen said, smiling at her favorite gun.

"Take what you need, but try your best not to let my place get all chewed up."

Wen took a couple pistols, and the MP7, and stuffed several extra mags in her pockets and pack. Chase grabbed an AK47 and a Desert Eagle pistol.

"You sure you want to fight here?" Dunbar asked. "I can get you to the airport."

"Airport seems risky while the Cherokee is coming."

"I could fly you in my helicopter."

"You've got a helicopter?"

"Howard Hughes left me a *lot* of money," Dunbar said. "I got a private plane at the airport, too."

Chase laughed. "You're quite a remarkable fella."

"Oh, not really. I just accidentally led a colorful life."

"What do you think?" Chase asked Wen.

"I should warn you, I'm not the best pilot in the world," Dunbar said before she could reply. "But I can fly. My pilot is out of town right now."

Wen looked at him. "If you will allow me, I'm a very good pilot."

"She can fly?"

"She's a damn good pilot," Chase told him with a hint of pride.

"Excellent." Dunbar called ahead and asked them to get his jet ready.

"We'll need to file a flight plan, once we know where we're heading," Wen said. "Let's get to your helicopter."

"That could be a problem," Dunbar said, pointing to a bank of security monitors above the gun racks. "Our friends in the Cherokee just pulled up."

Chapter Forty-Nine

Chase, Wen, and Dunbar took positions on the veranda, then quickly spread out into the trees. Chase got the first shots off as the Cherokee pulled through the circular driveway. He unloaded the AK47, the bullets ripping across the hood and tearing into the side, taking out two tires and injuring one of the men.

"I don't think they have a spare," Chase said, knowing Wen had already flattened one of the tires back in the forest.

"They better not try to take my Mercedes," Dunbar muttered.

"Circle around," Wen said. "They're going to try to come through the gates."

"I'll hold them off while you get to the chopper," Dunbar yelled after them.

"We can't leave you!" Wen shouted, running back toward him. She paused and fired at the gates where the three assailants were taking cover.

Dunbar fired an M16 machine gun as if he were a soldier on the front lines, further destroying the Cherokee. At the same time, Chase kept suppression fire coming from the other side.

"Come with us!" Wen yelled.

Chase joined them back on the veranda. "Can we go yet?"

They ran toward the helipad, located behind the main house, concealed behind a row of spruce trees. Wen hung back until the last moment to keep the shadow people pinned down. As much as she wanted to fully engage and defeat them, she didn't want to risk Dunbar's life, or the data from Cristina.

Two minutes later, Wen had them airborne. She resisted the urge to circle over the Cherokee and let Chase take some shots for the same reason she didn't advance on them at the house.

Twenty minutes later, they were at the airport.

"I'm not going to go with you," Dunbar said as he showed them his turboprop. "Just in case someone shoots you out of the sky or something. My plane is insured, but I'm not."

"We understand," Chase said. "Thank you for everything."

"I said I'd help," Dunbar said with a slight bow. "Good luck to you."

Wen hugged him. "Thank you. You've done more than anyone else could have."

"If you ever need anything," Chase said. "And don't worry, I'll get some money to the Police Department to replace that car. Hope Jack's all right."

"He's fine." Dunbar started to walk away, but stopped and turned back. "One thing. I won't ask you now, but one day I'd like to know what you actually did get at my hardware store. It'll make for a good story."

"Someone hid flash drives with critical data on them—big secrets. They should help us stop something . . . "

"I thought it could be something like that. Makes me feel like I'm in a James Bond movie. Were the people in the Cherokee after the same stuff?"

"We don't exactly know yet," Wen said.

"I'll let you know how the story ends," Chase told him. "Wish we could have seen more of your home. This is a beautiful area."

"You're always welcome. But maybe next time, don't bring guys with guns."

"Promise we won't," Wen said.

"And we'll have someone bring your plane back," Chase said.

"In one piece." Dunbar laughed.

They boarded the plane.

"We caught a break today," Chase said as Wen prepared for takeoff. "What are the odds a nice guy like that picks up two billionaires in a lifetime?"

"Hope he doesn't pay for helping us," Wen said.

"Yeah . . . they might be waiting for him. They may want to find out if he knows where we're going."

"I'm sure he'll go with Jack and a crew of deputies," Wen said, checking the gauges.

"That's exactly why I didn't tell him where we were going."

"You *still* want to do Halloween?" Wen asked, surprised.

"The Astronaut promised the kids. Tu and Leon have their hearts set on it."

"*The Astronaut* has his heart set on it," Wen corrected.

"We're still waiting for that report," he said, "so we can

just go on and find out. I've already arranged for the security."

"I know," she said. "We've got an eight team security detail—ex-Secret Service, special ops . . . "

"I think we can do it safely."

"You think it's worth the risk?"

"Sometimes, in the midst of all the chaos, danger, and craziness, the only thing we can count on is the hope, innocence, and joy of the children. It's the future. They're the future."

"Sounds pretty sentimental to me," Wen said, and gave him a kiss.

Chapter Fifty

A couple of hours later, Wen landed Dunbar's plane in Des Moines. Chase rented a car under an alias, as usual.

Even before they left the airport, Wen pulled out a special portable computer—not much bigger than a cell phone, and more powerful than any laptop.

"First time using it?" Chase asked, referring to the custom-built device.

"Yes, but The Astronaut gave me good training." She pushed the first flash drive in. "HaPPI," she said. "Look at this. Specific data points. And there's codes to some of their server farms. I wonder if those are still good."

"Even if they're not, we can put those into SEER, which will extrapolate what the codes are from there."

SEER, an acronym for Search Entire Existence Result, employed advanced photonic quantum information processors and utilized deep learning, AI, quantum algorithms, and virtually every data point in digital existence, to predict the future with stunning accuracy. It was still something that gave Chase constant pride, even when running for his life.

"And look. It's a complete profile."

"Of who?"

"Walter Hooper . . . not sure who he was."

"Was?"

"He killed himself," Wen said, reading. "Looks like Bargo systematically destroyed his life until he couldn't take it anymore."

"Not so HaPPI."

"I'm going to upload all this to The Astronaut." She stuck the next drive in and started skimming. "These files are CIA."

"How do you know?"

"MSS training, remember? That's what I do. They taught us to spot this encryption."

"Can you break it?"

"No, it's source codes into their files. But there are keys. I think The Astronaut can get in, but the point is this is our CIA link to HaPPI."

"Any contact division or name?"

"Not yet. Maybe in the encryption." They were both thinking of Tess. "The Astronaut will find it if it's there."

She put in the next drive, frowning at what she found.

"I think it's time we had a talk with Tess . . . "

"Why?" Chase asked.

"Look at this list."

He checked the small screen and saw eighteen names. The third one down had an asterisk next to it, and he wasn't surprised that it belonged to Tess Federgreen.

Bull and Dez had spent hours digging into everything they could extract about HaPPI after Bull detected several strings of code connected to Bargo. The Astronaut was then able to expand those series into an echo pattern, before inserting them into servers of major tech companies, social media platforms, search engines, and online shopping sites.

"The most links are in ShowUp," Bull told Dez as he handed her one of his specialty homemade green tea energy drinks. She took it without checking, sipped, frowned, and handed it back without looking at him. He had her kind in his other hand, and placed it in her still outstretched hand. Another failed attempt to wean her from what he referred to as "concentrated, refined, *dangerous*, unhealthy, junk."

"No surprise," Dez said, knowing that ShowUp, the world's largest social network, boasted 1.6 billion daily active users, and had made its founder one of the world's richest people.

"The Astronaut said ShowUp was started by the CIA."

"I thought it was started by a couple of college kids?"

"That's the cover story—aka 'legend'—they want us to believe. But doesn't it seem a little too good to be true?"

"I guess, but Chase and I started in college."

"Sure, so have lots of entrepreneurs, but starting something like ShowUp, something that *billions* of people around the world use to share all kinds of personal details, something that connects you to *everyone* you know, *everything* you like, *everywhere* you go? It's irresistible to the intelligence agencies."

"That means ShowUp is a major source for HaPPI," Dez said. "Meaning the CIA is involved as supplier *and* end-user. They control the whole chain."

"Yeah," she said, lighting a cigarette. "And we need to find a way to break the chain before we all wind up living our lives *in* chains."

Chasing Risk

Tess found Susan waiting in a conference room at the CIA headquarters in Langley, Virginia.

"Your program isn't under control," Susan said.

"It's *entirely* under control," Tess shot back.

"Then why do we keep having crisis meetings?"

"You know why. HaPPI is not some toy; it's far more complex than you think."

"I know what HaPPI is, and what it can do," Susan said incredulously. "But Chase Malone presents a big risk, and you can't handle him."

"He isn't a problem. The bigger issue is—"

"It's just you and me here, Tess. The *issue* is HaPPI."

". . . I know."

"Then answer this . . . are you able to fix it, or are you going to put us all in jeopardy?"

Chapter Fifty-One

It was nearly a three hour drive from Des Moines to Clinton, Iowa, a small city along the Mississippi River. Chase tried reaching Boone several times while they were driving to let him know their progress, but hadn't been able to get through. Chase normally switched phones every few days, but had kept this one longer than normal because it was the only number for him Boone had.

"I'm getting worried about Boone," Chase said as a semi passed them. "Especially after seeing what happened to Walter Hooper and all the other stuff Cristina told us."

"It *is* surprising he hasn't checked in," Wen agreed, inspecting Chase's phone. "We really should ditch this."

"Not until we hear from him."

"Maybe I should text your mother and see if she knows anything."

"I don't like to worry her . . . but Boone is never out of pattern, and with the HaPPI situation . . . Go ahead."

As she was typing the text, Chase's phone vibrated.

"That's not Boone," she said, looking at the caller ID.

"Only eight people have this number. Answer it."

"She tapped the speaker button. "Yeah?" Chase said, careful not to identify himself.

"Chase, I'm in jail."

After hearing his brother's voice, Chase pulled the rental car onto the shoulder. "Are you okay? Why are you in jail?"

"They've got me on like a dozen charges—at least those are the ones they've *told* me about. Apparently more are coming."

"More what?"

"More charges. It's like I'm in some Third World country. They grabbed me like I was a violent criminal, handcuffed and shackled me—*shackled*!"

"For *what*?"

"First they wouldn't tell me anything, then when they finally gave me charges—are you ready for this? — attempted murder, murder, conspiracy to *commit* murder—"

"Murder!?"

"They even charged me with bribery *and* forgery!"

"Who?"

"You mean who do they think I killed, or who's charging me?"

"Both."

"State *and* federal charges. I'm telling you, it was like storm troopers came into my home. Busted down the door, threw me on the floor."

"It's got to be Bargo," Chase said. "I'm sorry, man."

"Hey, it's not your fault. Well, I guess it kind of is . . . Yeah, they're doing this because of you."

"That's where they screwed up. They messed with the wrong guy." Chase pounded the steering wheel. "I'll have an army of lawyers on this as soon as we hang up. Has anybody set a bail hearing?"

"No bail."

"*No bail?* What the hell?"

"No," Boone said. "Apparently I'm *too dangerous*."

"They're obviously trying to pressure Chase by hitting you with all these charges and keeping you in jail," Wen reasoned. "Hang in there. We'll get them. And if not, we'll come get you out."

"Can you call Mars?" Boone asked. Mars, an ex-lawyer, was like an older brother to Chase and Boone. He'd been sent to prison years earlier, but had figured out a way to work the system. He'd created a mini-empire from inside, actually earning more money than when he'd been free. Mars was also instrumental in helping Chase and Wen stay a step ahead of their many pursuers.

"Great idea," Chase said. "I'm sure he can help."

"Where are they holding you?" Wen asked.

"Pelican Bay State Prison," Boone said.

"Wow," Chase said. "We were so close. Crescent City."

"Yeah, I can smell the sea air, just can't see the ocean."

Since their call was being monitored, Chase gave Boone his new cell number through a series of coded questions and statements only Boone would know.

"Are you okay? I mean physically?" Chase asked. "Have they roughed you up or anything?"

"Just the initial arrest. Nothing too awful."

"Don't worry, we'll get you out."

"The first question for the lawyers is why I was transferred *straight* to a state prison. No stops at a jail, no hearing, no nothing."

"It's a scam," Chase said. "This whole farce is—"

"Chase . . . I'm facing *life* in prison . . . no possibility of parole."

Chase, filled with a rage he hadn't felt since his father

had been killed, looked at Wen. The look of determination he saw on her face calmed him a little. He could already see her calculating the mission.

"If they're able to do this to me," Boone said, "they can do this to anybody. Anybody that disagrees with them, anybody that tries to stop them . . . you know what I'm saying?"

"Yeah. I do." Chase wanted to say a lot of things. He wasn't sure he could keep those promises, but he needed to echo what Wen had said. They weren't just going to let Boone sit there, even if they had to break him out. Finally, he simply said, "We will *not* let you rot in prison. It's never going to happen."

"I know. Just be careful. And *you* break it to Mom, okay?"

"Sure, give *me* the tough job."

Chase knew enough from dealing with Mars to ask Boone for his inmate number. It would make things easier for Mars to get help and for Chase to fill Boone's commissary account.

"I'll call some people in the government."

But they both knew it was bigger than that.

Chapter Fifty-Two

As soon as the call ended with Boone, Chase attempted to get ahold of Mars. It started with a call to his lawyer, which set off a convoluted series of steps that would eventually get to Mars. Then he could call Chase from one of his hidden cell phones—illegal for convicts to have. It usually took awhile for a message to reach him, since Mars had been moved to a federal prison in Virginia, and direct calls in to a federal inmate were impossible. He was also still establishing himself with the guards, so it might take even longer.

"It could be days until Mars gets that message," Chase said, frustrated.

"Are you going to call Tess?" Wen asked.

"I don't want to, but I have to."

Chase hadn't spoken to Tess since she'd failed to get a pardon for Mars after he had risked his life escaping from prison to save Chase and stop a major terror threat. He blamed her for not only failing to get his old friend released from federal prison, but also for the additional year added to his sentence.

Tess answered the phone. She knew what Chase was going to say even before hearing his voice. "I don't know anything about it."

"Don't know anything about what?" Chase asked, not surprised by her preemptive denial.

"Your brother. I'm sorry."

"But you do *know* about it."

"I am kept abreast of all things related to Chase Malone."

"You have to get him out."

"We went through this with Mars," she said defiantly.

"Mars *deserved* freedom, and instead you got him an extra year in prison!"

Wen shot a fierce glance of disapproval his way, silently saying, *Keep your cool if you want anything from her.*

"He was facing five to ten more years. He was lucky to just wind up with an additional twelve months."

"Yeah, *thanks*," Chase said calmly, sarcastically. "And why did they move him to a federal prison in Virginia?"

"You'd have to ask the Federal Bureau of Prisons."

Chase wanted to scream at her, but Boone's situation was too dire to burn this bridge right now.

"Tess . . . I need your help. We're talking about my brother. My *innocent* brother."

"I don't have those kinds of connections with the Justice Department, or, in this case, the California State Police."

"Don't give me that, you've got connections to *everybody*. This isn't about Mars doing some extra time, this is about my brother's *life*."

"Did it ever occur to you that he might be guilty?"

Chase wanted to hang up. He wanted to reach through the phone and grab her by the throat. But he needed her too much. She was his best hope to save Boone. "No. It didn't."

"Of course not. And I bet you didn't stop to think that this might be bigger than me. Bigger than *everything*."

Just as they hit the last stretch of interstate that would lead them into Clinton, Iowa, Chase received a call from a restricted number. "Mars?" Wen guessed after reading the screen.

"Maybe we got lucky."

"What's the latest emergency?" Mars asked, used to Chase and Wen's adventures.

"Boone's in prison," Chase began, and proceeded to tell Mars a condensed version of the events that had brought them to that point.

Mars didn't interrupt once. Always an instant away from getting caught with a phone, he made every syllable of a conversation count. Once Chase finished, he finally spoke.

"Are you going to get him?"

"If we have to," Chase said.

"You might. The system can screw people. It swallows them, and it's corrupt."

"I know."

"And that was *before* this HaPPI monster you told me about. This is *end of the world* stuff."

"Can you send Boone some help until we figure a way to get him out?"

"Yeah. I know a guy at Pelican Bay. And don't worry, Boone's tough. He can handle this."

Coming from a guy already seven years into a long

sentence, Chase wasn't about to whine that one day in prison was too long.

"You got him a lawyer?"

Chase told him the names.

"Four of the best," Mars said. "Good. Meantime, I'll try to make it as comfortable as I can for Boone, but they've obviously locked him up to pressure you, so they may put him in solitary. If that happens, I won't be able to do much good."

"Let's hope it doesn't come to that. I've also got Tess Federgreen working on it."

He scoffed. "She didn't do me any favors."

"I know. I'm forever sorry about that," Chase said bitterly. "How are you?"

"Oh, just dandy."

Chase knew the power Tess wielded. Getting a sentence reduction at the minimum and a pardon were both within her realm, and he'd added her refusal to help to a list of unforgivable offenses she had committed. The episode had further complicated their relationship, which had her switching from nemesis to savior on a regular basis. And yet he had to count on her again. This time though, there was unbelievably more urgency.

"There's no way Boone will survive a life sentence," Chase said. "We don't even know the full list of charges, or the details around them. How big is the frame job?"

"It doesn't matter. They want *you*. Comply with their wishes, and Boone goes free."

Chase would do anything to save Boone, and Boone knew it, so did Mars, and, apparently, so did Bargo.

"But you can't let them win," Wen said. "It's a long game . . . we can win if we don't rush it, don't fall into their trap."

Chapter Fifty-Three

Tess hastily arranged another meeting of Elevation. Gathered were the same grim faces who had been navigating the crisis from the start, their collective clout enough to take any action necessary, including war.

"We have several new developments," the director began. "Some of you are aware that Chase Malone's brother has been taken into custody and charged with numerous crimes, including counterfeiting, conspiracy, murder . . . there's a bit of a laundry list here."

"Is this legitimate?" a man from the NSA asked hopefully.

"No," Tess replied for the director. "This is a HaPPI operation."

"HaPPI has three main modes," Susan added, getting everyone up to speed. "There's the first one, simply referred to as 'rating.' It's similar to China's social credit system, where HaPPI scores individuals and businesses based on long criteria, which you should all be familiar with."

"Kind of like a super-credit bureau," Mary said.

"FICA on steroids," someone added.

"Yes," Susan said. "This will not be popular with privacy advocates." She looked around the room, ignoring Tess's strained expression. "HaPPI's second mode is more invasive: dynamic intervention and eviction. Bargo sometimes calls this 'die.'"

"Sounds pleasant," a man from Homeland Security quipped.

"Once a die order is issued," Susan continued, "HaPPI cannibalizes a person's assets and takes action to impact a target's personal life. It can be rather ugly."

"And there's a *third* mode?" a woman from the FBI asked. "Something *worse* than die?"

"Erasure," Susan said simply. "A subjects' entire existence is wiped."

"What's that mean? Wiped?"

"Officially, they never existed. They can't obtain a driver's license, open a bank account, collect government benefits, get a job—nothing."

"When would that ever be appropriate?"

"There is also a fourth mode," Tess said before Susan could answer. "A mode that we are just now seeing for the first time, where they can essentially use the same process to put someone—anyone—in a situation of a crime. Or, in this case, a series of them."

"All this is something out of Kafka or Orwell," a man said. "I can see where all these tools would be effective if properly engaged with oversight and strict parameters—perhaps something like a FISA Court. However, the system seems incredibly abusive. In this case—"

"In *this* case," the director interrupted, "it's being used to prevent a disaster. Chase Malone, as noted in prior meetings, has removed himself from the grid, and, therefore, is immune to HaPPI, or any normal channels of activity. He has also proved himself quite elusive to physical attacks, so—"

"This time," Tess cut in, "Bargo has used a family member to get to Chase."

"Putting an innocent man in prison . . . " The man who the director had interrupted looked around, as if soliciting support. "To leave this much power in the hands of a corporation . . . How soon until they come for you?"

"Don't be so dramatic," the director said. "*We* are in charge. Bargo is a vendor."

"For how long?" the man asked. "And what of the Malone brothers? Do they expect Chase to come out of hiding and do something about it?"

"Yes, that is the idea."

"What do they think he'll do?"

"Perhaps he can still be wrestled in as an asset," Tess said.

"Have you made any progress on that?" the director asked.

"What little progress we were making has been completely upended by this latest move by Dag."

"So you don't agree with it?" Susan said suspiciously.

"I'd rather handle these things myself."

"Of course you would. But when you're in bed with Dag, *he's* driving."

Tess was annoyed by the implications and mixed metaphors put forth by Susan, a woman who she didn't believe understood what they were trying to do with HaPPI. However, she was someone who also had a great deal of power, and, therefore, could not be dismissed.

"I think we need to strongly consider removing this threat once and for all," the director said.

"My group can handle that if Tess isn't willing," Mary said.

"I'd be willing if I thought that was the *correct* course of action," Tess said. "But I don't believe it is, and I'm not signing off on a kill order."

"Well, we need to do *something*. I've read his file. This guy is allegedly running around with a former top MSS agent. The two of them have amassed quite a track record since she defected to the West. I doubt they'll stand idly by while his brother sits in prison, especially on phony charges."

"Then what?" Tess said. "If you have a suggestion, I'm listening."

"The director just made a suggestion," Mary said. "Let's take this guy out."

Tess glared at both Mary and Susan. "First, you have to find him."

Chapter Fifty-Four

Chase called Tess again, unable to contain his outrage. "I know everything happening to Boone is related to HaPPI."

"So?" Tess replied, glad to have another chance to track him.

"I also know that *you're* behind HaPPI."

"Really?"

"You need to get him out, or our relationship is going to turn very ugly."

"You're not threatening me, are you, Chase?"

"You should know me better than that. Like you, I don't make threats."

"I know you like to play out of your league, but don't let your past successes confuse you into believing you're able to compete with me and my resources."

"We have too much history," Chase said. "We both know what we're capable of."

"You have *no idea* what I'm capable of," Tess snapped. "You've been lucky. With your money, The Astronaut's abilities, and Wen's training and experience, you think you're more than you are. But you risk becoming overconfident." She paused to allow that to sink in. "I have a *thousand* Wens at my disposal, we've got Astronauts, and *our* money? Oh Chase, our money makes your billion dollars look like chump change."

"I'm impressed," Chase said sarcastically.

"Be careful Chase, because although you like to pretend otherwise, and rarely believe what I say, I've been helping you from the very first day we met. I've saved your ass more times than you know."

"You want a thank you note?"

"You turn on me, and your life is going to change like you would never believe, and I can assure you I won't even show up at your funeral, because they're never going to find your body."

"So who's threatening who now?"

"You're not *hearing* me."

"Nobody knows where I am."

"I have found you. And I *keep* finding you. Don't let the jeopardy your brother finds himself in cloud *your* judgment. You *can* get him out. You've done the impossible before. I know you're upset, so I won't take offense at your threats and bad attitude, but I'm not the one your battle is with. There are others you have to tangle with."

Chase thought of Dag and grew angry.

"They know," she said. "*They know.*"

"You're talking about Bargo."

"I told you before, I'm not familiar with them."

"Yeah, well, I didn't believe you then, either. I know Bargo is working with a secret division of the CIA. That sure sounds pretty similar to you and your operation."

"Apparently you aren't aware of how many secret divisions there are within the CIA."

"I don't care. Even if by some chance it *isn't* you—and I know it is—either way, you are involved. Bargo isn't news to you."

"You're being reckless and jumping to conclusions. If you think Bargo is an issue, then I suggest you do some more homework."

"You're supposed to be keeping the world's corporations in check. Well, Bargo is a *massive* company collecting astronomical amounts of data on everything and everyone. How can you *not* know about them?"

"What I'm telling you, although I owe you no explanation, is they aren't on my radar in any *official* capacity."

"Really? You're saying the CIA considers them clean?"

"We don't grade companies. When there's trouble, we move."

"What do you need to move on Bargo?"

Tess remained silent for a moment as she studied the data on a large screen regarding Bargo, furious at Dag for inadvertently catching Boone Malone in their web. Now she had *this* mess to deal with, and there was no question that Chase could make big problems for Bargo *and* HaPPI *and* her.

"We'll take a look as a personal favor to you, but no promises. If we don't find anything, I've got other things to do."

"I guarantee you, you're *going* to find something."

"Wishing isn't going to make it so," she said. "And even if we *do* find something, I can't help you with Boone. You're on your own there."

"What you're going to find will help with Boone."

"If you're so sure I'm going to find something, why don't you send what you have?"

"Tess, the CIA is in bed with this company. You already

know everything I know. HaPPI is a CIA fantasy come true, and you and I both know this didn't happen by accident."

Tess had a crew attempting to track Chase. She needed to know where he was, needed to know what he knew, and there was a good chance she was going to have to throw him under the bus this time. If he got too close to HaPPI, even she couldn't save him.

Linda Moore, her assistant, signaled to her from across the room. As she approached, Tess muted the call.

"We've zeroed in on him," Linda reported.

Chapter Fifty-Five

Tess smiled, seeing Chase was in Iowa. "Chase, can you give me a number where I can reach you?"

He gave it to her.

"Give me a little time to check in on this. I see you've already made a healthy deposit into your brother's commissary account," she said, looking at a screen accessing the California Department of Corrections. "Don't worry, he's safe where he is right now. They have him in Short Term Restricted Housing."

"He'd be safer at *home*."

"Just don't do anything to piss anybody off, or they may wind up sliding him into gen pop, and that would be a *lot* less fun for him. Remember, it's a supermax. Not a lot of *nice* folks in there."

Once again, Chase wanted to scream at her, but he swallowed it down. Boone was caught in a cruel game of greed and power, and Tess was the game master.

As soon as the call ended, Wen shook her head. "Tess is still lying. And she knows *we* know that she's lying."

"She's probably got Dag sitting in her office *with* her."

"The worst part is she doesn't care that we know."

"What am I supposed to do?" Chase asked. "Call her a liar?"

"Don't let her play you like that."

"We don't need an enemy like Tess right now."

"Yes, with friends like that . . . "

"She said she'll look into it."

"She's *not* going to help. She's part of it. Tess and Bargo are the same."

"We'll just have to exhaust every other means, and if we can't get him out peacefully, then we'll have to decide."

"Decide what?" Wen asked.

"Which to do first . . . detain Tess, or break Boone out."

"Well, it's about to get real, then," Wen said, fire in her eyes. "We better be ready before they do put him into the general population—or worse, solitary—because Tess just telegraphed their next move. If we start squeezing too hard, that's what they're going to do."

"We need to find out everything we can about where they're holding him."

"Pelican Bay State Prison," Wen began. "Opened 1989, California's only supermax, the highest security classification. The two hundred seventy-five acre facility is located just south of the Oregon state line, and has a rated capacity of two thousand and eighty inmates. However the current population is closer to twenty-seven hundred violent male prisoners, more than forty percent of who are serving life sentences."

Chase was impressed with her memorized facts, and felt instantly sick.

"As Tess just told us, Boone is being held in short term restrictive housing. The grounds are divided, with half sectioned to maximum security inmates in General Population. The other half contains an X-shaped cluster of buildings. The barren ground offers no cover. An electric fence surrounds the perimeter. Inside the windowless eight by ten cells, made of poured concrete, the walls—"

"You already have a plan to get Boone out, don't you?"

"I'm confident we can help him escape, but I need to ask Mars a few things, and we'll need to hire a crew."

"Crew?"

"I know some people," she said with pursed lips, squinted eyes, and a furrowed brow, gazing distinctively ahead. He knew she was thinking brilliantly, and he loved her. "But you think we're wanted *now* . . . If we go in full force and extract a high profile inmate from a supermax prison, they aren't going to be happy."

"Who isn't?"

"Those in power. Those who think we're in the way of their HaPPI ending."

Linda Moore, Tess's deputy, stared at the monitor in Mission Control, then turned to Tess. "This could be a major catastrophe."

"Tell me something I don't know."

"He knows you know," she said.

"Of course he does."

"And he knows you can get his brother out. One phone call gets that done."

Tess nodded. "*Damn* Dag for putting us in this position."

"Everyone who's ever underestimated Chase Malone, has lost."

"I know that."

"What are you going to do?" Linda asked, watching the satellite images showing Chase in Iowa. Another display had detailed views of Pelican Bay Prison. Eight others were filled with HaPPI data.

"There are times in this business when you need to act decisively. When bold action will make all the difference," Tess said, watching different screens. "This is not one of those times. This is a 'wait and see' situation."

"Oh," Linda said, surprised, having never heard her boss take that approach.

"I don't have enough information yet."

"But aren't you worried?"

"About what?"

"About how much damage Chase and Wen can do in the next twenty-four hours?"

"I'm worried about what they can do in the next *three* hours. That's why I'll be monitoring everything they do."

"And you're going to make sure that nothing bad happens to Boone Malone while he's in custody? Because as long as he's safe and communicating with his brother, we have a chance to make this thing work out right."

"That only buys us time."

"Because you don't really think Boone is getting out . . ."

Tess shook her head slowly.

"Because Chase isn't going to leave HaPPI alone?"

"Chase Malone was born to destroy HaPPI," Tess said. "Every day of his life has been building to this fight, to this moment. He's everything that Dag Kirrem fears."

"So Bargo will destroy him?"

"If Chase and Wen don't destroy them first."

Chapter Fifty-Six

Parked several houses away from where they would be meeting Tu and The Astronaut, Chase and Wen continued to strategize while waiting for them to arrive.

"We need to find a way to stop Bargo," Wen said, pulling on a jacket against the evening's chill.

"I don't think that's going to be possible," Chase said, staring down the street at a few specific houses, seemingly in competition with their elaborate Halloween decorations. "These people sure take Halloween seriously. I've never seen so many lights and phony graveyards, spiders and witches and—"

"And you were saying?" Wen said, trying to get him back on track.

"Sorry, yeah, maybe we can slow them down long enough to get Boone out of prison and repair his life, but . . . Wen, I *really* love peanut butter cups. I haven't had one in *years*."

"We could put together a team, get some help from WOLF," she said, referring to The Cause, an underground movement started by a few radicals, intellectuals, and activists intent on bringing about income equality throughout the world. The group had quickly evolved into a full-fledged revolutionary movement, seeking to bring down the current world order run by the elites.

"And what? Blow up their offices? Kill their executives? Destroy their server farms?" Chase had always been leery of WOLF, especially its militant wing.

"Yes, that's what I'm saying. Once HaPPI gets fully established, it will be much harder to defeat. I'm not a chocolate fan, but I do like black licorice."

"You do? Not sure that's a big Halloween treat." He squeezed her hand. "Even if we *could* do what you suggest," Chase said, "that's only a temporary solution, and it brings great risk."

"Risk is what this is all about," Wen said, watching a van cross an intersection down the street.

"You're right," Chase said. "They want to control everything by assessing what risk people pose to the system . . . What if we could turn that around?"

"What do you mean?" she asked, watching the van slow in front of a house at the end of the block.

"We use it against them," Chase said. "I've got to call Bull."

Bull listened to Chase's idea while smoking a cigarette on a long balcony overlooking the Pacific Ocean. It was a brisk night in California, but Bull had enough caffeine and nicotine in her system that she didn't notice. "We would need their key codes," she said, "but even if we get those, it might not be possible. I would need to talk to The Astronaut."

"He'll be here soon. I'll have him call you. But you think it *might* work?"

"If we get the codes, and I'm as good as I think I am, we may *possibly* be able to pull it off."

The van drove up the street a little too slowly for Wen's liking, passed them, and finally disappeared around the corner.

After finally having time to fully review the materials from Cristina's drives, and with at least ten minutes before Tu and The Astronaut arrived, Chase and Wen decided to contact Cristina hoping to get a little more information. She was safely concealed off the southern Florida coast, on Siesta Key.

Chase called one of the security people. After a couple of minutes, she handed her phone to Cristina.

"I'm calling to make sure you're comfortable and happy with your living arrangement."

"I can't say that I'm *happy*. I'd prefer to have my old life back, but it is workable. Thank you for protecting me, and for trying to stop them."

"It's what we do," Chase said. "We appreciate your bravery."

"Well it's not what *I* do, and I wouldn't call it bravery. I'm scared to death."

"That's what courage is, facing fear."

"I once heard it's about being generous. I guess we're both trying. It's just astonishing to me that Bargo would actually do this. I mean, it's something out of a bad science fiction movie. They really are trying to know everything about us, to control everything we do. I couldn't sit and let that happen."

"A lot of people would have," Chase said. "In fact, a lot of people are doing just that."

"I know," she said, thinking of Dag, Marta, Reggie, and the rest of them.

"Listen, after going through the drives . . . I know you've had some help. Who gave you this? Who helped you get this data out?"

"I'd rather not say. I trust you, but we made a deal that I wouldn't reveal them."

"We need to talk to the other person. Whoever it is, they're in great danger, you *know* that. They'll kill them. We can help."

"I guess it's better if I tell you. A lot has changed since this began. His name is Mitchell Landes."

"Where can we find him?"

"He's no longer with the company, either. He's in Kansas."

"Kansas?"

"Outside Topeka. He grew up there. It's in the middle of nowhere."

"Then they'll find him."

"He was adopted, so he said they couldn't trace him."

Wen rolled her eyes. "You have a phone number?"

"He has no phone. He's scared. He knows the phones are the first way they track you."

Chase looked at his disposable burner phone, thinking it wasn't just the first way, it was the *main* way. "Okay, an address? Something?"

Cristina told them all she knew. Then Wen asked her one final question.

"Who would have the key codes?"

"That will never work," she replied. "They have too many protections against hacking."

"Hacking isn't exactly what we have in mind."

"Whatever it is, I think you're wasting your time. But most of Bargo's IT department is based in Chicago. The executive VP who runs it answers directly to Dag. His name is Sheldon Reams. There's a list on one of the drives you have that contains all the executive's names, phone numbers, home addresses, salaries, etcetera."

"We can fly out in the morning," Wen said, after they finished with Cristina. "We'll have to fly to Chicago, then to Topeka, assuming Dunbar doesn't mind us keeping his plane a little longer."

"As long as we don't get it blown up," Chase said, imitating Dunbar's low drawl.

"It's insured, remember?" Wen said, smiling

"But *we* aren't." He winked.

A few minutes later, The Astronaut drove up to the house, trailed by an SUV containing a large security team Chase had brought in to keep Tu safe for the night.

As Tu got out of the car, Chase and Wen both beamed, saying simultaneously, "There's Tu!"

Chapter Fifty-Seven

Boone sat in his prison cell, feeling two days beyond dead. *The only thing worse than prison,* he wrote in a letter to his wife, *is being in prison for a crime you did not commit. And the only thing worse than that is being in prison for a crime you did not commit when the authorities know you are innocent. The powers have changed our life in one moment. All they had to do was flip a switch and take everything away from us, then they flipped another one, and took away the one thing I had left: my freedom.*

He was already fighting to keep himself from spiraling into a deep depression. A man used to climbing to the tops of skyscrapers and mountains, accustomed to doing whatever he wanted in life, had suddenly found himself caged like an animal.

A place like Pelican Bay, considered by some to be one of the most dangerous prisons in America, could strip the life from you, leaving only a hollowed shell.

Boone, facing the possibility of never getting out, had been fighting tears since the correctional officer had closed his cell door.

After surrendering to the rage, a few hours later, a different guard appeared outside his cell, and the door slid open.

"Looks like you've got important friends, Malone."

For an instant, Boone felt ecstatic relief, thinking they'd found the mistake, that Chase had pulled the right strings, or some magic had occurred and they were about to release him.

Instead, the guard tossed in two cartons of cigarettes, mesh bags containing food, a deck of cards, and a couple of paperbacks.

"Thanks," Boone said, deflated, "but I don't smoke."

The guard smiled. "Cigarettes spend like cash in here."

Boone nodded, glanced into the mesh bags, and saw all kinds of goodies that weren't on the authorized commissary list. "Are you setting me up?"

"Now, if we were setting you up, we would just plant a bunch of drugs, or another inmate's corpse. This is a gift from Mars. Does that mean something to you?"

Boone smiled slightly. "Yeah. Thanks," he said sincerely.

The guard nodded once, turned, and went on his way. Immediately the door slid closed again. That deafening, loud, locked *clank* sent chills throughout his body.

"What is it?" his cellmate asked, raising his head off the thin mattress covering the lower concrete bunk.

"Care package."

"Cool," the heavily tattooed gang member said, a little more life in his voice. "Share that stuff."

"Sure," Boone said, happy to have something to help win over his burly cellmate who, thus far, had looked at Boone more as an annoyance than anything.

Boone looked inside the bag more closely and saw, among the other treasures, ten packs of peanut butter cups.

Mars knew they'd been his favorite candy as a kid. He had to admit that even as an adult, he occasionally snuck a few. There was even a six pack of Mexican Cokes. He preferred them in glass bottles, but that never would've been allowed in the prison.

Boone handed his cellie a can of Coke.

"Damn, they let you have *soda*? That ain't allowed at all. Must have cost at least five-k to get that in here. You got juice, dude."

The food was a nice treat, and he had to figure out how to best make use of the cigarettes. If he'd had a match, he would have lit one up right then, even though he hadn't had a smoke since his teenage years.

However, it was more than the food that lifted his spirits. Mars was out there, looking after him. Mars and Chase were working to free him, the two guys he loved the most in the world, and two people who knew how to get stuff done.

Maybe there *was* hope. Maybe, somehow, they'd find a way to beat the odds, to beat the system.

Marta and Reggie stood in the corridor. A newly installed stone waterfall at one end, surrounded by small palm trees, made the setting more relaxed than the urgency of the meeting.

"What do you have for me on WOLF?" Dag asked Reggie, who'd been in charge of the project.

"Revolutionary group also known as 'The Cause.' A woman, Margot Ariesen, leads them. They've successfully eluded US intelligence agencies. The French had something on them, but it's loose ends now. They were based in

Amsterdam for a while, but they've managed to stay under the radar quite effectively."

"And Chase Malone is involved?" Dag asked as they paced the corridor.

"It appears so. We don't know to what extent."

Dag turned to Marta. "And what does the CIA think of this *cause*?"

"They don't have much on the organization, either."

"I don't believe that," Dag said. "They just aren't willing to share it with us."

"Correct," Marta said. "And Chase Malone has been in touch with the agency about his brother."

"Very interesting. When might we expect a call from the great Mr. Malone?" Dag asked.

"It's hard to say. He may be employing more covert methods on us."

"Such as?"

"He got to Cristina."

"Damn," Dag said. "Where is she?"

"She's disappeared," Reggie said. "She was running scared before any of this started."

"Yeah, but how did we *lose* her?"

"She had help."

"You think Chase has her somewhere?"

"Our sources at the CIA suggest we should not underestimate him," Marta said. "And that's just what we're doing."

"Not anymore," Dag said. "If they won't take him out, we will."

Reggie looked concerned. Marta nodded.

"It will be expensive," she said.

"I don't *care* what it costs," Dag barked. "See to it!"

Chapter Fifty-Eight

Chase scooped Tu off the carpet and hugged him tight. They had waited until Tu and The Astronaut had gotten settled inside Leon's house before joining them.

"Chase Bank," Tu said, returning the hug. "You came!"

Then he saw Wen. Chase reluctantly handed him over, and she kissed his forehead. "I've missed you!"

Leon, a nine-year-old autistic boy who The Astronaut had unofficially adopted as a kind of nephew a few years earlier, ran around in his dragon costume.

"Do I look scary, Uncle Nash?" Leon asked.

"Yes," The Astronaut replied. "A magical kind of scary."

Sarah, Leon's mother, smiled as she took photos. "Thanks again for doing this. He loves it so much."

"Not as much as I do," the math savant said. This was the fourth year he'd taken Leon trick-or-treating. They also usually got together once or twice every summer, but Halloween had been The Astronaut's favorite holiday as a kid, so Chase understood the importance. It had become

Leon's for much the same reason young Nash had once discovered; he could pretend to be someone else, pretend to be normal, as the whole world slipped into a kind of autistic sense of reality, everything a little bit more magnified, highlighted, different. The Astronaut liked to say, "Halloween is reality slightly askew, with extra attention on the surreal."

This year, in spite of everything going on, Nash did not want to let Leon down. Nor did he want to miss it himself. Things were extra-special this time, because he had also promised to bring Tu along for his first trick-or-treating experience.

Tu had never dressed up before, and still didn't understand exactly why he was, or what this crazy *Halloween* holiday was all about, but he had, for some reason, become very excited to go. After months of thought, Tu had finally decided on a costume.

"I want to go as an astronaut," he'd announced one day.

It had made Nash Graham immensely proud. Even though he was not a real astronaut, it had been a tribute to him.

When Tu first walked out in his costume, The Astronaut's eyes filled with tears. He knew how important a child's costume decision was, even if Tu did not understand. He could have chosen to be anything, but instead of being a Star Wars Jedi, an old-fashioned ghost, vampire, Frankenstein's monster, or even an American cowboy for his new land, Tu had chosen to honor Nash.

Tu and The Astronaut shared the same kind of bond with Leon. Not that Tu was autistic, but he was different, special. With his unique abilities and analytical mind, he did not fit into the standard world. Tu already knew his life was going to be unusual.

Because of Tu's connection, Chase, Wen, and The

Astronaut had spent quite a bit of time together. It hadn't taken long for Tu to realize that The Astronaut was like him, at least a little bit.

"Do you like my costume?" Tu had asked excitedly.

The Astronaut pulled himself together and readily agreed that it was a fine choice, and that he looked like "a very brave Astronaut."

They headed down the first block of the out of the way, self-contained neighborhood, Tu and Leon leading the way. Chase, Wen, Leon's mother, and The Astronaut kept extra vigilant. The kids were unaware of the eight-member security detail trailing them.

Even though The Astronaut had explained the holiday customs to Tu, he was still surprised when they knocked on the first door and the people answered in costume.

"Trick-or-treat," Leon said loudly.

Tu followed with his own, softer, slightly altered phrase. "Tricks and treats." He didn't really understand the trick part. All that mattered was that he was going to get a treat. Still confused, Tu stuck out his tongue. Everybody laughed, which confused him even more, but then a Snicker's bar dropped into his bag and he believed he must have done it correctly since he'd received the coveted treat.

It continued like that, house after house, up and down the streets. Tu tried different pieces of candy as they went. He *kind of* liked most of them, but didn't love any until he received a box of Dots. The squishy, colorful candy gels impressed him.

"I like the gummy feel of them between my teeth and the artificial flavors on my tongue," he said.

Chase and Wen were delighted to see Tu happy, finally getting the chance to act like a 'normal' kid.

"Tricks and treats, more Dots, please," he said at the next house, as if he finally understood Halloween.

"This neighborhood sure goes all out for Halloween," Chase said, as they stood before a yard filled with an entire graveyard, crawling with zombie babies. "Those tombstones are a little *too* authentic."

"What about the ghosts and spiderwebs hanging from the trees?" Wen said.

Leon delighted in this area, clapping and laughing, then he sang the names of the ghouls. He also explained to Tu which decorations were new and which ones were reappearing from last year.

"This is all very strange . . . and a little scary," Tu said as creepy music filled the air at the next house.

"That's the idea," Chase said, appearing behind them. "Strange and scary."

"But why? Isn't there a more efficient way to give out candy?"

"Hershey and Mars seem to think this is a pretty good way."

"Hershey's annual revenue is seven point nine-four billion dollars," Tu said. "Mars is a private corporation, they bring in around thirty-five billion, but that is not all derived from candy."

"No, of course not," Chase said, as if he knew this.

"Americans spent roughly ten billion last year on Halloween. About a quarter of that was on candy, the rest was decorations and costumes."

"That's a *lot* of candy," Chase said.

"But isn't it fun?" Wen asked him.

"As long as they keep giving out Dots!"

"Look at *this* place," Chase said, pointing to a house they came upon filled with a big cemetery and a whole pack of skeletons, tombstones, goblins, giant spiders, and the scariest witch on a broom Chase had ever seen.

"Oh, this is Jack's house. It's a favorite on this block. He goes all out every year. This guy is obsessed with Halloween, with making kids giddy with excitement and feeling the joy of this all Hallows Eve," the Astronaut said. "Even the adults dress up in this neighborhood."

"Come on, Tu!" Leon shouted. Tu ran off to join him at the next front door, hopeful for more of his favorite chewy treats.

"Chase Bank, I got a peanut butter cup for you!" Tu cried excitedly as he ran back to Chase, throwing the orange wrapper up in the air. Chase caught it, and Tu ran back to Leon and the next house.

"How do we look?" Chase whispered to Wen as he opened the wrapper to the peanut butter treat.

"All clear. So far so good."

The security team was keeping their distance to avoid making the children nervous, but Tu had noticed them. Wen was dressed as a witch, her broom a modified machine gun, and concealed under her capes were several other weapons. If anyone found them, it would be an ugly scene.

A large van rolled onto the street. "Are we a go?" the driver yelled into the back.

Grimes closed his eyes for an instant, then opened them, turned to Shelby, and said, "Ready?"

She nodded. "Let's take them!"

Chapter Fifty-Nine

Darkness had fully enveloped the neighborhood when an SUV came toward them. Wen aimed her broom and spoke into the headset sealed under her gray wig and witch hat. "Positions everyone," Wen said tensely.

Chase, shocked they'd been found again, was angry at himself for being surprised. Now they had Tu, Leon, and the other kids on the street to worry about.

One of their security detail stepped into the street to slow the vehicle. Another member of the team approached the driver's window of the SUV.

"False alarm, clear!" came the response Wen had been holding her breath for.

"Who's that?" Wen asked as a dark gang approached the other end of the street.

"Just some teenagers dressed in black with skeleton faces," a woman on their team responded.

At the same time, a monster answered the next house's door. Leon squealed at the elaborate costume.

Three of the eight security detail were equipped with

night vision. However, Wen quickly realized that in this neighborhood, with its overabundance of glowing Halloween lights, haunting scenes, monster recordings, strobe lights, and over the top decorations, *anything* could be lurking in the shadows—especially shadow people.

The Astronaut stood behind Tu and Leon, beaming. Chase and Wen had never seen him so happy. Dressed as a pirate, complete with an eye-patch, gold hoop earrings, and a pretty convincing peg leg, The Astronaut seemed a different person than the rigid math savant they knew. After each house, Tu and Leon would immediately show The Astronaut their new "loot."

Wen and Chase were content to wait in the road for the boys to return. Chase received a text. "Dez sent a chartered jet," he told Wen. "It'll be here in an hour, so you won't have to fly tomorrow."

"More important is if they're tracking Dunbar's plane," Wen said.

Chase nodded. "He sent an extra pilot to take Dunbar's plane back to Colorado."

A vampire, Gandalf, and Darth Vader, all under four-feet tall, walked by.

"Look, Uncle Nash," Leon said. "Another Baby Ruth. Don't they know I don't like Baby Ruth?"

"Not everyone knows you as well as I do," The Astronaut said.

"Why not?" Leon asked. "I don't have any secrets."

The Astronaut smiled.

"Why do they make them?" Leon persisted. "And who *does* like Baby Ruth?" Leon looked at Tu.

"Not me," Tu said. "I like Dots. It says on the box they are Americas number one selling gumdrop brand."

"I don't like Dots," Leon said.

Tu looked at him as if he were crazy. "Only one hundred thirty calories per serving, and twenty-one grams of sugar, what's not to like?"

"Corn syrup. I don't like corn syrup, or Red 40, or especially not Yellow 5."

As they rang the next doorbell, Leon said a little too loudly, "I hope they don't have Baby Ruth."

The man who answered laughed. "I couldn't agree with you more about Baby Ruth. They shouldn't even make them. Don't worry, I've got Milky Way's, Three Musketeers, Snickers, and Reese's Peanut Butter Cups."

Tu wondered if he should ask if they had Dots, but he was unsure of the protocol.

Baby Yoda, Harry Potter, and a little Ruth Bader Ginsburg ran across the street.

The next house was the least decorated in the neighborhood. "I think that means they will have the best candy," The Astronaut theorized.

Tu assumed that meant they'd have a big bucket full of Dots, and certainly no Baby Ruth bars. However, as soon as the door opened, he knew they weren't going to be getting any candy. He had learned in his younger years of confinement in China to identify mean people, and the ones opening the door were *very* mean.

Tu, Leon, and The Astronaut were all pulled inside. The door slammed and locked behind them.

Chapter Sixty

Grimes looked at Shelby, stunned. "What just happened?"

"The kids got grabbed," Shelby said, straining to see out the windshield.

"Are we sure?"

"Chase and the woman are moving like hell itself just opened."

"Go!" Grimes yelled to the driver, then turned to another man who was monitoring something on a laptop. "Find out who this is!"

Tu and Leon both screamed at the sudden assault. Finding themselves caught in large tight nets, Tu thought it might be a giant spider's web. *A Halloween nightmare.* Rough hands dragged them down a short hall. *Slick wooden floor.*

"Help!" Tu screamed as they were hoisted into the air and slung over shoulders like sacks of grain.

The Astronaut, who thought of himself as a mind ninja,

had no practical fighting skills with which to defend himself against guns and brute strength. Before he could complete a protesting sentence, they slammed him against the wall. His face hit a framed family photo, sending it crashing to the floor, glass shattering. It felt as if his wrists were being broken when they handcuffed him.

Tu struggled to see The Astronaut and screamed Chase's name before a cloth was shoved in his mouth that tasted like dirty socks. They moved in continuous motion through the house to the back door.

Tu felt the night air only for a few seconds before they were thrown into the back of a van. He accidentally kicked The Astronaut when he was shut in with him. The van pulled away onto the street behind the house just as Chase and Wen reached the front door.

"It's solid metal!" Chase yelled.

"Go around back," Wen directed the security team from her headpiece.

Chase found a large rock bordering a flower bed and smashed the front window. Barely breaking out enough glass before he went through, Chase unlocked the front door to allow two of his detail to enter.

Wen met him at the back door. "Van moving west," she said with the cool, determined reporting of a trained agent instead of the horrified scream that a parent would have used. "Get the vehicles onto the back street." Wen never stopped moving, running toward the distant taillights. "Too dark for me to make out color or model. Can anyone see it?" she asked, knowing some of them had night vision. She finally stopped when it turned the corner. "Unit Four where are you? Do you have them?"

"Eyes on the van," came the response. "And we have the boy's mother."

The security crew had three vehicles which had been stationed strategically in the neighborhood. One of which had been following down the street.

Chase and one of their team picked Wen up.

"Shouldn't we have someone check the house?" Chase asked.

"There won't be so much as a single fiber inside that could help us," Wen said.

"This was such a bad idea," Chase said, knowing Wen was thinking the same thing, but would never say it. Her philosophy was to always keep moving forward.

"Can't you go faster?" Wen asked from the back seat.

"I'm trying not to kill a bunch of innocent trick-or-treaters."

"We're going to lose them," Wen said, thinking of other options.

"Because they don't care about mowing down children," Chase said. "Look out! Black Panther and Iron Man!"

"I see them," the driver said, swerving as the superheroes jumped out of the way.

"We're going to have to call in local police," Wen said reluctantly.

"Sure you want that?" the driver asked.

"They've got two kids and a high-value intelligence asset," Chase said, pushing the emergency number on his phone. "I don't *know* the address," he snapped after telling the dispatch of the kidnapping. "We were trick-or-treating."

The driver told him the name of the street.

Chase relayed it to dispatch and gave their descriptions, with and without costumes, his contact number, and a phony name.

It didn't take long for them to see police lights. They continued to pursue in the direction the van went while coordinating with the other security cars fanning out to close in on the assailants.

"Finally," Chase said. "We're out of the neighborhood. No more kids."

The driver floored it, but Chase knew the kidnappers were certainly doing the same.

"If they're shadow people," Chase began, "I don't understand why they're leaving *us* behind."

"They aren't after us," Wen said.

"So it's MSS after Tu?" Chase asked, even more panicked, knowing that Tu could already be dead.

"No. They're after The Astronaut."

Chapter Sixty-One

"Roadblock!" the van driver yelled in Arabic. "Police, police!"

"Run it!" another one yelled in the same language.

The van rolled over spike plates twenty feet before the squad cars. With all four tires flattened, they slid to a stop inches from impact.

The driver and his fellow kidnappers began shooting immediately. The police returned fire. The bloody shootout lasted less than a minute.

"Ten-nine-nine-nine. Officers down. Three officers down," an injured survivor radioed in. "At least one of the assailants fled on foot. Officers in pursuit."

"There," Chase said, pointing to the flashing lights.

"I see it," the driver said.

Seconds later, Chase and Wen jumped out as another vehicle arrived with more of their team. They raced to open the back of the van while some of their security detail helped the fallen officers, and two more ran in the direction the injured officer indicated.

The sirens of an approaching ambulance and additional police cars added to the confusion. Chase pulled the terrified kids out while Wen helped The Astronaut. She grabbed a radio and handcuff keys from one of the downed officers

"Let's disappear," she said to Chase.

Before anyone else arrived to ask more questions, they were heading to the airport. Police dispatch called Chase's phone repeatedly, but he didn't answer. It was time to dump that phone anyway.

Wen spent part of the drive soothing the kids and trying to learn more about the assailants from The Astronaut, but he seemed unable to speak. She continued to monitor the police frequency, hoping to discover what the cops were learning about the attackers, and heard an officer had killed the man who'd fled.

Leon's mother met them at a fast food place near the airport. Chase apologized profusely for putting him in danger. Leon was physically unharmed, but was still trembling as one of the team drove them home.

Chase called on the way to the airport and asked Dez to have the pilot stay on the plane, refuel, and be ready to take off immediately. "I'm going to need another plane to meet us in Chicago," Chase added, without giving Dez more details than needed in case someone was listening.

By the time Grimes and Shelby arrived at the crashed van, Chase, Wen, The Astronaut, and the kids were already gone. "Where would they go?" the driver asked.

"Airport," Grimes said. "Get there as fast as you can."

"We don't want to get pulled over."

"Don't worry about that. Every cop within fifty miles is either here," he pointed to the roadblock scene, which now involved nine cruisers from two jurisdictions, "or on their way here."

"You're sure they'll go to the airport?" Shelby asked. "Seems too obvious."

"I've spent *two years* tracking and studying Chase and Wen. They'll be at the airport."

"That's her name?" Shelby asked. "When did you learn it?"

"Yes, her name's Wen Sung, and it's unimportant when I discovered it."

Shelby knew it was actually *extremely* important when he'd found that out, but let it go, because she also knew Grimes well enough to be certain he wouldn't reveal his source unless he had to.

And soon he *would* have to.

Once the HondaJet leveled off to a cruising altitude, Wen and Chase changed out of their costumes. Tu and The Astronaut had no other clothes with them, and would have to wait until they reached their final destination.

Wen asked Tu and The Astronaut for more information on the men that took them.

"They spoke Arabic," Tu said. "I hear them talk about Mumford Grimes."

"Why would the shadow people come after The Astronaut, and leave us alone?" Wen asked.

"They also say 'Malone' many times," Tu said. "And they definitely talk about Bargo."

"So what's connecting Grimes, the shadow people, Bargo, *and* the CIA?" Chase asked.

The Astronaut had remained extra quiet, as if the whole episode had been more traumatic for him than Tu.

"Are you okay?" Wen asked gently, knowing The Astronaut was on the spectrum, and couldn't stand to be touched. "It must have been horrible."

"I did not want that," The Astronaut said.

"I know, but you're safe now."

"I did not want that. I did not want that," he repeated, while shaking his head. She reached over to touch his hand, but he recoiled quickly. "Those are *not* good people," he said angrily.

"It would be good if you could help us find them."

"I do *not* want to find them. I did not like that. I don't need to see them again. I need to stop them from ever doing that again. So that they don't come after us. They came for me. Leon and Tu were hurt because of *me*."

"They're not hurt. Everyone is fine," she said, not mentioning the injured officers.

"They *are* hurt. Leon is *very* hurt," he said. "I do not want to see those horrible people."

"You don't have to, but we need to know what the connection with all of this is."

"They came for me. They are always looking for me because they want my brain. They don't care about The Astronaut. They just want my brain. *I* need my brain, too." He looked at her helplessly. "It's all I can do . . . is use my brain."

"That's what I need you to do," Wen said. "Use your brain. But you don't have to do it now. It's the way to get back at those people and stop them. You can do it with your brain, and you won't have to see them. We'll keep you safe."

"I don't care about those people."

Wen knew he would help later, but he needed to be calm now. She left him sitting there, rocking back and forth, muttering to himself.

Meanwhile Chase and Tu were breaking down the common denominators between Bargo, shadow people, Grimes, and the CIA.

"It's possible Grimes is working for Bargo *and* for the shadow people," Tu said, fully absorbed in the challenge with no fear. "Maybe shadow people are even bigger than you think."

Chapter Sixty-Two

Wen moved over next to Tu and gave him a hug. "You don't have to work on this, honey."

"I like to," he said. "I get those jerkos."

"I want to make sure you're okay."

"Oh, I'm good. But I could use some more Dots."

Chase laughed. "I think we're all out of Dots. You ate them all."

"Maybe we'll get you some more when we land," Wen said.

"You mean they have Dots *outside* Iowa?"

"I think they've got Dots everywhere."

"They have no Dots in China." Though still in his astronaut suit, his helmet had gotten lost somewhere. "At least no one ever gave me Dots. Maybe I had to wear a costume. Do you think that's it, Wen? I could've gotten Dots all the time in China if I dressed up?"

"I don't know. Maybe. But China is different."

"I want to catch up on the Dots I missed."

Chase shook his head, laughing.

They'd arranged to have a car waiting when they landed. Chase sent a text to see if the driver could pick up a bag of Dots.

Wen reached into her pocket and handed Tu the shell and rock she and Chase had picked up for him back on the beach in Brookings. "For your collection."

"You remembered!" he said, smiling, excited to have a new addition to what he called his 'nature collection.' It consisted of pretty rocks, shells, sticks, and especially sea glass. "Thank you!"

"We'll take you there sometime."

"I would like that," Tu said thoughtfully. "You have a lot of money, Chase Bank. Why don't *you* hire Mumford Grimes?"

"That . . . actually might be a good idea," Chase said.

"Pay him to not work for anyone but you."

They discussed the possibility of trying to get information from Grimes.

"I wish I could have checked them for tattoos," Wen said, speaking of the kidnappers.

"There are too many factions," Chase said.

"Exactly why we need to put the puzzle together."

"There was a tattoo," The Astronaut said, breaking his long silence.

"The same?" Wen asked. "Finale?"

"Yes," The Astronaut said. "Two of them had it."

Wen nodded, knowing The Astronaut was coming back, but that his mind would be strained if the conversation went further.

"They came for me," The Astronaut said.

"Yes."

Wen's eyes met The Astronaut's and lingered for a long moment. They had both already figured out that the abductors had wanted Tu and The Astronaut for different reasons—for different *clients*. It was a terrifying realization, and one they did not want to discuss in front of Tu.

The HondaJet landed at Chicago Midway International Airport, where a GulfStream and three men from WOLF were waiting. Wen knew the men; two of them would take Tu and The Astronaut immediately to the west coast aboard the GulfStream. Dez and Bull would meet the plane and take them to a new safehouse, where Wen's grandmother would be waiting. The HondaJet and its pilot would fly Chase and Wen to Topeka in the morning after they finished their business in Winnetka, a wealthy Chicago suburb, with Sheldon Reams, the executive VP in charge of Bargo's IT department.

"Are you okay?" Wen asked, hugging Tu.

"I'm okay, but I'm sorry The Astronaut not okay," Tu said.

"I'm fine," The Astronaut told him. "Just needed some time."

"They were bad people," Tu said, "but we safe now. Can we come with you and Chase?"

"No, because Zǔ mǔ has been waiting for you, and you must explain Halloween to her," Wen said.

"Anyway," Chase added, "Bull and Dez need you and The Astronaut to help us figure this whole mess out."

"I already figure out," Tu said. "You hire Grimes, send him against other shadow people, CIA, Bargo."

"Maybe," Chase said, hugging Tu tightly, wanting so much to keep him near.

"It work, you see."

Chase and Wen waited until the Gulfstream took off before they left the airport. The third man from WOLF drove them to a hotel. He would pick them up in the morning and assist with the visit to Sheldon Reams' home.

"I can't sleep," Wen said as she lay next to Chase in the impersonal hotel room.

"Dez will text as soon as Tu arrives."

"I know. It's not that. It's Bargo. They're about more than just checking identities."

"Yeah?" Chase said, unsure where she was going with the rehash.

"They are part of a plan to manipulate and control the population," Wen said. "You can see they've projected this thing out. It's not just about ending crime and making people act good, it's about making people do what the authorities want them to do."

"It's always about control . . . money and control."

"Right, but if the CIA is behind it, why is Dag acting like the one with everything to lose?"

"It's a big contract."

"No, it's an overthrow. Once HaPPI is fully operational, that's the end."

"Of what?"

"Of a free government," Wen said. "The corporations will have control. *Total* control."

Chapter Sixty-Three

The Bombardier jet carrying Grimes and Shelby landed at Chicago's O'Hare twenty-nine minutes after Chase and Wen arrived at Midway. A man was waiting for them, and handed Grimes a phone. Grimes knew it would be Belfort on the other end of the line.

"What happened?" The impatient voice of his contact with the cartel, echoed his own irritation and frustration.

"We were seconds away," Grimes said, as if he were throwing verbal punches. "One of *your other teams* moved on them and botched it."

"*You* were late."

"We were *seconds from them*," Grimes shot back. "You bring in amateurs, and you get amateur results."

"Finale are *not* amateurs."

"They are for this type of work. I would think that California, Paris, Brookings, and the mountains would have taught you that by now."

"If you would do *your* job, I wouldn't *need* the others."

"Then let me *do* my job," Grimes said. "Where are they?"

"They split up. Malone and the woman are still in the area. I'll get you details within the hour."

"An hour? They could be anywhere by then."

"I doubt that."

"And the others?"

"Flying to California."

"Interesting."

"Yes, it is. You'll need to split up as well."

"Why don't you have more teams moving?"

"Act as if you are the only one."

Grimes knew that meant he was not. "Anything else?"

"Chase Malone is the priority. Understand?"

"Of course. The sooner you get me his whereabouts . . . "

"One more thing," Belfort said. "This is the one."

Grimes grimaced, nodded, and ended the call.

"What did he mean by that?" Shelby asked. She could see that the unflappable Grimes was quite shaken.

"Nothing. You need to handle Malone and the woman."

"What about you?"

"I'm going to California."

"When?"

"Now."

Carl, the man from WOLF, picked Chase and Wen up at sunrise. The brisk air on the first day of November helped keep them alert after so little sleep. Dez had called a few hours earlier to let them know that he had Tu and The Astronaut.

"There's a large safe under some kind of incredible pool table," Carl told them while handing out thick paper cups of hot coffee.

Chase was impressed that WOLF had discovered such information in so short a time. "How'd you get that?"

"Bargo paid for the install, WOLF found the record. Some hack or something."

"Specs?" Wen asked.

He pulled papers from his coat and handed them to her as he steered the car out of the parking lot.

"And we're assuming he keeps the key codes in this safe?" Chase asked.

"That's the hope," he said.

"What about security?"

"He has people at night, but during the day it's just a system."

"What kind?"

"We don't know."

"How are we going to get *in*, then?"

"Scrambler," Wen said, checking the road behind them. "Tell me we have one."

"Yeah, in the trunk. A seventy-five, eight-thirty," Carl replied.

"Good," Wen said, still watching the road, looking for trouble.

"What's a scrambler?" Chase asked.

"A scrambler jamming reset device, created by the CIA. It'll give us a certain blackout time."

"Okay. Who's going in?"

"You," Wen said. "I'll need to cover the outside in case we have company. You're the SEER expert, and you have the tech skills to deal with whatever you may find."

"And what will Carl be doing?" Chase asked.

"I have to keep the scrambler operational," he said. "*And* . . . I'm driving the getaway car."

Ten minutes later, Chase was inside as Wen walked the perimeter.

"I see the pool table," Chase said.

"And the safe?" Wen asked through her headpiece.

"This is the craziest thing I've ever seen . . . translucent felt of some kind, and below it are tropical fish. It's got to feel like playing pool under water—a *pool* of water." Chase laughed.

"*The safe*," Wen hissed.

"All that's under the table is a rack with a ton of pool balls."

"There has to be a safe."

Chase studied the area. Nothing else under the table revealed any sign of the safe. He tried to push the rack of balls out of the way, but it wouldn't move.

The rack is the safe. Chase looked for an opening. *It's the balls . . . very clever.*

"Any idea what the combination is?" he joked.

"Open it," Wen said impatiently.

"Dez, do you hear me?"

"Got you, partner," Dez replied.

Chase held his phone in over the balls. "See it? The numbers on the pool balls must be arranged to input the combination."

"Yeah, ingenious." Dez clicked a button and the video feed from Chase's phone went into SEER, which had already been given everything they could find on the home's owner, including date of birth, blood type, his internet browsing history, and a million other details. As Chase had said, "We're going to HaPPI him."

"Anything?" Wen asked, worried about how long it was taking.

Chase continued inspecting the rack while Dez worked the delicate options within SEER.

Almost two minutes later, Wen was considering drastic measures, thinking there must be a way to blow the safe without damaging the sensitive electronics and drives inside. "Chase, we don't have forever."

"It takes time," Chase said, now lying down under the fish tank/pool table, trying to get a better look at the safe. "Problem."

"What?" Wen and Dez asked simultaneously.

"I think the safe requires a voice-activated combination."

"I thought it was the balls?" Wen said.

"It's *both*."

"Security approaching," Carl reported. "Get out of there!"

Chapter Sixty-Four

Susan and Tess had been battling it out on an internal email chain with everyone in the Elevation group. The CIA director convened another meeting of them all after their contentious words had boiled over.

"I don't give a damn about your disagreements," the director said. "We've *got* to hold the line here. HaPPI is moving forward." He lit up a screen at the end of the room. "You can see the implementation has spread."

"We're about to enter into the conspiracy theorist view —otherwise known as the independent Internet media," an NSA man said. "Once we're in their field of vision, they'll pick this up, and it's going to snowball like nothing we've ever seen. You think people were upset about the Patriot Act or Snowden's revelations? Word gets out about *this*, and things like WikiLeaks and the Panama Papers are going to look like comic books."

"We need to have this on solid ground," the CIA director said. "Our friends in the media are not going to be able to sweep all of this under the rug."

Tess shuddered, recalling the seventy-year-old CIA program controlling the media in the United States. First known as Operation Mockingbird, the ultra-classified campaign had been started by Cord Meyer and Allen W. Dulles to influence and manipulate public opinion, recruiting leading American journalists. Before it was exposed by US Senator Frank Church in the mid-1970s, the CIA, through Mockingbird, had spread its covert influence into student and cultural organizations, political campaigns, magazines, newspapers, radio, and television. Although then CIA director George H. W. Bush claimed to have ended the program, it was simply secretly renamed "Pocket-Watch," and remained ongoing to this day. The latter version of the covert media operation was light years beyond what was achieved by Mockingbird, and now included disinformation campaigns, falsification of historical events, infiltration of social media, and full review and control over all major media operations in the United States.

Tess had no doubt they could bury anything that came out on HaPPI, and any Internet sites that tried to enlighten the public would be branded conspiracy theorists. However, there was always a slim chance that a movement could build steam. "If people are allowed to form a negative impression of HaPPI," Tess said, "we could have a storm of trouble that would slow everything down. It's best if we don't trip the algorithms in the beginning. We don't want any more Boone Malones."

Susan laughed. "It would be an obvious problem if we suddenly have hundreds or thousands of people losing their jobs, their homes, or being erased."

"Why don't *you* try to figure it out, then," Tess said to Susan.

"This is going too fast," Susan shot back. "Tess is playing a dangerous game here."

"If it weren't for Susan's screw ups—"

"If it weren't for *you*, Chase Malone wouldn't be a factor here."

"Then we should have moved on him sooner," one of the men said.

"I didn't block you from protecting Chase Malone from the beginning," the director said.

"Need I remind you, I've got two IT-Squads out there looking to take Chase out," Tess said. "And *your* people haven't had any more success than I have."

"We'll get him."

"When I told you he was a valuable asset, I warned he was resourceful and not easy to track. I think that has now been demonstrated."

"Yes, he might have been worth keeping on our side," the director reluctantly agreed. "Unfortunately, he seems intent on jeopardizing critical operations."

"Yes," Tess said.

"Which is my point," Susan continued. "We should reassess not only the program, but Tess's involvement."

"Look, we're all on the same side here," the director said. "I'm extremely confident that Chase Malone will be taken care of in the next six hours." He let out a weary sigh. "Getting back on track, each of you has received a new list of potential opposition. Run them through. And let's get those taken care of *before* anyone bangs open more of these doors."

Tess left the meeting knowing the choice she had been dreading for two years was finally before her:

Kill Chase Malone, or betray my country . . .

Chase knew he couldn't leave without the contents of the safe. "Where are we, Dez?"

"Almost there."

"How are we getting past the voice recognition?"

"SEER found some voice samples."

"Where?"

"I don't know—webinar, zoom, YouTube—does it *matter?*"

"*Get out,*" Carl repeated urgently. "Security entering the driveway."

"We've got the combination," Dez said. "Waiting to synch voice."

"Where are you, Wen?" Chase asked.

"East side yard, near the guest house."

"Do you see them?"

"Yes, but I don't have a shot."

"Dez?" Chase asked.

"Here we go!" Dez said. "Ready?"

Chase placed the phone near the tiny mic he'd found in the pool rack. "Go."

"The security car has stopped," Wen said. "Two officers exiting the vehicle."

The voice of Sheldon Reams began reciting a series of numbers. The pool balls moved until the numbers lined up to match the combination.

"It's open," Chase said, sliding the heavy lid out of the way.

"Security approaching the front door," Wen said. "You need to get out *now.*"

Chase snatched the only thing in the safe—a shoe box

sized computer drive—and rolled out from under the aquarium/pool table.

"Another car," Carl announced. "Approaching the driveway."

"Looks like Reams is coming home," Wen said. "Chase, are you out?"

"No. I'm heading to the back door."

"Stop," she said. "One of the security team just went around the other side."

"Where should I go?"

"They've surrounded the house. This was a setup."

"Is there *anywhere* to go?" Chase asked.

Wen didn't respond.

No way out, he thought as the front door opened.

Chapter Sixty-Five

Dag sat on the terrace of his ninety-foot mansion yacht, more than ten thousand square feet of pure luxury. The palatial boat measured forty-two feet across, and could comfortably hold two hundred people.

"This is magnificent. Pharaoh-like, really," the CIA official meeting with him on one of the outdoor decks said, overwhelmed by the pure opulence. She and her team had flown in twenty-five minutes earlier, landing on the yacht's helipad.

Although they weren't staying overnight, each was given a stateroom to relax and freshen up in before the meeting. Dag was more interested in talking about his new boat, which boasted one hundred forty solar panels capable of outputting 20 kW of renewable power.

"I've got a five thousand gallon holding tank for freshwater *and* a desalinization plant on board," he said when one of the intelligence officials remarked about how long one could survive in open seas on a boat like this.

"Don't you get tired of being out at sea?"

"That's the best thing about my little boat," Dag said, smiling, as if describing a cabin cruiser. "There are four eighteen-foot hydraulic legs. Each has a lifting capacity of a million pounds."

"What for?" the man asked, trying to be polite.

"When I'm in shallow water, the entire structure can stand up and look more like a small beach house or a bungalow on stilts."

"It's like an island."

"Except if a storm comes up, I just float away. The alloy finish is impervious to just about anything."

His visitors decided to skip the eight person hot tub and game room in order to go straight to the indoor theater for a presentation on HaPPI. Afterwards, they moved up to the chef's kitchen and dining space, which appeared more like a high-end Manhattan Café—except for the floor-to-ceiling windows that offered them panoramic views of the sparkling ocean.

The question-and-answer session found Dag at his most charming.

"How close are we to full implementation?" the CIA woman asked while waving off an offered cocktail. She tolerated Dag's eccentric ways because he had put together a truly remarkable collection of companies, databases, apps, and algorithms. Yet, as the head of the project and knowing of his schemes, she felt fear for what kind of future they were creating. A future when a man such as this could create a corporate force with unlimited power.

"Soon," he answered. "Don't be nervous. As we consolidate control, the world will experience new stability." Dag smiled, not like a salesman, but like a doctor who'd just said *'This won't hurt a bit.'*

We're actually putting the world more at risk, she thought.

Dag's wealth, the ease of his power, had more and more convinced her that her superiors in Washington were fooling themselves into believing their quest coincided with his.

"What safeguards are there during the initial rollout?" one of the analysts asked, referring to the time when the public would first become aware of HaPPI. "We expect to face pushback on the perception that the program is weakening the protective safeguards which had grown organically or intentionally in society for decades."

"I'm most interested in your public relations efforts and plans," the woman added, tired of his boasting and rambling about all that they had.

"We definitely have a full frontal in place for that," Dag replied. He touched his smartwatch; a glass screen descended from the ceiling. Although translucent, a series of visuals appeared, supplementing the comprehensive program they had already seen in the theater on the lower deck. "You'll see in addition to a ninety million dollar ad campaign, there will be hundreds of media reports supporting our position, and no critical mainstream coverage."

The woman knew the CIA, through its control of the mainstream media, also had a massive propaganda program ready to supplement Bargo's campaign which would convince the masses of the necessity and benefits of HaPPI.

The CIA representatives smiled at the convincing presentation of the measures that were to be employed. Dag had thought of everything. His demonic smile was only added to by his dark, bushy eyebrows, lending a comical, sinister, and light-hearted way about him. Those attributes did not hide or embellish his cutthroat edge. In fact, he was one big secret; a dangerous, cunning man who did not show emotion unless he slipped—which he did, concerning the success of the meeting. It was going to work. Everyone in the world wanted a safer, more peaceful existence, and as the post 9/11 era and patriot act had proven, they would trade almost anything in exchange for that promised security.

"Once the new reality becomes the accepted norm," Dag began, "we will implement Phase Two."

That made her particularly nervous. This data would all come directly to the corporate structures, and relied on friends, neighbors, and family members providing information on each other, surrendering all the little details of their daily lives, unwittingly sharing information on those closest to them. It would create what Dag liked to call a 'three-dimensional view into each person.' The algorithms would be able to form a predictive model of what a person was thinking in real time, based on their actions and those of their family, friends, neighbors, coworkers, etcetera. *One step closer to the thought police, she thought with a shiver.*

"The two-way vision is what they were thinking and what they were doing," Dag said, knowing he really shouldn't be going into the details of Phase Two just yet.

"What are those?" one of the analysts asked, noticing what appeared to be large guns mounted above them.

"Defensive systems," Dag said hesitantly.

"By *'defensive systems,'* you mean anti-aircraft, anti-ship guns?"

"It's not fun to be a sitting target for pirates and other threats. I can't just rely on some ex-agents with machine guns now, can I?"

The woman in charge was clearly annoyed, but it was an acceptable explanation, and under normal circumstances it might've been a good enough answer. In this case, though, it gave her more cause for concern. More and more she saw these corporate CEOs as modern day Emperors, establishing their versions of armies. She knew they already controlled the future of warfare with technology and big data. The US government, as well as those of other countries, were falling behind. It seemed only China had a chance at keeping up with the corporations, but that was dependent on how long they could keep their massive population satisfied.

She had not asked to be put in charge of this project. It, like so many other crises, had dropped in her lap because of her specialized division's abilities.

"I do hope you're not recording our meeting today," she said, smiling tersely at Dag.

"Of course not." The question insulted him, as it was meant to. Her people had digitally and electronically swept the boat upon entering it.

Unfortunately, none of them knew what lay beneath.

Chapter Sixty-Six

Chase looked around, saw a shadow pass one of the windows, and knew it was too late to leave. He had no gun.

The front door opened. Two sets of footsteps echoed on the marble floor. "Sheldon, we have exposure on this," a female voice said.

"Dag has it covered," a man responded. Chase assumed him to be Sheldon Reams, the Bargo vice president whose home he was currently trying to escape.

"The CIA isn't the most trustworthy ally," the woman said as she walked down the hall. "They could turn on us."

"Chase, did you get out?" Dez asked in his ear. Chase didn't answer.

"Dag is using them, not the other way around," Reams said. "I'm sure the CIA is using *us*, too, but Dag is so far ahead of them. HaPPI has stuff on all of them. When the time is right, he will implement 'Ever After,' and they will cease to be a threat."

"And Bargo will control the CIA?" she asked, their voices getting farther away.

"Bargo will control *everything*," Reams said.

"Ever After, as in HaPPI-ly ever after. That's cute."

"As long as you're not Little Red Riding Hood," Reams said, laughing. "When your sweet little grandma turns out to be a wolf."

"But Bargo isn't the bad guy in the fairy tale. We're going to make the world better."

"I know, it was a bad analogy. I was just going with the 'happily ever after' theme."

She laughed. "One thing though, why does . . . "

Their voices became too muffled to hear. Chase knew he had one chance to escape without them discovering him —the front door.

He whispered Wen's name as loud as he dared just before he turned the knob. No response. He'd taken four steps outside when a security officer yelled, "Hey!"

Chase turned in time to see the man draw his gun. His first thought was to protect the data vault in his left hand as he dove into a boxwood hedge. The security guard took a bullet in his chest before he could fire at Chase. That shot ignited a firefight. Bullets seemed to be flying from every direction as Chase moved through the landscaped flower gardens and hedges toward the entrance.

If I can make it to the car . . .

"Wen? Carl?" He tried to raise them as he ran.

"Chase, where *are* you?" Dez asked.

"I'm in a war zone," Chase replied as a bullet ricocheted off an Italian marble fountain he was hiding behind. "I don't know where Wen is."

"Do you have the data vault?"

"Yeah," Chase said, "but I'm getting shot at, and have no idea if Wen is okay."

"Bull's working on something. We *need* that data," Dez said. "It's going to be a big upload. You should be able to use Wen's satlink from the car."

"I've got to *get* to the damned car first," Chase said. "Wen? Carl?" *Where are they?*

He reached the outer ring of the circular driveway, but would lose his cover if he tried to cross it. Chase crouched and picked a route to the other side. The shooting had lessened. He looked back at the house. Reams and the woman were standing in the front door.

Why aren't they afraid of getting shot? he wondered.

Two security officers standing near them both fell to the ground. Reams and the woman disappeared into the house. Chase took the opportunity and bolted. He negotiated through more hedges and a stand of trees, the area manicured like a city park. Finally, he had the car in sight.

He reached it a few seconds later, and found Carl's body on the ground on the other side, a bullet hole in his forehead.

Chapter Sixty-Seven

Rick Zinner, an operative paid by the Cause, had been a mercenary for seventeen years, having seen plenty of action in South and Central America. It wouldn't have mattered if he agreed with WOLF's mission, he would've taken the assignment either way. Money is money, after all, and his skills were generally available to the highest bidder. However, his hardened experience and jaded outlook on life, after seeing so much war and death, had left him open to be seduced by the ideas of the Cause. Zinner believed in right and wrong, but he knew how complicated they each could be.

Henry Fikes was not unlike Zinner. He was an American who'd served two tours in Afghanistan before an honorable discharge and going freelance. After that, he'd been recruited by WOLF, and the two of them had done several jobs together. Margot, the leader of WOLF, called them her "tough team."

"I've seen a lot of wrong in the world," Zinner said as they were flying in for the deployment. "Enough to know firsthand that money makes the war, and war makes the money."

"I can't tell you how much that sickens me," Fikes agreed "All this waste."

"You member Raul?"

Months earlier, Zinner and Fikes had served together on a covert operation in Venezuela, along with a close friend, Raul, who didn't make it.

"That wasn't over nothing but money," Fikes sneered. "Venezuelan oil reserves, rare-earth minerals, corporate interests, whatever."

"Freakin' waste," Zinner said. "I can't take much more of it."

But he had to. It wasn't the money, really. "Soldier work" was the only thing he was any good at, and if it weren't for that, Zinner knew he'd be in a VA psych ward somewhere, or maybe a homeless shelter.

However, the Cause showed him that other people were fed up, too, and they were trying to stop it, trying to *fix* it.

Zinner and Fikes dropped into the ocean in full SCUBA gear. A waterproof unipack held the operation's equipment. They surfaced under what, to them, appeared to be an oil rig platform. They knew it was actually Dag Kirrem's super yacht.

"I found a dry corner," Zinner said, bobbing in the air chamber below the main platform. He did a quick sweep, checking the area. "Do you believe this stuff?"

"I wish we'd brought some Gruelly," Fikes said, referring to Gruell-75, a top-secret military grade explosive. The patented and classified manufacturing technique, combined with tactically engineered components, resulted in a lightweight and pliable material which packed eighty-seven times more force than any prior forms of compound-explosives. "I would've liked to have blown this whole platform—and the people on it—out of the water. Quicker route to end some of the world's misery."

"We wouldn't be much better than them then, would we?"

"Yeah, well, I agree with the Cause. They don't want to use some slow, nonviolent methods. We should sign a few thousand people, drop them in the right spots in the world, and we could finish this."

"Let's just take care of today, shall we?"

"If we *don't* do it, you know how many operations are going on right now around the world? *Thousands*."

They swam to the end of the open channel. Zinner mounted brackets and meticulously added pieces, connecting a complex transmitter base. On the opposite side, Fikes wired up other monitoring equipment.

Fikes signaled Zinner. He nodded, donned his mask, and they both submerged under the hull. Zinner knew Fikes was thinking it would be a great place to put explosives with a delayed detonation. They'd worked a similar job in the Persian Gulf, but this was a different mission.

They came up on the outer edge of the platform, still hidden from view. Zinner looked up into the sky. They had a high altitude surveillance drone they could control from their current location, its flight level high enough that it would be difficult to spot by those on board, but it wasn't foolproof. If Bargo's security people were trained well enough, they might conduct aerial surveillance. If so, then Zinner and Fikes' hotline experience, and the few weapons they'd brought with them, would be the only things to determine if this would be their last mission.

Chapter Sixty-Eight

Chase saw the shadow before he realized he wasn't alone. Hoping it was Wen, he turned around, smiling.

"Hello, Chase Malone," Shelby said, pointing a submachine gun at him. "Remember me from the beach in Brookings?"

Why aren't I dead? was his first thought.

Where's Wen? was his second.

"Are you going to kill me?"

"Don't you think I would have already done that?"

"Depends on your objectives," Chase said, trying to buy time.

"Get in. You drive."

Chase looked around.

"No one's going to save you," Shelby said. "Get in. NOW!"

Chase stepped over Carl's body and opened the driver's door. He took one more glance around and slid in, setting the data vault on the passenger seat as Shelby got in behind him.

"Did you kill Wen?" he asked, dread tightening his chest.

"I didn't have to. One of the security people got her. Now drive."

Chase didn't want to believe her, but Wen hadn't answered, he hadn't seen her, and, most telling of all, she hadn't rescued him yet.

He took a deep breath.

"*Move it*," she ordered, pressing the gun to the back of his head. "It won't be very pleasant for either of us if we're still here when the cops show up."

Chase pulled the car onto the quiet street. "Where are we going?"

"Airport," she lied.

Suddenly, a security van blasted out of a hedge bordering the end of the Reams property and blocked the road. Chase slammed the brakes and stopped inches before crashing into its side.

"Back up!" Shelby yelled.

Instead, he turned off the car and opened his door. Before he could escape, Shelby's window exploded. In a blur of confusion, Shelby collapsed onto the backseat as her door opened. Chase jumped out as Shelby's body hit the seat, then Wen was climbing in on top of her, shoving her limp body against the door and out of the way.

"Come on!" Wen shouted. " We need to go!"

"How?" Chase asked, getting back in and starting the car. He drove up into the grass and destroyed more of the hedge to get around the van. "What happened? Is she dead?"

"I don't think so," Wen said. "I hit her with my gun. Hopefully she's just unconscious."

"Where *were* you?"

"Fighting through," she said wearily. "I don't know where they all came from."

Chase looked at her in the rearview mirror. "Is that *your* blood?" he asked, seeing the dark red stain on her shirt.

". . . apparently," she said.

"Are you okay?"

"I don't think so."

Zinner and Fikes waited underneath the mansion yacht. "We're not connecting," Zinner said.

"I thought we had a clear on the satellite uplinks from the site," Fikes said.

"We're gonna have to do it hard," Zinner muttered, meaning they would need to bring the audio and video data out with them.

They stationed themselves back underneath the hull and watched the video feeds. There, they were able to communicate with a WOLF boat in the distance. Zinner described the video.

"Six visitors on the vessel—two women, four men." They had already intercepted a transmission that said these were CIA representatives.

The drone picked up the first videos and limited audio from the conversation as Zinner relayed the highlights to the men on the surveillance boat. *Typical CIA operation,* he thought, *in bed with corporate assets.* He'd long held the opinion that the CIA was willing to use anybody to get what they wanted. He'd seen it all over the world, where they would develop assets, using them without regard to the consequences. If an asset were discovered once the operation ended, they simply cut ties and moved on. He'd been guilty himself of facilitating that kind of systematic shame.

"They're talking about a phase two," he said. This was new information. He went quiet to listen to the appalling description of the secondary stage operation. He then relayed the information that the ship carried anti-aircraft and anti-ship guns. It wasn't information directly needed—they'd been sent to find out about HaPPI—but Zinner knew that a future mission might attack the vessel.

Fikes listened to the report, and wanted to get topside for some "mission expansion." He'd already decided that, when they got back, he was going to find out if there was a branch of WOLF that was splitting off to pursue more violent means, and, if so, he was going to join it. *I'm not a patient man*, he thought, before returning to concentrate on the dialogue they were monitoring.

There were a loud series of pops in the audio. Zinner made an X signal with his arms, pointed up.

"*What?*" Fikes mouthed.

"*Drone*," Zinner replied in a hoarse whisper, Fikes couldn't hear. Then a little louder added, "Our drone just got hit!"

"They know we're here!" Fikes yelled, looking at the edge. "Go now!"

Chapter Sixty-Nine

Fikes went to his bag and pulled out two machine guns in waterproof cases.

"What are *those* doing here, man?" Zinner asked, surprised by the presence of extra weapons.

"I don't go anywhere without my babies," Fikes said. "Why don't we just take this party out?"

"We don't have orders for that. Stand down."

Fikes made his decision, and pointed up.

"No way," Zinner said. "We're outgunned. Let's go before we're out of time."

"They've made us. We're already out of time," Fikes said, donning his mask. "Screw it, man. I'll do it alone if I have to."

"Nah, come on. Let's go. We've got enough information here . . . Wait, they're sending—"

Two divers appeared from below. Zinner had heard them being deployed through the audio monitors. Those seconds gave Fikes the slightest edge. He'd grabbed the second machine gun and fired from his air pocket, turning the water underneath the floating mansion red.

"Dammit!" Zinner said, swimming to the other end of the platform. "Two more coming down."

"Where?" Fikes asked.

Zinner pointed.

Fikes took them out. Zinner got to the end of his area and engaged with four more as they came into the water. Fikes yelled, "Dog, dog, dog! Let's get up top and see what damage we can do."

"You got it," Zinner said, knowing they were in it now.

"We live through this one, I'll buy the beer for a month."

They both climbed onto the deck and sprayed machine gun fire using a periscope technique. Two of the CIA officers went down.

Dag and the woman fled below deck.

"Who the hell is attacking us?" the woman asked breathlessly as they hurried down the hall.

"Must be friends of yours," Dag said. "But don't worry, I've got two indestructible safe rooms."

"Great, we can sink in an airtight chamber."

"No," Dag said proudly. "If the mansion sinks, both the safe rooms convert into submersibles, and will jet out. We are a thousand percent safe."

"Well, we've got to *get* to the rooms first," she said. "And what about my people on deck?"

"There's plenty of security devices up there," he assured her.

Fifteen seconds later, they were locked in a room together. Dag wanted to continue the meeting, but the woman wouldn't consider it until she knew what was going on with her people.

"We can monitor the action topside," Dag said, flipping on a large screen, showing sixteen views. "Look." He pointed. The split-screen showed two of her team being ushered down by Dag's assistant to the other safe room.

The woman pointed to another view. "Those are terrorists," she said as Zinner and Fikes came on board.

"Not to worry," Dag said.

They watched as Fikes was immediately cut down by motion activated artificial intelligence guns concealed in one of the exterior walls.

"Yes!" Dag cheered. "That was money well spent."

Zinner barely got any farther before the ship's captain activated a laser netting system.

"This lucky bastard will be taken alive," Dag said proudly. "I *do* hope more will be coming. I have so many tricks we haven't even used yet."

The woman could not hide her annoyance.

Zinner had never encountered such defenses as this modern castle contained. *This isn't a luxury yacht or a mansion, it's some sort of futuristic warship*, he thought as the lasers descended on him. He was about to turn the gun on himself, determined not to be taken prisoner by these sci-fi corporate lords, but before he could get the gun spun around, the lasers incapacitated him, and he blacked out.

Chase turned in his seat to look at Wen. "Hold on, I'm going to pull over."

"No, we need to get clear."

"How bad is it?"

"I'll be okay."

He didn't believe her.

"You have to drive. Do you see the satlink?" she asked.

"Yeah, it's on the floor," he said, looking at the high tech box under the dash on the passenger side.

"Plug in the data vault. Get it to The Astronaut."

Chase fiddled with a pouch of cables on top of the box, while keeping his eyes on the road. "How's the sniper?" Chase asked.

"Still out."

"And you?"

"Still breathing."

"I've got to pull over," Chase said. "I can't find the right cable."

"Find somewhere out of view."

A few minutes later, Chase found a church and pulled into the back parking lot. He plugged the data vault into the satlink, then checked on Wen. "Oh my god—you got shot in the stomach!"

"I think it's above the abdomen, closer to my liver, but it missed it or I wouldn't still be conscious."

"I'm taking you to a hospital."

"No. I've got most of the bleeding stopped for now. The bullet exited. I'll live long enough to make it to the plane."

"Then what?"

"Call Margot."

"Okay." Chase hoped that since they were so close to Chicago, the leader of WOLF would be able to get a doctor to meet them at the plane. He found some zip ties in Wen's pack and secured the sniper's wrists. "She's still breathing."

"Good, we can question her later."

Chase wondered if 'later' was actually going to come.

Chapter Seventy

Zinner, handcuffed awkwardly to a brass deck rail, refused to give them his name. But with his military background, having access to CIA databases, and after scanning his fingerprints and sending them to Langley, the IDs for both Fikes and him, plus their complete classified files, landed on the CIA woman's phone in almost no time.

"Richard Zinner," Dag said. "You're some kind of soldier of fortune, huh?"

Zinner gave him a cold, blank stare.

"Who are you working for?"

More angry poker face.

"I'll take care of this," the CIA woman said. "Listen Zinner, I've just brought in Naval assets to find out where you came from and who else you've got out there, so soon you won't be as useful to me."

As if on cue, two US Navy choppers flew overhead. Zinner remained silent.

"You think messing with Bargo was a big deal? You have no idea what you've stepped in with *me*, Zinner." She walked over to one of her team, and came back with a pistol.

"Hey, what are you doing?" Dag asked nervously.

"Tell me who hired you," she said, pressing the gun against Zinner's forehead.

"Do it," he growled, his eyes burning into hers. "You'd be doing me a favor."

She stared at him for a moment, slowly moved the gun away from his head, then shot his right hand.

Dez, Bull, The Astronaut, and Tu had been working on their plan all day, and as soon as the contents of the data vault arrived, they knew immediately it could work.

"Are they okay?" Bull asked Dez when he came into the room to give Tu a sandwich.

"Fine," Dez replied, giving her a look as if to say *sort of fine*, but not wanting to upset Tu with news about Wen.

"We don't have everything," The Astronaut said. "In order to make this work, we need the enigma core."

"What's that?" Tu asked.

"In advanced AI programs, there's something that is the power source for the ultimate coding. If we get the one they're using, we will be able to alter HaPPI. If we don't have it, we can do nothing."

"Where can we get it?" Bull asked.

"Someone else on the inside," The Astronaut said.

"What about Mitchell Landes?" Dez asked.

The Astronaut reviewed the corporate records that had been in the data vault, finding Mitchell's file. "He didn't have direct access, but he *was* in the department that developed it, so . . . "

"So that might explain why he's in hiding," Dez said.

"He is?"

"Yeah. Chase and Wen are on their way to meet him."

"They may not find him in time," Bull said. "We only have until midnight."

"Why?" Tu asked.

"The formats will all shift at midnight—part of their security protocols."

"I better call Chase to let him know the deadline," Dez said. "That's not much time."

"We should keep working," Tu said, sounding like part of the team. "In case Chase and Wen don't find him in time, we need to get a way to crack it."

"Cracking the enigma core isn't something you do in hours," The Astronaut said. "If it's possible at all, it will take years."

"What was *that*!" Dag yelped.

Zinner grimaced and spit, but otherwise gave nothing. Two of his fingers were gone, his trembling hand a blood soaked mess.

"*Eight* people are dead," the woman snapped, "including two of my operatives. I'm going to kill this traitor unless he tells me everything I want to know."

"All this blood . . . " Dag said, not knowing what else to say, but wanting to mask his shock.

Dag had fed Zinner and Fikes' names into HaPPI, and less than ten minutes later, they had an unbelievably comprehensive profile on them. But Zinner was a hardened warrior, and not easily harassed, or susceptible to enhanced interrogation methods.

"I'll ask one more time," she said. "Who do you work for? How much did they hear?" She knew the drone meant someone serious, even before one of Dag's people had brought up the transmission equipment. She shook her head, appalled that part of their meeting may have gotten out.

What they didn't understand about Zinner was that he was already past the point of no return. One too many kills, one too many buddies dead in front of him; the cost versus reward ratio for the mission he was on no longer existed.

"You have a good service record, Zinner. A brave soldier. What happened to make you betray your country?"

"Ask yourself the same thing. The CIA is *not* my country."

"Do you want another bullet?"

He laughed a demented laugh. "It doesn't matter what you do to me, I'm already dead."

She shot him in the head. "I guess you were right."

Chapter Seventy-One

Bull and The Astronaut stared at their respective screens. The room appeared as if it had been tossed in a police raid —piles of empty energy drink cans, overflowing ashtrays, stacks of paper, odd scribblings, mostly from The Astronaut, a tipped over waste can filled with countless urgent, crumpled equations and messages, things strewn about, stacks of hard drives, a dish full of flash drives, and others randomly scattered everywhere.

A series of monitors representing different target computers covered a large folding table behind them. Tu studied the scene as a detective might, looking for anything that made sense in the chaos.

Bull had two more tables crowded with laptops that were all in various stages of hacking into Bargo and related firms. The Astronaut had nine computers working a long string into government systems, and two separate drives running on Heaven, the ultra-classified US intelligence network.

"We gotta figure out how they're collecting the data in

the government pool," Bull said. "They can't just be blending them."

"There has to be an overriding algorithm working," The Astronaut theorized.

"Leave forced algorithm," Dez said, coming back from a SEER session. "Chase made one to four different arenas, and we still haven't yielded any satisfactory results." He opened the window a little wider in an effort to vent some of Bull's cigarette smoke. "You aren't supposed to smoke in here."

"I know," she said, exhaling a gray cloud and stubbing her current cig out.

"What if we put a different launch objective and add re-on inputs from the social media profiles?" The Astronaut suggested.

"Worth a try," Bull said, taking her hands from the keys and fishing through an empty pack of cigarettes, hoping the final one might miraculously reappear, before she continued typing commands. "Do you see before the posts are merged?"

"Yeah," Dez replied. "Do you think that's possible?"

"I *might* be able to make that work by modifying the round." She smiled briefly, as if the idea appealed to her, that it might be the solution to something that had been bothering her.

"The other way is open," The Astronaut said.

"I can't get in," Bull muttered back, the four words she most despised leaving a bad taste in her mouth.

"Change calibration sequence," The Astronaut said. "If you invert the tangle, it'll open."

"You think this is my first day? I've *tried* that."

"Try again," The Astronaut said. "And this time, do it *right*."

Tu laughed as Bull moaned in frustration.

"I *did* do it right," she said, reaching for the empty pack of cigarettes again. Tu saw a new pack on the other side of the room, but said nothing.

"Humor me," The Astronaut said. "Try it again."

Bull rekeyed all the entries, which required her to upload a series of concurrent downloads before the string would take. "It's got to come in that way," she said, "but it's exactly how I did it before. And see, noth—"

"I see it worked this time," The Astronaut interrupted. "It's amazing the results one can achieve when they do things in the proper order."

Tu laughed again.

"You changed something."

"No. *You* changed something," he said. "You did it correctly this time."

She knew The Astronaut did not play games. His matter-of-fact tone assured her that it was, in fact, *her* mistake. Normally she didn't deal in failed strings or error messages, but she was tired. They'd been working too long.

Bull pushed the button to steer her wheelchair across the room. She rummaged through one of her backpacks, with its many zippered compartments and velcro pouches, for almost a full minute. Tu tried not to giggle, still looking at the new pack of cigarettes sitting on the shelf behind her.

"Finally!"

"Did you get into the server?" The Astronaut asked absently, staring at half a dozen screens at once, thinking she had achieved a breakthrough.

"No, but I found another fresh pack of cigarettes."

"Well, isn't that just wonderful for us."

"It'll keep me working longer," she said, flicking her lighter multiple times, getting nothing but sparks.

"It'll keep us working until we die of smoke inhalation."

"I thought you were going to say lung cancer," she quipped, finding another orange lighter, this time getting a flame.

"No, it'll take years for your lung cancer to kill you. Meanwhile, secondhand smoke will give me any number of unpleasant ailments and shave several points off my productivity."

She sat back at the screen, happy in her nicotine-induced calm, a fresh blue haze floating around her head as she squinted at the monitor. "What's this?"

"I think we just established it's a cigarette, which means a slow death."

"No, I mean this series of numbers. I think we've gotten through—at least on the micro level."

"The micro level is where we need to begin. Can you verify?"

"I'm trying." Her fingers on one hand flew across the keyboard while her other worked the touchscreen.

"I think we're getting much closer to determining Bargo's methods."

"It's still a long way to go," Bull said, exhaling smoke. "But there certainly is a path."

"They've made this all hack-proof," the Astronaut said.

"*Nothing* is hack-proof."

"Bargo is obviously anticipating full attacks once HaPPI becomes public. Makes our job harder," he said.

"But also more fun," Bull returned. "I don't hack because it's easy. I do it because it's hard."

"You can be sure they planted some land-mines."

"Yeah, but they may be counting on the fact they can destroy the hackers, or at least their friends and family. That's a major deterrent. They can penetrate any screen name. We're not susceptible to that, though," Bull said, winking at The Astronaut.

"They have government support," The Astronaut said, "at the highest, most secretive levels. They can extort and control all their opponents and enemies."

"Our only way into their house is to burn down their house."

Chapter Seventy-Two

The plane was there in the private hanger, but Chase didn't care about that. All he wanted to know was if the doctor had made it. His question was answered when two men emerged from the plane as soon as he got out of the car. Both were members of WOLF, and one was a surgeon.

They helped get the still-unconscious sniper on board while Chase carried a very woozy Wen. The doctor began examining her before they even took off.

"She's lucky," the doctor said. "There's an exit wound. The bullet appears to have missed anything vital, but she's lost a lot of blood."

"So she'll be okay?"

"Yes, but in order to aid her recovery, she'll need bedrest and no exertion."

Chase knew that was not going to be easy.

"I gave her a sedative," the doctor said. "That should help for now."

"And her?" Chase asked, pointing to the sniper.

"I'll take a look at her next."

The other Cause member, who had been keeping an eye on her in case she woke up, moved to another seat to give the doctor room.

After examining the sniper, he reported that she was suffering from a serious concussion, but should be fine.

Once they landed in Topeka, Kansas, the doctor and other Cause member stayed with the plane and the sniper.

Wen was still groggy as they started the hour-plus drive to Mitchell Landes' house. By the time they were half an hour out, she was feeling clearer.

Margot had sent a text to inform them that a raid on Dag's floating mansion had gone bad.

We lost the operatives. Company official present. Some data still recoverable. Soon.

Wen read the cryptic text, knowing "company" meant CIA. "Was it Tess?"

"Who else," Chase said, partially regretting it was her, and partially furious.

"If Bull and The Astronaut get in . . . " Wen began.

"I know. Tess will be targeted."

"Her life will effectively end. Full erasure."

Chase looked out at the dry, post-harvest wheat fields, and thought that Mitchell Landes might have picked a good place to hide. "He's either going to give us more information about the government's involvement, or another way in," Chase said.

"With the key codes, all we need are the AI cells," Wen said.

"Cristina was sure he had gotten away with them. Can they change them, or in some other way lock—"

Chase's phone rang.

"I didn't think we were still in range," Chase said, knowing only a handful of people had this new number.

"Who is it?"

"Restricted."

"Couldn't be," Wen said, wondering if Tess had found them.

"Hello?" Chase said hesitantly.

"Stop the car!" Tess said. "Get out of the car right now!"

"Tess, what are you—"

"Damn it, Chase, do it *now*!"

Chase and Wen exchanged a glance. Could they trust her? Wen readied her gun and quickly scanned the area. They were seemingly alone for a million miles.

"Do it," Wen said.

Chase jerked the car over. "What is it?" he asked Tess.

"Bomb! Run!"

Another shared glance, as if it might already be too late. They sprang out of the car, running for their lives. An instant later, the car erupted into a fireball. The force of the explosion knocked them to the ground.

"Are you okay?" Chase yelled.

"Yes."

"What the hell?" he said, climbing to his feet.

"Let's get away from here," Wen yelled, clutching her side.

"Tess," Chase said into the phone, then looked at it. "She's gone. We're out of range."

"Scary," Wen said, walking around what used to be the car to join him. "Was she trying to kill us?"

"Didn't she call to save us? Wait . . . Wen, stop. You're bleeding."

"I'm okay. It's just the movement, keep going. How did she know? Someone in the government, or Bargo . . ." She turned around again to look at the burnt wreckage, which shifted sideways in her vision. "That wasn't a car bomb, that was a drone strike," she murmured as blood seeped through her fingers and blackness crawled over the flames. She dropped to the ground, calling for Chase.

Chapter Seventy-Three

Dag swallowed down bitter bile at the sight of Zinner's slouching, twisted body, still cuffed to the rail. Blood ran freely down his face, the mangled, bloody hand smeared on the gunwale. "Was that necessary?"

"Apparently," the woman said, then turned to one of her people. "Get him out of here."

The man motioned his head out to the ocean. She nodded.

"Wait, you're *actually* going to throw him overboard?" Dag asked, irritated.

"Unless you want to keep the body for some reason. Sharks got to get fed."

He shook his head.

"I thought not," she said. "Now we need to clean up the rest of your messes."

Dag thought of the blood all over his beautiful floating mansion, but she meant something else.

"Boone Malone needs to die in prison."

"*Yes,*" Dag agreed enthusiastically, happy it would be

something accomplished far away from his sight. *People should die in prison*, he thought.

"You never should've locked him up, especially in a place like Pelican Bay," she said in a curt tone. "But, now that it's done . . ."

"I thought Boone would be a bargaining chip against his brother."

"Ah, yes, Chase Malone . . . the *real* mess."

"HaPPI may still find a way to destroy him."

"We're past that point," she said, watching Zinner's body plunge into the ocean. "No, Chase has already destroyed himself."

"So you'll kill him, too?"

She looked at him as if he were a fool.

"Isn't that what spies do?" he asked.

"Listen 007, this *isn't* a James Bond movie."

"But you're going to do it to Boone."

"Boone is in prison. It's an easy task, happens every day. No trace, no mess," she said as his phone rang. "Chase will have to be dealt with another way."

He looked at his phone.

"Go ahead," she said.

"We've located Cristina," Marta relayed after he'd answered.

"I don't want to know where."

"What do you want us to do?"

"Make the problem go away," he ordered.

"Consider it done," she said.

"And the other *thing*," he added, knowing she would understand who he was referring to.

"Already taken care of."

"Excellent," he said, relieved. "No issues?"

"None."

Marta pushed the button to end the call. "Good work on Cristina," she said to Reggie. "I must admit, I was skeptical."

"What do you mean?" he asked, knowing exactly what she meant.

"Thought you had a sweet spot for her."

"I have a sweet spot for *me*."

She nodded. "Let me know when she's done."

After the call, Dag looked out to sea for a moment.

"Everything all right?" the woman asked.

"Yeah, yeah."

"Good, because we have another matter to discuss."

"What?"

"InDive."

He couldn't hide his shock, which, remembering how she'd just put a bullet into the head of a laughing man, quickly turned to fear. He shook his head, as if unclear what she meant.

"InDive," she repeated firmly. "Your *secret* intelligence division."

"Yes?" he said with a dry mouth.

"Another reckless move. Hiring ex-MSS, ex-CIA, and others—did you *really* think that would escape our notice?"

"It's merely a precaution—"

"Don't insult me, Dag. You're setting up a future for when Bargo will be more powerful than the United States' government. Than the CIA. You think you won't need us, but you will."

"No. I, uh . . . "

"It doesn't particularly bother me. I know what's coming, and you aren't the only one. But there *are* those within the agency who don't like your expansion plans. People who want you to provide HaPPI services as nothing more than a trusted vendor. But you and I know better, don't we?"

He nodded hesitantly.

"You and I will be partners, *won't* we?"

"Yes." His voiced cracked.

She patted his stomach with her gun. "Good. First, we have to make sure Chase Malone goes away, and takes another problem with him."

"Another problem?"

"The only other person who can stop Bargo. A person who would happily destroy HaPPI."

"Who?" he asked, alarmed.

"Tess Federgreen. She must go down with Chase, and it must be *today*," Susan told him. "And I'll need your help."

"What can I do?"

"You get to pull the trigger," she said. "Figuratively speaking, of course, but nonetheless, it will end them *both*."

Chapter Seventy-Four

The Astronaut was asleep on the couch. Bull looked at the time. He'd been dozing for more than an hour. Tu was nestled into his side, also asleep. She didn't want to wake him, but this was too important to wait. She rolled her wheelchair over next to the couch and gently nudged his shoulder. If it'd been one of her old hacking buddies from back when she was a certified outlaw, she might have sprayed beer or Red Bull across his face, but she had too much respect for The Astronaut. He was different.

"What? he asked in a beleaguered voice.

"Shh." She put her finger to her mouth and pointed. The Astronaut gently slipped from Tu, letting him stay asleep. "I found something," Bull said.

"You better have found the enigma core," he said, as if it was unacceptable to wake him for anything less.

"I did. I mean, I *think* I did. Well, there's a *really good* chance I found it."

He sat up in the way a parent might when their young

child wakes them to tell them they're *certain* Santa Claus is on the roof.

"*Really*. You *need* to look," she urged, seeing that he clearly didn't believe her.

"What time is it?"

"No idea," she lied.

"How long did I sleep?" he asked. "*Did* I sleep?"

"At least two hours, maybe three," she lied again.

"Your credibility is only diminishing the more we talk, so let's just see what you think you found."

She rolled back over to her workstation. He got up and followed her.

"I've immortalized it on Henry Ford," she said, referring to the name of one of their main servers. Each was named after a different inventor: Alexander Graham Bell, Thomas Alva Edison, Nikolai Tesla, the Wright brothers, and so on. "But I'm running it live on Tesla." It was her favorite, and most powerful machine. She believed Elon Musk was going to change the world, and she was rooting for him.

"When did Tu join me?" he asked.

"Not long after you went to lie down. You were out in minutes. He sat next to you as soon as you dropped off, then curled up in your arm and fell right asleep, too. It was cute."

"The enigma core's base artificial intelligence program links together all the other algorithms, apps, and programs encompassed in every database from social media, to the government, the private businesses, credit agencies, insurance companies, banks, *whatever*, and twists it all into HaPPI results."

"I know."

"I know you know, but *that's* the way in," she said. Bull hadn't even been sure the enigma core existed. Even Dez had cast doubt on The Astronaut's theory, arguing that the individual algorithms could blueprint to each other without a central unifying program needed. Although, when he wrote the code to demonstrate how it would work in a simplistic way, the sequence parentheses had collapsed. Dez claimed they lacked the constant expanding data yields and uprising parameters that HaPPI's operating platform would contain.

"Do you see?" she asked, pointing to the largest monitor, which was filled with streaming code. Few people could make any sense out of it if it were still, and no one she'd ever met, other than The Astronaut, could remotely grasp it while moving.

"Is this live, or the memorialized?"

"It's the backup."

"Okay," he said, still studying the rolling characters as if reading a trigonometry textbook. "Slow it there." He pointed.

Bull keyed in the commands so the stream slowed.

"Okay . . . and pause." He pointed to another spot on the screen. "Yes . . . you might be onto something," he said, connecting patterns too fast for a normal human brain to see. "Of course, it could be something else entirely."

"What numbers? It has to be deliberate," she said.

"How did you find it?"

"I used their own response templates, and then I multi-layered them, then slid that into the external indicator programs that they've been feeding. After that, it was simple to multiply—"

"The template quantifiers by seven," he finished, a rare bit of excitement in his voice.

"Well, yes. I mean, I used six first because—"

"Because it was the obvious choice, but not the correct one."

"Right, but after I burned *that* forty-five minutes I'll never see again, I figured it had to be seven, and I was right. *Was* I right?" she asked. "I mean, it's *right*, isn't it?"

"It is quite possibly correct. I think almost *certainly* correct. But that does not mean it is the enigma core."

"It *has* to be."

"Have you applied it?"

"Just one initial round to see, and it came back positive. But I haven't had time to go the full way. I thought I should wake you."

"So I could tell you how brilliant you are?"

"That would be nice."

"Well, let's run a full overview and see what it does."

"It'll take *hours* to run a full board," she said.

"Then we'd better get started."

"What are we going to do if it works?"

"Smoke a celebratory cigarette," The Astronaut said with the hint of a smile.

"Why, Nash Graham, I *do* believe you are developing a sense of humor."

"Oh. I thought I was just being mean."

"I guess it was a dumb question," she said. "Obviously we call Chase and Wen, and then try to work it into a full response against Bargo."

"The timing is the question," The Astronaut said. "But let's not get too far ahead of ourselves. This may not work."

"It *is* going to work, and I've always found it's a good idea to get ahead of myself. Then I'm ready for when it hits the fan."

"For you, that is a wise strategy."

"Maybe we should call them now, in case this is the best time to start."

"Let's wait a little longer. In the meantime, we need

more ways into Bargo's servers. You said yourself you've never seen a network so protected."

"True, but defenses are only there to be attacked and taken down."

"Well, if you're so sure of your brilliance, then show me."

Bull smiled, opened a fresh energy drink, lit a cigarette, cracked her knuckles, and immediately began to play dual keyboards as if she were a concert pianist. "Dag Kirrem better get ready, because here I come."

Chapter Seventy-Five

Wen flagged down the pickup truck. It had only been the fourth vehicle they'd seen in nearly half an hour. Chase had tried to get the first two to stop, but the flaming car in the distance might have spooked them. Her gunshot wound had started bleeding again, but she had it well covered, even though her hand was drenched in sticky blood. Chase was worried by how awful she looked.

A ruddy old farmer pulled over. "That your fire back there?"

"It was our car," Chase told him. "A rental."

"What the heck happened?"

"Don't know," Chase said. "The engine suddenly caught fire. We barely got out before it exploded."

"Damn foreign cars," the farmer griped. "They can kill you five different ways."

"Ain't that the truth," Chase said.

"Climb on in, I can take you as far as the crossroad. Where you heading?"

They lied and said Mitchell was Chase's cousin. Luckily the farmer didn't know him too well.

"It's only about twenty minutes or so up the road," the farmer told them. "You all right?" he asked Wen.

"Yes. The fire and everything really shook me up."

"I'll bet," he said, and for the rest of the drive proceeded to tell them a story about when one of his tractors caught fire and it spread across a dry cornfield.

The farmer dropped them off on the main road and pointed. "It's just down there, a hundred yards or so. There's a big thicket of what used to be a hedge, now it's all brambles and whatnot. Be on your right."

"Thanks," Wen said.

"Yeah, sure. Got a stack of tires marking the driveway, can sometimes be overgrown. You'll find it."

"Much obliged," Chase told him.

The man pulled off, leaving a dusty cloud to follow them as they made their way down the narrow road, which seemed to be a combination of broken pavement, gravel, and dirt.

"We're lucky," Wen said. "We're not here much later than we would've been."

"Yeah, it's kind of nice. Your car blows up, and you still make it to the appointment on time." He smiled, having amused himself.

"Let's just try not to do it again," Wen said. They were both still somewhat shaken and a little giddy to have survived. They'd been close to death before, but this time it felt like it'd brushed past them just a hair closer. Less than a second more, and they would've been part of the horrendous explosion.

They found the bramble hedge and the stack of tires, just like the driver had said, and made their way down what otherwise would have been an old, unmarked country lane.

"Looks like no one's been down this way in years," Chase remarked.

"That's a good sign," Wen said, keeping her hand concealed in the bag with a submachine gun, and the other hand pressed against her wound. Chase had the Glock under his coat. "There's the house," she said after a few more minutes of walking through increasingly taller weeds.

"The yard is so overgrown, like it's doing its best imitation of a jungle. Are you sure anyone lives here?"

"I think that's what he's going for here, a deserted, don't-bother-me-everybody's-long-gone type of look."

"He's doing a damn good job of it," Chase said as they picked their way through high weeds, thistle, and mullen. "The house looks like it might fall down any minute."

Soon they reached some scattered, cracked concrete that might have once been a sidewalk. At the end, Chase climbed up a set of creaky steps onto a splintered porch. Gray flakes of paint on the edges showed what color it might've been in its last lifetime.

"Still no signs of life," Chase said. "But I guess that counts." He pointed to an old dog limping from around the side of the house. It growled lowly.

"He's more scared than anything," Wen said. An empty flowerpot filled with dirty water caught her attention, and she cleaned her bloody hand in it.

As they approached the door, Wen raised her machine gun. Chase took the cue, pulling out the Glock and readying it. Wen glanced to the side of the building where the dog had come from, now whimpering. Apparently the guns made it nervous.

Wen tapped on the door with the barrel of her MP7.

After ten seconds or so of silence, they looked at each other. Chase pulled open the screen door, which might've fallen off if not for the duct tape-reinforced hinge configuration—one rusted and ancient, the other shiny and new. Chase pounded on the door, waited a second, and then reached for the knob.

Wen shook her head and held up a hand, then pointed over the roof, as if indicating the back of the house.

Chase nodded.

She held up her hands, signaling ten seconds, then dropped over a rickety edge of the porch and headed back along the side of the house. Ten seconds later, Chase tried the knob. It was unlocked. Cautiously, he went inside. At the same moment, Wen entered the back door.

It was a small, ranch-style, single level house, not more than a few rooms. They met in the central hallway.

Wen waved her gun through the rooms, ready to shoot anything that moved. She'd been there before; not *that* house, not *that* day, not *that* asset, but she'd been in that situation enough times to know something was wrong. The dog, the doors, the energy of the place—there was a viable feel to it.

Her intuition shifted into defensive mode.

She pointed to the back room, the only one without an open door. She moved swiftly down the hall, knowing a dying man could still provide valuable intel.

Chase looked in each room as they went by, but Wen already knew. She got there first and confirmed it when she opened the door and found Mitchell staring back at her, hanging by a rope from the ceiling, dead.

Chapter Seventy-Six

Chase looked at Mitchell's body, dangling from the rafters. "We're too late."

Wen stumbled backwards, but caught herself and leaned against the wall.

"It's a long walk back to town," Chase said, seeing how exhausted she was.

"How did he get here?" she asked, walking to the window. She looked around the property and spotted an old, dilapidated barn on the far edge. "I'm willing to bet he has a car stashed in there."

Chase ran out to check.

While he was gone, Wen searched the house for anything helpful, but came up empty.

"Turns out it's a nice one," he yelled out the window, driving up to the back door.

She got into the silver Jaguar. "Our best hope is the sniper," Wen said as Chase drove through the weeds and found the road.

A few minutes later Wen nodded off. He woke her only as they approached the airport.

"How are you?"

She smiled weakly. "The sleep helped." But her shirt was soaked in blood.

They found the sniper awake when they got on the plane. After the doctor changed the dressings on Wen's wound and admonished her about needing bed rest, she asked him and the other WOLF member to wait outside so they could interrogate their prisoner.

"Who do you work for?" Wen asked as nicely as she could once they had the plane to themselves.

"You're wasting your time."

Wen nodded, staring at her for a few moments. "You're probably right. And I'm not in the mood to waste time, so here it is. I'm going to kill you if you don't tell us who you work for."

"Then kill me."

Wen thought about it for a second, actually considered just *doing* it, but a look from Chase brought her back from the brink. "Mumford Grimes," Wen said.

The effect was visible. The sniper was obviously surprised.

Wen smiled. "We already knew."

"Then what is *this*?"

"Who hired Grimes to kill us?"

"We weren't trying to kill you."

"Really? It sure looked like you were."

"Wen, you're much smarter than that. If I wanted to kill you, you'd have already been dead five times."

"Okay, I'll play. Then what were you doing?"

She shook her head.

"We want to talk to Grimes."

"Good luck with that."

Chase felt his phone vibrate—an urgent text from Bull. "We need to answer this," Chase said to Wen.

"Don't go anywhere," Wen told the sniper as she followed Chase off the plane. "What is it?"

Chase saw the doctor and the other man sitting in a small open lounge at the other end of the hangar. "Bull and The Astronaut are ready to reverse."

"They found the enigma core?" Wen asked. "Without the data from Mitchell Landes?"

"Yeah."

"So we're done?"

"If it works."

"So, Tess?"

"We need to be sure," Chase said. "I mean, she just saved our lives, and we're about to erase hers."

"She knew where we were, therefore she knew our destination. The drone attack was just to delay us."

"But why let us live?"

"I don't know, but it may not matter. We can destroy her, Dag, the other top executives, and wipe HaPPI out of existence. We should just do it."

"Okay," Chase said, thinking about his long, complicated history with Tess. Although he wasn't directly ordering her death, a complete erasure almost always resulted in some kind of life-ending horror.

He called Bull, discussed the final details, and then gave

the word. "Full reverse," he said, using their term for reversing HaPPI back on its architects and, ultimately, on itself. Using the key codes and the enigma core, Bull, The Astronaut, Dez, and even a few suggestions from Tu, handing Dots to all who would take them, had reengineered the program. It would fully erase all the top executives of Bargo, and Tess Federgreen, whom they believed to be their inside source at the CIA.

"Underway?" Wen asked as he ended the call.

"Yeah."

"Let's go finish beating up the sniper."

The sniper was waiting. "Shall we continue?" she said. "I'm in kind of a hurry."

Chase couldn't help but laugh. "Really?"

"I have a plane to catch."

"You're not leaving here until we know where to find Grimes," Wen said, seething. Wen noticed again that the mention of Grimes sent her face into a flurry of emotions.

"No."

"Fine. We can skip Grimes for now. Tell me what you know about Finale."

She surprised them with a detailed account of the secret group of elite mercenaries, including the admission that many had specifically been recruited to hunt them. During her explanations, Chase received two texts—one from The Astronaut, with the identity and government file of the sniper, the other from Bull. They were three minutes from initiating full reverse.

"Good. We appreciate the cooperation, Lena Shelby,"

Wen said as Chase showed her the screen with Shelby's data.

Shelby was, again, surprised.

"Still don't want to talk about Grimes?" Wen asked.

Shelby shook her head.

"Okay, then help us out on what you know about HaPPI and Bargo."

"What about it?"

"You tell me. How deep is Dag Kirrem in with the government?"

"Dag's ambitious. He's planning to circumvent the government."

"The US?"

"*All* of them. He's been recruiting for his own intelligence network for at least two years."

Wen glanced at Chase. "Go on."

"I'm sure you know about his plans for using HaPPI to totally control society?"

Wen nodded.

"The CIA is giving him the power initially, but they don't realize how quickly he will render them obsolete. That's his plan."

"Do you think he will achieve it?"

Shelby looked at them both carefully. "Depends on you."

"How so?" Chase asked.

"You're trying to stop him, and you usually win."

"Do you know who his contact is at the CIA?" Chase asked.

She squinted, as if deciding whether to answer, or what to ask for in return. Finally, she just answered. "Susan Shields."

"What?" Chase said a little too loudly. "Are you *sure*?"

"Positive."

"*Not* Tess Federgreen?"

"No," Shelby said, puzzled. "CISS is trying to stop Bargo, just like you are."

Chase instantly pushed Bull's name on his phone, wondering if it was already too late.

Chapter Seventy-Seven

Bull answered the phone on speaker. "We've initiated. It's working . . . it's *working*!"

"But it's not Tess."

Her celebratory mood suddenly deflated. "What?"

"Tess *isn't* the CIA contact."

"I . . . I don't know if we can stop it."

"Find a way!" Chase understood better than any of them that once an AI script departed from its programmers, it took on a life of its own. Something as sophisticated as HaPPI meant it could be impossible to unravel. He heard Bull and The Astronaut arguing back and forth.

"We may be able to supplement it," Bull said.

"Yes . . . yes, that could work," Chase said. "How about substitution?"

"That would help," The Astronaut said. "But Tess will *have* to take a hit."

"We can fix her later, just like we're doing with Boone," Bull said.

"If you have another name, give it to us now," The Astronaut said.

"Susan Shields," Chase said. "CIA."

The Astronaut keyed the name into the database. "Got her. And you're *sure*? Erasure?"

"Yes, she's the CIA contact."

"She's about to lose her job," Bull said. "And a whole lot more. No more CIA, no more car, no more home, education history gone, social media wiped, bank accounts, brokerage accounts . . . Wow she has a $4.9 million stock portfolio—well, not any longer. Vacation home in Hilton Head transferred away, online shopping accounts vanished—"

"Thanks, I don't need a play-by-play," Chase said, uneasy with how susceptible people were in a digital world, how much the government and tech companies knew about us, how easily it could be manipulated, taken away. "What about Tess?"

"Scary," The Astronaut said.

"What?"

"She had a cocoon."

"Meaning she somehow had protected herself?"

"Yes," he said. "She escapes unscathed."

"Because Tess knows," Chase said. "She knows what's coming. She understands the threat we're facing from the surveillance state, the corporate data police, the social credit demons."

Wen found Chase outside the plane. He filled her in on the situation with Tess and Susan. In return, she shocked him with her new plan.

"You want to let Shelby go?" Chase said, stunned. "She's tried to kill us!"

"She is in love with Grimes . . . and he is most likely in love with her."

"*So?*"

"She will never give him to us."

"Okay, but we can't *release* her."

"If we kill her, we'll never turn him."

"You really think we can?"

"It isn't his mission. He's just a hired gun."

"But don't these types of people have reputations to protect? Some code they live and die by?"

"You've seen too many movies, but you're right. He won't want to betray the people who hired him. They're clearly an extremely powerful group who he wouldn't want as an enemy."

"Then how—"

"Our first act of good faith is to release Shelby."

"So she can try to kill us again."

"We send her with a message to Grimes."

"Which is?"

"It's been two years. Time to talk."

"And we agree to meet?"

"Yes."

Chase shook his head. "He'll think it's a trap."

"It won't be."

"He may trap *us*."

"No."

"If it works, and he meets us, what's the play?"

"We offer much more money than they're paying, and we guarantee him the shadow people won't come after him."

"How do we do that?"

"By destroying the shadow people."

"With his help?"

"Exactly."

"What if she just disappears, and the next time we hear from her or Grimes, it's in the form of bullets aimed at us?"

"Then I would have been wrong. I'm *not* wrong. I see it on her face, in her eyes. She and Grimes can be turned."

"Okay, but let's have The Astronaut and Bull use everything we have to track her," Chase said, wondering if they were crazy. "We'll plug both of their files into SEER. If either one of them so much as crosses a street, goes out to lunch, buys gas, turns up *anywhere* there's a camera, we'll know where they are."

"It may take a while," Wen said.

"This might be the dumbest thing we've ever done," Chase said.

"Play it safe, or take the risk. You can't get anywhere in life without taking a risk."

Epilogue

Boone was released from prison within a few days of the collapse of Bargo. Bull and The Astronaut managed to get all his charges switched to Dag Kirrem, who was assigned a tired public defender since he had no assets, no job, and a long rap sheet of prior criminal convictions.

Two months after Boone's release, Bull and The Astronaut were still working to rebuild his digital life. His business had been completely ruined by HaPPI, but Chase had given him the money to start over.

Chase and Wen did not celebrate the victory of HaPPI because they knew another version of the social credit system would be back. "It's like stamping out a fire," Chase said. "There are still flames burning somewhere, and unless the public calls for change and protections, and demand their privacy back, sooner or later, it will engulf us all."

Reggie, in an effort to protect himself, ordered Cristina killed, but a WOLF team rescued her in time. After being erased, Reggie took his own life. In the weeks following Marta's erasure, she was caught shoplifting at a Whole Foods Market in Denver.

Sixty days after Bull eliminated Susan Shields, the former CIA official's whereabouts remained unknown.

"It's been eight weeks since we let Shelby go," Chase said to Wen. They watched Tu racing waves on a deserted beach.

"We'll hear from them," Wen said emphatically.

"How can you be so sure?"

"Because the shadow people have been pursuing us for two years, and Grimes is the best they have. I have The Astronaut and Astaria hunting them."

Chase picked up the binoculars and scanned the horizon, zooming in on a ship in the distance.

"Anything?" Wen asked.

"I don't think so."

"It may not be today, or next week, or even next month, but sooner or later, we *will* meet Shelby and Grimes again."

Tu ran up to show them a particularly beautiful shell he had found. They each told him how much they liked it, and Wen said she would hold it for him. He smiled and returned quickly to the surf.

"Nothing in the future is guaranteed," Chase said. "All we have for sure is this present moment." He looked at her for a second, and then back to Tu, twirling and running at the edge of the water. "And it's a wonderful moment."

Next in the Chase Malone Thriller series

vinci-books.com/chasing-mind

Imagine if they knew your every thought... How far would you go to keep your mind your own?

When fugitive billionaire Chase Malone and ex-spy Wen Zhou uncover a sinister plot to control humanity through advanced mind-reading technology, they are thrust into a terrifying world where even their own thoughts can't be trusted.

Turn the page for a free preview…

Chasing Mind: Chapter One

Nine black-clad operatives moved into position, their leader confident. "The day has finally come," he said to himself, lining up the sight of his sniper rifle, as a gentle snow fell. "The last day of Chase Malone's life."

Chase Malone sipped an earthy concoction of tea and coffee, bitter and good, gently waking up his tired brain. His thirty-second birthday not far off, he looked and felt older than that. "It's been a while since I used these parts of my mind," he said, smiling at Wen, taking in her beauty framed by a view of jagged peaks and blue skies in this gorgeous slice of Utah. It was as good as any place to hide—not that they *were* hiding, or at least that wasn't their initial objective, but in reality the pair was always on the run.

"Alpha ready," an operative said, beginning a relay of check-ins.

They were there trying to solve a problem with Chase's latest invention: OvR-sITe, a program designed to keep the government in check. Chase, a brilliant engineer and AI expert had made a series of tech breakthroughs during the prior ten years.

"Bravo ready," an operative reported.

"Charlie ready."

Chase and Wen had come to Dan Shaw's mountain estate because, like Chase, he was an expert on machine learning. The two old friends had spent the previous thirty-six hours looking for a way around the ever-changing government firewalls and writing code.

"Delta ready."

Wen, svelte, muscled, alert, checked out the window, a habit the former Chinese MSS agent couldn't seem to shake. Although no one knew where they were, someone always seemed to anyway. She made eye contact with Chase, an unspoken *all clear*.

"Echo ready."

"Foxtrot ready."

Dan Shaw, whose net worth at 7.3 billion made him almost seven times wealthier than Chase, glanced up from his computer. "I think it's in the autonomic computing," he said, excited. "If we use Heuristic search techniques, we should be able to get it to work."

Chase smiled, his rugged good looks belied his geek mind. "Let's put it in the predictive model."

"Golf ready."

"Hotel ready."

Chase started to walk toward Dan, excited that they *finally* had an answer, wondering if it would really work. The model would be critical in stopping the governments of the world from further abusing their power.

"Go," the leader said into his wrist.

The mansion erupted in gunfire.

"Down!" Wen yelled, rolling away from the window under a storm of splintering wood and shards of glass.

Chase dove under a table, where somehow Wen slid him a submachine gun.

"Dan!" Chase shouted, wondering where his friend was as the opulent room of a minute earlier was shredded by an unrelenting hail of bullets.

No answer, but moments later he appeared in the hall, wielding a shotgun.

Wen executed a man as he entered the blown-out south window. Dan got three shots off and managed to badly wound one of the intruders before a stray bullet caught him in the head.

Chase saw his friend fall, but Dan was already dead by the time he reached him. "Sorry, man," Chase wheezed painfully, sounding as if he'd been shot himself. Then he twisted in a blur and finished off the man who'd killed his longtime friend, a kind and generous man, light years ahead in technology.

"We've got to get out of the house!" Wen yelled.

"Wine cellar?" Chase replied.

"You read my mind."

They both continued shooting while retreating to the large kitchen. A sliding door, partially concealed inside the walk-in pantry, opened onto a narrow wooden staircase. Had it only been twelve hours since Dan had proudly showed them his wine cellar?

Chase closed the pantry door behind them and rushed onto the first step. Wen found the light switch as Chase slid the paneled door shut, wondering how long it would take for their escape route to be discovered.

"Where's that door?" Chase muttered as they reached the bottom of the stairs. The stone façade archways led off in three separate directions. Chase recalled Dan's enthusiasm as he'd shown them his prized six thousand bottle collection.

"Over here," Wen said, choosing the center corridor.

"Of course *you* remember," Chase said quietly, knowing Wen's first task upon entering any new place was to scope out every possible exit, anything which could be used as an advantage. "While I was looking at the bottle of 1945 Chateau Mouton-Rothschild, you were making mental maps."

Wen unbolted the heavy exterior door and opened it slowly, peering out, leading with her gun. "Come on," she said. "You go first, get the car."

As snow continued to fall, Chase darted across the driveway, knowing Wen would be covering him.

He made it into the front seat and turned over the engine before the first shots came his way. Hitting the accelerator, Chase steered the Mercedes-Benz GLS 580 SUV back toward the side of the house where he'd left his long time Jedi-like sweetheart at the entrance to the wine cellar, but she was no longer there.

Keeping the SUV moving, the submachine gun on his lap, he scanned the area, trying to find Wen. He finally spotted her on the other side of the heated outdoor swimming pool, heading for the trees. He'd have to drive around the far side of the circular drive and across a wide section of lawn to reach her.

The operatives swarmed into the open like vultures circling roadkill. Chase punched the gas, then saw what had prompted Wen to run.

Seven armed men were closing in on her.

She's going to die, he thought, an instant before a sudden burst of gunfire sprayed across his windshield.

Chasing Mind: Chapter Two

With the front and side windows blown out, Chase swerved the vehicle around a flagstone fountain and headed straight at one of Wen's pursuers, intending to mow him down, actually visualizing their bodies crunching under the Mercedes' twenty-three inch wheels. *They must be from the shadow people,* he thought angrily. The mysterious group had been trailing them relentlessly for more than two years, and they'd yet to discover why.

Blazing across the expansive lawn at close to seventy miles an hour, Chase zeroed in on his target. The man heard the 580's eight cylinder engine pumping 483 horsepower. He turned to shoot, but it was too late. The SUV steamrolled over him, bouncing over his crushed body as if it were little more than a bump in the road. Chase, whose driving skills were one of his greatest sources of pride, cranked the wheel and aimed for the next body, even though he cringed at the thought of killing another person. Grass and dirt flew as the heavy vehicle cut through the dried-out lawn, now slick with a dusting of snow.

Chasing Risk

The wintery storm suddenly picked up, flakes flying into Chase's eyes through the shattered glass, making it a trickier run at his next victim. This time the man fired quick enough to damage the grill and hood of the SUV, but not soon enough to save his life. His body broke upon impact, rolling across the bullet punctured hood, crashing through remnants of the shot-out windshield and plunging head-first into the passenger seat, his legs still dangling out onto the hood.

"You think I'm an Uber?" Chase asked, his sarcastic humor often surfaced during times of stress. He cut the wheel hard, attempting to line up with the next man when a Suburban SUV came barreling toward him.

Seeing Wen almost to the trees, and with no other choice, Chase turned wide and went heavy on the gas pedal. The Mercedes fishtailed as he tore up more of the lawn before sailing out onto a narrow dirt road lined by towering trees.

Snow and freezing rain blinded the already foggy air. The driver of the Suburban took full advantage of the tight lane and jammed into the back of the 580. Realizing he was now on an old forest service road coated in powdery snow, Chase drove as fast as conditions allowed, but couldn't break away from the powerful Chevy.

What would Wen do? he asked himself.

Before an answer came, the road opened onto an edgy canyon. He knew it wasn't safe to be traveling more than twenty-miles per hour on something with a drop that treacherous. Glancing down, he saw the speedometer was clicking in at fifty-four, just as a sharp curve raced up at him through the fog.

Chase pulled the wheel around, but it wasn't enough. The Mercedes soared over the cliff. All fifty-seven hundred pounds of steel, plastic, and leather dropped straight down. Chase, still buckled in, braced for the crash.

The driver of the Suburban also failed to make the turn, but the two-seconds of warning Chase had given him let him jump out just as the three-ton monster went off the edge.

Believing he was about to die, Chase had a sudden reprieve when the front end lowered, and below—

Big, beautiful, and hopefully deep water, he thought, pulling out his favorite weapon, a custom multitool.

A fast few moments later, the Mercedes smashed into the lake. In less than a tenth of a second, both front airbags deployed. The force of their impact slammed Chase back against the seat. Almost instantly, the windowless SUV began sinking. Chase punctured the driver's airbag with the multitool's blade, then slashed the seatbelt. As the Mercedes sank, he fought through the shifting, tangled body of his "passenger" to squeeze himself out through the open windshield.

The water, remarkably clear and incredibly cold, was also deep. The Mercedes appeared to be driving off into the depths without him. The Suburban came past him as if intent on continuing the car chase. He couldn't tell if anyone was left inside, and he looked around wildly, expecting a new attack.

Bullets filled the water like dozens of deadly micro-torpedoes.

Chasing Mind: Chapter Three

GUANGZHOU, CHINA

Lights from passing cars reflected off the painted cinderblock walls of a back alley, behind almost a mile of warehouses, in the old section of town. Chun had been waiting for ten minutes, surprised that Jin wasn't already there.

He's never been late before...

He looked at the clock on the dashboard. Jin was seven minutes behind schedule.

Seven minutes could be lost anywhere. No sense to panic yet.

Still, panic wouldn't necessarily be an overreaction. Jin could be dead, and if he was, Chun would also be dead soon. *Very* soon.

When Jin finally arrived, Chun noticed his disheveled hair and patchy stubble. "Please forgive my being late," Jin said in Mandarin, looking over his shoulder.

"Are you all right?" Chun replied in the same language, nervous himself. This was the riskiest operation they had ever undertaken.

Jin swallowed hard and nodded. "Yes, just tired." He kept looking around quickly, his eyes darting like prey.

Chun thought back to a time in his life when something like this would've been unimaginable, back when he was still married and his son was still alive. Chun, like most citizens of the People's Republic of China, considered risk a four letter word. He, along with all of his neighbors, coworkers, and the people he passed on the streets during his daily commute, followed the party line. It wasn't because he was afraid, but because everything seemed fine, as it should be. However, that illusion had come crashing down once his son had become involved in an antigovernment demonstration.

"Were you followed?" Chun asked, squinting his eyes, ready to take a blow, a habit fostered by too much bad news in his life.

"Of course not," Jin responded as if insulted, but Chun noticed how he kept checking behind him.

Chun didn't like to think about what had happened to his son, but something in Jin's mood and the eerie dark of the night brought the awful memories flooding back. He couldn't recall now if his son's demonstration had been about Hong Kong, or Taiwan, the Chinese President taking unlimited powers, or something else. But there had been a crackdown. His son had been sent off to prison for what was supposed to have been a two-year sentence.

Then, during his first few months of incarceration, he'd died.

"Do you have it?" Jin asked after apologizing again for being late.

"Yes," Chun replied, raking long, boney fingers through his thinning, spiked hair, thinking the question unnecessary. This was everything, the very thing he'd been working toward since they'd taken his son. More than likely he'd been murdered in prison by the Communists, but there would never be a trial, no way to prove any of it.

Unable to deal with the grief, Chun had left his wife soon after. Then, almost accidentally, Chun had met some people who knew things that he didn't, things that his son must have suspected or heard about. For the last six years, Chun had been a member of the underground, trying to bring down the communist oppression and corruption.

"And?" Jin asked. "How does it look?"

"It's pretty bad. The advances they've made are considerable."

"It's only been eight months since our last intercept," Jin said. "How far could it have gone?"

"I think the last round of data must've been older than we thought. Maybe the dates were calibrated wrong. *Something* was off, because it's hard to imagine they could've moved this far ahead in so short a time." Chun looked down the street as a car passed the opening to the alley. Both men tensed, as it seemed unusual for a vehicle to be there at that hour.

"It kept going," Jin said, relieved.

"You'd better get this down the line," Chun continued, not wanting to explain the disturbing information contained in the reports. More than the danger, it was a difficult topic.

Jin nodded. "With any luck, I will have this delivered by morning."

They had learned that the government monitored all communications, that even encryptions could not be trusted. Thus they moved data at night, and in person.

Chun recalled the images of the school children wearing headsets. The Chinese government had claimed it was a small program—simple monitoring, nothing else. *Lies!* Chun thought angrily, squinting again, breath shallow. Love for his son and pain for his loss intertwined in his gut in a numb, vicious knot.

But now they had evidence.

Jin turned to go before stopping and turning back to face Chun. "Is it the proof?" he asked hesitantly.

"Yes," Chun whispered, his passion getting the better of him. "The Mind Project has expanded. It now includes millions of children and factory workers."

"Then they *are* doing it?"

He nodded. "The government is building a database."

Jin's face was terrified, both from fear of getting caught with such sensitive secrets, and for the horror of what the Mind Project meant. "Exponential growth and machine learning . . . *that* is why it is accelerating at an astonishing rate."

"Yes. The Mind Project has developed a device that can accurately predict the thoughts of people." Chun paused, looked up the alley, then in a more urgent, but still hushed tone, added, "And they are planning to use it to take over the world."

Chasing Mind: Chapter Four

The driver of the Suburban had jumped out just as his vehicle followed the Mercedes over the cliff into the lake. Banged up and a bit woozy, he finally got to his feet and looked over the edge. Only the back end of the Mercedes was visible, while the Suburban was sinking twenty feet away. After seeing no sign of life, he fired almost a full magazine down into the water, then waited another couple of minutes. He snapped a few photos with his phone, then jogged back up the road, planning to help his comrades with the woman.

She had made it into the woods with five of them still on her. The Suburban driver expected her to already be in custody, until he stumbled upon the body of one of his team, almost cut in half by machine gunfire. Twenty yards later, he found another, neck snapped. And then Marcus, his close friend, leaning against a tree . . . at least he *thought* it was Marcus. It was difficult to be sure since his face had been shot. The mess that remained made him sick. Two hundred yards beyond that nightmare, maimed and draped over a dead log, was Drake, unclear how he died. Suburban shook his head in disgust and kept moving.

Finally, he saw the woman fighting with Pyle. Based on everything he'd just seen, he assumed Pyle had only seconds left to live. Fortunately, in the midst of their hand-to-hand combat, she hadn't heard his approach.

"Freeze!" Suburban yelled, firing a couple warning shots. "I'd like nothing more than to avenge my buddies and kill you."

Wen turned slowly to face him, furious she'd lost her gun in the last fight. "Why don't you then?"

"Don't tempt me."

"You're telling me that after all this, you weren't sent to kill me?" she asked, trying to buy time, concerned about Chase, figuring it was just these two men left, and knowing she could take them.

Just keep the conversation going . . .

A blow to her side knocked Wen off her feet. The man she'd been fighting stood over her, holding the heavy, four-foot-long log he'd used to club her. Before she could react, he hit her again in her leg. "Just in case you were planning to kick me."

Suburban used his boot to shove Wen's face into the cold, snowy dirt, while the other man duct taped her ankles together, then taped her wrists painfully behind her back.

"By the way, your boyfriend's dead," Suburban said. "I left him at the bottom of a frigid lake."

She writhed against her bonds, trying to gain contact with either one of them. "I could kill you with my bare hands if I were free!"

The man clubbed her in the gut. She had a high pain threshold, but he hit something that almost made her pass out.

"Where to?" he asked Suburban, dragging Wen by her feet. She struggled to turn her head to keep her face out of the snow and dirt.

"We need to find a ride."

"Where's the Suburban?"

"Bottom of the same lake."

"What about back at the house?"

"It's burning. Someone hit a propane tank or something," Suburban said, checking his GPS. "Rich dude had four cars in the garage, and they're all on fire."

"Not easy to find a ride with this cargo," he said as Wen's battered body bounced over the rough terrain.

"This way," Suburban said, looking up from the GPS. "We may get lucky."

"*Lucky*," Wen growled. "The only luck you can hope for is that I'll kill you quickly instead of slowly."

Suburban kicked her already tender ribs and stuffed a bandana in her mouth.

I will kill you, she thought, thinking of Chase, desperate to believe they were lying to her, that he had escaped or someone else had him. *Either way, you two are going to die.*

Grab your copy…
vinci-books.com/chasing-mind

About the Author

USA TODAY Bestselling Author Brandt Legg uses his unusual real life experiences to create page-turning novels. He's traveled with CIA agents, dined with senators and congressmen, mingled with astronauts, chatted with governors and presidential candidates, had a private conversation with a Secretary of Defense he still doesn't like to talk about, hung out with Oscar and Grammy winners, had drinks at the State Department, been pursued by tabloid reporters, and spent a birthday at the White House by invitation from the President of the United States.

At age eight, Legg's father died suddenly, plunging his family into poverty. Two years later, while suffering from crippling migraines, he started in business, and turned a hobby into a multi-million-dollar empire. National media dubbed him the "Teen Tycoon," and by the mid-eighties, Legg was one of the top young entrepreneurs in America, appearing as high as number twenty-four on the list (when Steve Jobs was #1, Bill Gates #4, and Michael Dell #6). Legg still jokes that he should have gone into computers.

By his twenties, after years of buying and selling businesses, leveraging, and risk-taking, the high-flying Legg became ensnarled in the financial whirlwind of the junk bond eighties. The stock market crashed and a firestorm of trouble came down. The Teen Tycoon racked up more than a million dollars in legal fees, was betrayed by those closest to him, lost his entire fortune, and ended up serving time for financial improprieties.

After a year, Legg emerged from federal prison, chastened and wiser, and began anew. More than twenty-five years later, he's now using all that hard-earned firsthand knowledge of conspiracies, corruption and high finance to weave his tales. Legg's books pulse with authenticity.

His series have excited nearly a million readers around the world. Although he refused an offer to make a television movie about his life as a teenage millionaire, his autobiography is in the works. There has also been interest from Hollywood to turn his thrillers into films. With any luck, one day you'll see your favorite characters on screen.

He lives in the Pacific Northwest, with his wife and son, writing full time, in several genres, containing the common themes of adventure, conspiracy, and thrillers. Of all his pursuits, being an author and crafting plots for novels is his favorite.

Acknowledgments

I dictated most of this book while walking a nearly deserted beach on the Pacific coast of Mexico. That experience determined the setting for the next Chase/Wen thriller, *Chasing Mind*. When we returned to the United States, the lockdowns were beginning. That experience has inspired many more ideas for Chase and Wen, and some other unrelated thrillers which may or may not get written. I hope they do, because their plots and characters are constantly running around my crowded mind.

To my wife, Ro, and our Teakki, who continue to put up with my crazy ideas and share my belief that Chase, Wen, Tess, and all the others are real. And for understanding that, obviously, *everything* isn't a conspiracy . . . but it *might* be.

My mother, Barbara Blair, is such a good editor, and thankfully has some kind of affliction that means she doesn't mind (or at least doesn't complain about) reading my books over and over, even in their roughest forms, even five times over the same page, even when she has to use four or more colors of ink to get her point across. Thanks Mom!

I'm always grateful to Melanie C. Hansen for cleaning up the final version, and Gil Forbes for another excellent "Forbes Treatment." Thanks to Jack Llartin, my copy editor, for getting the manuscript into top form, and for giving Tu and The Astronaut a place to go on Halloween. Thanks to the team for all the fast work!

And, finally, to Teakki, who patiently waited to talk politics and show me his most recent comic creations until I finished writing each day. Can't wait to read this one with you!

Most of all, I can never express enough gratitude to my readers. To all the ones that have read everything I've published, to the ones who have just finished their first Booker thriller or Chasing adventure, it means the world to me that you've decided to spend your money and time on my stories. Please drop me an email anytime – responding to reader emails is one of my favorite times of the day!

I'd also like to mention a few fellow authors who have helped or inspired me: Craig Martelle, Michael Anderle, Mark Dawson, Nick Thacker, Ernest Dempsey, Eric J. Gates, Dale DeVino, and Phil M. Williams.

A special thanks goes out to the following readers and members of the street team for either their support, kindness, reviews (I *love* reviews), suggestions, and/or encouragement:

Ken Friedman, Rob Zorger, Robyn Shanti, Bob Browder, Chis Bond, Melanie C. Hansen, Chet Keough, Sue Steel, Jacky Dallaire, Adam Tanner, Frank Murphy, Gil Forbes, Blake Dowling, Sam Rhoades, Karen Markovitz, Kyle Dahlem, Christine Moritz, Tom Strauss, Irene Witoski, Martha Heckel, Sandie Parrish, LA Dumas, Bob Dumas, John Nicholson, Peggy Gulli, Randy Howerter, Ingo Michehl, John McDonald, Kathy Creecy, Susan Norlund, Liz Miller, Cheryl Olson, Jan Dallas, Chuck Gonzalez, Justin Lear, Rick Ferris, Janice Gildea, Vivienne Du Bourdieu, Elaine Dill, Sharon Moffatt, Jean Sink, Julie Price, Judith Anderson, Terry Myers, Carl Howard, Chris Tomlinson, Judy Hammer, Satish Bhatti, Christopher Bowling, Michael Ferrel, Susan McGuyer, Bill Borchert, Samantha Jackson, Debra Harper, Dennis Lowe, Cathie

Harrison, Marcel Roy. Gerry Adler, Brian Schnizlein, Mike Lauland, Mark Perlmutter, Frank Fusco, Gene Leach, Ron Babcock, Leslie Royce, Michael Picco, Gillian Charlton, Sam J. Rhoades III, Stephane Peltier, Ron Babcock, and a double-extra thanks to whoever the reviewer "Serenity" is!

There is a goal among some authors to turn readers into fans, fans into super fans, and super fans into friends. I am fortunate to have been able to achieve that goal on numerous occasions.

Thank you.